THE
CINDERELLA
THEOREM

KRISTEE RAVAN

This is a work of fiction. Names, characters, places, and events either are products of the author's imagination or are used fictitiously. Any resemblance to actual events, locations, or persons, living or dead, is entirely coincidental.

The math in this book is entirely non-fictional. It is based on actual math that really does exist and is awesome. If you haven't already done so today, please take a moment to thank your math teacher for being a perpetuator of said awesomeness.

for Lisa who loves math,
for Kellee who loves Cinderella,
and for Jason who loves me

CONTENTS

If you want your children to be intelligent, read them fairy tales. If you want them to be more intelligent, read them more fairy tales.

- Albert Einstein

1

PRETZELS AND THE BOX

Lily," Mrs. Price, my guidance counselor, flashed a fake smile. "You have forgotten to put any fun in your schedule. Why don't I switch you out of Geometry and put you in Health and Careers? Lots of students say this is a *fun* class…" She let that last part dangle in the air, like a worm on a hook.

I don't like worms on hooks. "No thanks."

Mrs. Price shifted in her seat, still smiling. "And this class will help you discover what you're good at as you explore your career options."

Chatting with a woman who can't recite the Pythagorean Theorem isn't exactly how I thought I would be spending my first day of high school. "I know what I want my career to be."

PRETZELS AND THE BOX

Mrs. Price sat up straighter, leaning forward. "Oh, and what is that?"

"I want to do pure mathematics research at a major university or be a code breaker for the National Security Agency."

Her eyebrows arched. I think she thought I was going to say *I want to be a doctor when I grow up* or *I want to be an artist.*

"Lily," Mrs. Price said slowly, "Are your parents pressuring you to take more math classes?"

"No." I folded my arms across my chest. Mrs. Price has incorrectly assigned *two* parents to me. This can lead to an error in the equation of my family.[1]

1 Lily + 1 mother = the Sparrow family.
The Sparrow family ≠ 1 Lily + 1 mother + 1 father.[2]

"Lily, if you don't want to take these extra math classes, you don't have to. Your parents can't make you."

"I want to take Geometry."

----

[1] This is my least favorite error in the equation of my family.

[2] Whenever you see a + sign, read it as "plus."

= as "equal."

≠ as "does not equal."

It's pretty basic. I like math, so I tend to talk in equations. My mother is forever reminding me that not everyone finds the principle of ratios as fascinating as me, so I'll provide explanations of the mathematical elements whenever necessary. This equation is the one I always use to think about my family. I suppose the "1 father" would have been a part of it at some point, but in my mind he's never been there. He died in a train wreck two days before I was born.

2

"Lily," Mrs. Price paused dramatically. "Do you know that you can talk to me about anything?"

Is that supposed to make me open up to her? Mrs. Price has not equalized her equation. She assumes: one simple reminder of being able to talk to her = me sharing my deepest beliefs and ideas.

I sighed, rolling my eyes. "Mrs. Price, no one is pressuring me to take math classes. I just like math, that's all."

Mrs. Price frowned. "I had hoped you would agree with me, Lily, and change your mind about these classes, because I'm afraid I can't allow you to jeopardize your academic career with difficult classes that will cause you extra stress. Besides, our school district frowns upon students taking more than one math course a year. I'm going to switch you from Geometry to Health and Careers, from Statistics to Tennis, and from Pre-Calculus to Legendary Literature. This will be a much less stressful class load for you."

It was my turn to frown. Scowl, actually. "How exactly are Health and Careers, Tennis, and *Legendary* Literature going to help me in life?" I was especially disgusted with Legendary Literature. Tennis was at least active and I suppose Health and Careers could–*at the very least*–be informative.

"Lily, I'm sure you'll enjoy these classes. Other students in this school have rated these electives as some of their favorites. Now, run on back to class." She returned my schedule card, all marked up and practically math free.

Can I have a look at population and sample data used to arrive at this conclusion? Other students in this school do not want to be mathematics researchers. Other students in this school do not understand that

3

mathematics is fundamental to all life. Other students in this school do not *love* math. I *do*.

Mrs. Price called cheerily, "Oh, I almost forgot. Happy birthday, Lily!"

Yeah, what a great start to my birthday. Resigned to my mathless fate, I walked back to class figuring out how many days were left until I graduated and escaped to college.

4 years x the 180 days required by the state = 720 days – the ½ a morning I wasted arguing with Mrs. Price about the joy of mathematics = 719 ¾ days.[3]

~ ~ ~

My mother is a famous writer (in this equation, famous = distracted). For some reason, that I have not been able to calculate, being a famous writer makes it difficult to focus on any one thing for extended periods of time, including daughters' birthdays. Writing is not as exact as math.

To combat her distraction, I mark my birthday on every calendar in the house. It's not so much that Mom forgets my birthday. It's that she gets distracted while planning. This year, I took an additional precaution: I changed her screen saver to "LILY'S BIRTHDAY IS THURSDAY!!!!!"

So, having solved the problem of the distractedness, we are usually ready to proceed with normal birthday celebrations. I say *usually* because there

---

[3] Read x as "times." See? Math is fun!

are occasionally book signings or tours that cause further issues. This year, however, there were none of these kinds of complications.

That is not to say that there were *no* complications.

There was, in fact, a huge one.

I came home from school intending to go out to dinner with my mother. That is a normal, mathematical way to celebrate a birthday. I grabbed a handful of pretzels from a bowl on the counter and popped my head into Mom's office to say hello. (Mom's office = a cluttered, messy room full of unorganized paper scraps that contain notes about her stories.)

Mom smiled at me. "How was school?"

"Not enough math." I munched a pretzel. "What time are we going out tonight?"

"Going out?" Mom's voice was quieter, distracted. She was sinking back into her novel.

"For dinner? For my birthday?"

Eyes fixed on her computer screen, she answered, "No. Matt is bringing dinner."

"Matt? Matt who?" I quickly ran a mental index of my mother's friends, acquaintances, and contacts for a Matt.

Mom gasped, covered her mouth with her hand, and mumbled, "Oh! It was supposed to be a surprise! What am I—"

"Mom!" I grabbed her shoulders, crushing a pretzel in my palm. "Stop. Who is Matt? Explain logically."

She nodded. "Okay. Let's sit down." She led the way to the living room and sat beside me on the couch, patting me on the back. "The thing is, Lily, I don't want to explain too much without your father. He—"

"Wait. What?" I interrupted. "My *father?*"

"Oh! Fiddlesticks! I did it again! Matt's going to kill me. I do fine for fifteen years and blow it on the last day. Why am I—"

"Mom!"

"Right. Well," she took a breath. "To begin, I should say that your father is not dead."

"But, he *is* dead. You told me that he died—that the train he was on hit a cow."[4]

"No, Sweetie." She patted my knee. "He's not dead. He *is* alive and he's coming to dinner."

"I don't understand. The train wrecked, the cow died, Dad died. You showed me the channel 6 news footage."

Mom sighed. (Why is she sighing? Did she think that I would automatically understand? Did I miss the *Lily, your dad is not dead* memo?) "There was a train wreck, a cow did die. And it was on the news. But your father was *not* on the train."

I took a deep breath and tried to sort out the emotions that started crowding my brain. Shock and disbelief—what she's saying can't be possible—can it? Joy and happiness, too—my dad's alive!

But years of dealing with my mom have made me logical. One of us has to stay focused, so I pushed all the emotions down and focused on gathering more data. "Okay. Where was he?"

---

[4] If I seem a little slow to understand what my mom is telling me, keep in mind that fifteen years of believing my dad is dead is greater than 3 minutes of hearing he is alive. ($15 > 3$.)

"He wants to explain all this to you, and he should be the one to do it. Can we just leave it at: he's not dead, and he's coming to dinner tonight?"

"But why did you tell me he was dead?"

"It was safer for everyone if you thought that. But, Lily, your father can explain this a lot better than me." She stood up. "Now, I need to work on getting the prince to fall in love with the princess, and you should probably get your homework done before dinner. I'm sure you're going to have a lot to talk about with your dad." She turned to go back to the office.

Are you kidding me? *That's* the end of the conversation?

I followed Mom into her office. "But you *lied* to me."

She sank into her chair, sighing. "Lily. There will be a *lot* of discussion about this tonight. Please. Let's just wait until then." She added in a lower voice, "I wasn't supposed to have to do this alone. It was so stupid of me to slip up."

"So, we're not going to talk about it now?"

"Lily! I have a deadline. You have homework. Go do it!"

"Fine." I slammed the door on my way out.

~~~

Mom was wrong to assume I had homework. It was the first day of school. We wasted most of the day with passing out textbooks and going over rules. I spent my "homework" time analyzing the events of the afternoon.[5] Specifically, I needed to place Mom's shocking new variables into the equation of Lily's Life.

Lily = a 5 foot, normal, freshman girl, who has shoulder length blonde hair, green eyes, and a distracted mother.

The new variables that now had to be put into my equation are A = *my father is alive* and B = *my mother is a liar.*

A and B are dependent upon one another. For instance, my mother is proved to be a liar (B), because my father is alive (A). My father's being alive (A) was a secret because my mother is a liar (B).

How is that normal?

Statistically speaking, teenagers should have parents who create supportive environments for them to grow in during their difficult, formative years. This is the *mathematically* proven way of success.[6]

How are a dead father, who is not dead, and a mother, who is a liar, supportive? What teenager sits around on her fifteenth birthday trying to think of questions to ask her mother about her used-to-be-dead father?

I was led to believe my father died in a bizarre train/cow accident two days before I was born. I always thought of it like this:

---

[5] And putting all my emotions back in their neat boxes. Emotions cloud logical thinking. I try to keep all that illogical messy stuff put away so I can focus on analyzing, gathering data, and formulating equations.

[6] Statistics = Math done to prove something.

After the accident = (Amtrak − 1 train) + (Lily − 1 father) + (Farmer Jones − 1 cow)

But none of this matters now, since my father is *not* actually dead. How unfortunate there isn't enough time in the Plan of Lily's Life to have therapy discussing cows, liars, and fathers. I dug around in the bottom of my closet looking for *The Box* my mother gave me for my fifth birthday. It contains everything I know about my father and once upon a time, I thought it was the best birthday present ever.[7] When I was younger, I kept *The Box* beside my bed. I was very afraid of the dark as a child and having *The Box* next to me gave irrational comfort. (Mom leaving the hall light on helped, too.) But as I grew older and no longer needed *The Box* beside me to sleep, I put it away in my closet, getting it out less and less to look at the items and think about my father. And this past year, I hadn't even looked at *The Box* since my last birthday.

I blew the dust off, slowly opening the lid to hear the creak of the hinges. I like that sound. *The Box* has a tarnished keyhole, but the key was lost before I ever had it. I ran my fingers over the lid, feeling the words carved on the smooth wooden surface:

Our Only Protector
HRHMS

---

[7] But, now that I've gotten my father back from the dead, I guess this will rank as the best. *Obviously*, a not-dead father is a much better gift than a box of memories about him.

PRETZELS AND THE BOX

When I asked my mother about the words on *The Box*, she said she didn't know what they meant; Dad had never explained them to her. (She was probably lying.) There are three items in *The Box*–three tangible, mathematical facts about my father. The first is a solid blue marble, the color of a tropical island lagoon or something else that is blue.[8] My mother told me the marble was my dad's. He was so good at marbles as a boy that marble playing at his school stopped, because no one could beat him.

I decided that I, too, would become skilled at marble playing. I got pretty good, but marbles was not a game children played at my school, so I mostly played by myself.[9] (My mother would sometimes play with me, usually whenever she needed a break from her characters.) But I never played with the blue marble. In my elementary school mind, I reasoned that I would save the blue marble for the game I would one day play with my father. (At seven, mathematical facts, like the surety of death are not overly important.) I do, however, find considerable irony in the fact that, now (apparently), I can play that game with my dear old dad.

---

[8] Color descriptions in the mathematical world are simpler. To me, the marble is blue. To my author mother, the marble is blue, the color of the sky after hearing that the king of the land has fallen in love, or some other strange description that has nothing to do with colors *or* marbles.

[9] The kids at school usually wasted their time playing non-mathematical games like Chase the Cute Boy, Dodgeball, or Tag. Based on what I've seen in math tutoring, they would have better spent their time at marbles with its emphasis on geometry and probability.

The second item in *The Box* is an antique brass doorknob my father used when he proposed to my mother. He said, "I am giving you the doorknob to my heart because you are the only one who can open it," or something else equally sugary and romantic. Even though romance is too abstract to be mathematical, I always thought this was a tremendously clever way to say "I love you." (Evidently, so did Mom.)

The third item in *The Box* is a letter from my father to me. It was written the day before he "died" or whatever the new story will be. (For all I know, my mother could have written the letter. She is, after all, a *writer.*) This is what he "wrote":

Dear Future Sparrow Child:

I wanted to take a moment to write down what I am feeling at this moment. I am rather excited and pleased that in a few days (or maybe less!) I will officially be your Father! I wanted to let you know that you are coming into a wonderful family. Your mother will dream up wonderful stories to tell you, and I will help you explore this New World of yours. We are going to have a grand adventure together. I can't wait to see you! I am counting the minutes until I can be

Your Father

Now that Mom has given me new data to consider, I'm not sure what to think about the letter anymore. Did he know he was leaving when he wrote it? How could he write such a letter of excitement and then leave? And for that matter, why did my mother say it was safer for everyone if I thought he was dead? Was he dangerous? I lean towards a "no" on this issue. (In my experience, which is limited, dangerous people do not propose with doorknobs.)

There are no pictures of my father in *The Box* or in the house for that matter. My mom does not like to answer questions about pictures. It makes her very defensive and bothered.[10] And I've given up looking for them in her closets or in the attic. There are just no pictures of my father.

I had been working on a theory that Mom burned all of them in some sort of grief cleansing after he died. But now he isn't dead.... Could he be a spy? Or maybe he was a tortured, drug-addicted musician? Both of those theories would support Mom saying, "It was safer for everyone if you thought he was dead."

I shook my head. Speculation is not mathematical and the trouble with looking for tangible facts about my father in *The Box* is that the equation *The Box* sets up is this:

what I know about my father = M(1 blue marble + 1 doorknob +1 letter +1 old box)

M = what my mother says about my father

---

[10] Here is a list of reasons she has given to explain why there are no pictures of my father:
1. A random car fire ruined her camera.
2. His parents were against the marriage, so they had a very quick and simple wedding, with no photographer.
3. *Her* parents were against the marriage, so they had a very quick and simple wedding with no photographer.
4. They dated only a short time, so there weren't many opportunities for pictures.
5. They were just so in love that they never bothered with taking pictures.

We can reasonably conclude that the M is tainted (by my mother's lies) and thereby taints the whole solution, but if you take M out, you'll have no information at all. Multiplying by zero equals zero. Zero stories about my dad. Just a box.

And for the first time, looking through *The Box* had made me angry. All of these things I "know" about my dead father were probably lies. Just one of Mom's stories made up to entertain her daughter.

I shoved the blue marble in my pocket. Then I put *The Box* away and checked the clock. Almost five. Five o'clock is *always* suppertime in the Sparrow home. I don't know how this kind of a schedule works with a distracted mother, but somehow it does. She always has supper ready at five, no matter what the characters in her story world are doing.

I saw no signs of supper in the kitchen. Nothing. I looked in the office. Mom was still busy writing. What are the odds that on the day I find out my dad isn't really dead, my mom also forgets to cook supper?

I wanted to ask my mother about supper, but I didn't want to ask about my father specifically, because that would be weird, and I didn't want to lash out at her. (Cool, rational thinking wins the day.) I didn't want to say, for instance, "Hey Mom, you may have lied to me for fifteen years, but don't you need to be cooking something? It isn't everyday Dad comes over for dinner." so I said instead:

"What are we having for dinner tonight?"

Mom continued writing for a moment, then realized I had spoken, "I don't know, whatever your dad brings home."

I stood shocked for a moment. Let me see if I have my facts straight: a man I have never met, a man who has been "dead" my whole life, is bringing home my special birthday dinner. HE is bringing it HOME? *To our home?* We have a leaky faucet that has lived here longer than he has. This is *not* his home. Home implies permanency.

Mom looked at me. "Why are you staring like that, Lily?"

"What do you mean 'he's bringing dinner home'?"

"Try to understand, Lily." Mom patted my arm and spoke slowly as if she were talking to a three-year-old or a crazy person. "Your dad is coming home for your birthday, and he is bringing dinner with him."

I stared at her. "You mean he's coming *over* for dinner, right? He can't be coming *home*, because he doesn't live here."

"Lily, he'll be here in less than five minutes. Do we really have to discuss whether he's "coming over" or "coming home," at this exact moment?" She started stacking her notes in different piles, a sign that writing was done for the day.

"Yes." I folded my arms. "You don't get to just lie to me and then say a stranger is coming home and then try to neatly stack me up like one of your writing notes!"

"Lily." Mom's voice was stern. "We are not doing this now. If you need to go back upstairs to calm down—fine. But I don't want your father coming home to us screaming at each other."

I could tell I was on the verge of becoming irrational so I stomped upstairs to brush my teeth.[11] (I

---

[11] I had been about to stomp my foot and yell some more. I don't like to lose control. It's unmathematical and embarrassing.

tend to brush my teeth when I get annoyed.) What does she mean, *coming home?*

On the landing, I stepped over the mini-vac Mom had left (through her distraction) plugged in. Most likely, this morning, when she was supposed to be vacuuming the stairs, inspiration seized her and she abandoned cleaning for writing.

I stomped into the bathroom, annoyed with my adult role model. How am I supposed to grow up in this abnormal environment?

Just as I finished angrily squeezing toothpaste onto my toothbrush, the shower curtain was pushed back by a fully clothed man standing in the bathtub.

"Lily!" he said. "Happy birthday!"

2

LUBCKER

I screamed and threw my toothbrush at him. Not waiting to see if my aim was good, I rushed out, slamming the door behind me.

"MOM!"

The man opened the bathroom door. "Lily, let me ex—"

"Stay back." I grabbed the mini-vac off the floor and revved it at him. I could hear Mom rushing up the stairs.

"Lily? What's going on?" Mom stopped when she saw the man. "Matt! Welcome home!" She threw her arms around him, kissing him.

I dropped the vacuum.

"Lily," Mom said, pushing the tub-man forward a little, "this is your father. Matt," she started tearing up, "this is Lily."

Will nothing in my life ever be mathematical or normal again? Not only is my father not dead, but I meet him while brushing my teeth, and my mother greets her husband that she hasn't seen in fifteen years like he just came home from a day at the office.

Tub Man handed a present to my mom. Then he hugged me. I pulled back a little from the hug, but he didn't notice. He just squeezed tighter and said, "I've missed you so much, Lily. I've been looking forward to this day ever since you were born."

I couldn't think of any response to this, so I stared at him, studying his features to form an equation.

My father = a tub-loving, blonde-haired, tallish man, who is not dead, but apparently has a loose definition of what it means to be a family man.

My mother interrupted my analysis. "Let's go downstairs," she said. "We'll be more comfortable. Lily, don't forget to put the vacuum away."

Tub Man beamed as he put his arm around Mom.

I picked up the mini-vac, stuffed it in the closet and followed my "parents" to the living room. My mother sat next to my "father" on the couch. I sat in the chair opposite, processing what had just happened. How did he get in the bathtub? If he came to our house after school, I would have heard him coming upstairs. If he had been in the house since before I got home, why did my mother act like she had seen him for the first time upstairs? *And why was he in the bathtub?!*

"I can't believe this day is finally here." Tub Man flashed a bright smile.

"I'm so glad we're all together." Mom gazed at him with the same stupid smile.

It doesn't make mathematical sense for her to react this way. Wouldn't they have grown apart over fifteen years? Shouldn't she be bitter or something? I am a reasonably intelligent person: Why don't I understand any of this?

"Why don't I understand any of this?" I asked.

"What don't you understand, Lily?" Tub Man turned his smile to me.

He has to ask what I don't understand? I filtered through my questions and had just decided to ask, "Why were you in the bathtub?" when we heard a voice calling from upstairs:

"Should we bring the dinner down, sir?"

The fear I felt in the bathroom was back. I grabbed the arms of my chair. "There's someone upstairs!" I hissed.

Tub Man, instead of rushing up the stairs to defend his wife and child from the intruder, turned to my mother and asked, "Perhaps we could do this better over dinner? What do you think, Ginnie?"

My mother, instead of being confused about the voice and upset that her husband was not protecting her, answered, "That's probably a good idea. Will they need any help?"

I began rapidly thinking over and over again: *What is happening? Who are 'they'? What is happening? Who are 'they'?*

"No. They should be able to handle it." To the voice upstairs, he called, "Sure, Lubcker. Bring it on down. We're just moving to the dining room."

"Who is Lubcker?"

Tub Man grinned mischievously. "Lubcker is my personal chef. I asked him to prepare a special dinner for tonight."

That was not a satisfying answer. So as we sat down, I asked, "Why is he upstairs? Wouldn't it have been easier to bring the food in through the door?"

"Well..." Tub Man began to answer as the door to the dining room opened. In came a person, about the height of a five-year-old, holding a steaming dish of food. He wore all red: red shirt, red pants, red shoes that looked like they were made of cloth, and to top off the whole outfit, a red beret on top of his white hair.

"A very happy birthday to you, Princess Lily!" He put the food on the table.

Before I had time to respond, six more little people entered. They all had white hair and were each dressed in a different color: orange, yellow, green, blue, purple and brown. Each placed their dishes of food on the table, while wishing *Princess Lily* a happy birthday.

When all seven dishes were on our table (and that was something of a mathematical feat, because the area of our table was only slightly larger than the area of the food[12]), they lined up in the order they had appeared along the wall of the dining room, like a rainbow of short people.

The little red man asked, "Shall we stay and serve, sir?"

---

[12] You know what area is, right? Area is simply the size of a surface. The formula is area = length x width.

Tub Man, in no way put off by the rainbow people, answered, "No. Thank you, Lubcker. We shall manage just fine tonight."

Lubcker bowed. "As you wish, sir." The others left with Lubcker. The man in brown winked at me as he went. I was as confused as I imagine a non-math-lover would be in a trigonometry class.[13]

"I'll get some plates and silverware." Mom jumped up from the table.

Tub Man grabbed two of the dishes. "These are dessert." He left me alone in the dining room with five dishes that magically appeared from upstairs.

"Well," Tub Man said, when he came back. "That was Lubcker. Does that answer your question?"

Are you kidding me? "Are you kidding me?" I asked. "Seven small, short, *whatever* people appear from upstairs and bring down food. How does 'that was Lubcker' answer any kind of question? Not to mention you are supposed to be dead and you just show up in the bathtub! The *bathtub!* What is that about?"

Mom brought in the plates, silverware, and glasses. She looked a little surprised by my outburst.

Tub Man smiled. "Take a deep breath, Lily. Let's go through this logically. Your first question was 'Who is Lubcker'? That was sufficiently answered by his entrance, I think. (And they prefer to be called dwarves, you know. Not 'small' or 'short people.') Now, as to

---

[13] Trig is, according to my mother, the worst math class ever. I haven't officially taken it yet, but I bought an old college trig book at a second hand book shop. I had fun going through it. It's mostly about triangles and angles and who doesn't like that?

why he was upstairs and who was with him, it might be better for me to just explain everything, and then, you can ask questions if necessary. How does that sound?"

"How did you get in our bathtub?" I asked, narrowing my eyes.

"Believe me, Lily, I understand your frustration. A lot of new things have been revealed today. You're overwhelmed with questions. Your mother and I are going to do everything we can to answer them for you." He looked at my mother and smiled. "I was in your bathtub because, the only way to get from *my* world, E. G. Smythe's Salty Fire Land, to *this* world is through the bathtub."

I just stared at him. What in the world (and I mean *my* world) is going on here? Why can't I just have a normal father, like a trash man, or a zookeeper, or something?

3

MARVELOUS MIDAS CREME

Over the salad, I learned Tub Man is the king of E.G. Smythe's Salty Fire Land.[14]

"You see, Lily," he said, "because there is so much magic in fairy tales, myths, and legends, the characters, places, plots, and story lines were able to channel that magic and become living as well."

---

[14] *Smythe* is pronounced "Smith." Apparently, *Smythe* is just a fancy "Smith."

"That isn't possible," I interrupted. "You're talking about fictional characters, right? They are not alive, and therefore cannot create anything."

King Tub chuckled. "Straight to the hard questions. You weren't kidding, Ginnie." He smiled at my mom. "She's bright." He looked back at me. "That's a deep, philosophical question, Lily. We aren't sure why they're alive, living 'happily ever after' in E. G. Smythe's Salty Fire Land, but they are. The impossible is sometimes possible."

"That's not possible. The laws of physics are concrete. They don't change. A ball is always going to fall downwards. It is impossible for it to fall upwards."

"Except in space," King Tub argued. "If a place exists where gravity doesn't work the way it does on Earth, can't there be a place where what I'm telling you is possible? For the sake of our discussion, let's just *assume* that what I'm saying is true and possible."

"Fine." I took a deep breath and realigned my thinking.

Math, however lovely and wonderful, could not explain this situation to me. No equation was going to balance out the things my father was saying. No equation could explain tub travel. And if I couldn't form an equation to explain something, then I simply needed more data. Solid questions were the only way I would be able to gather enough information to understand this bizarre birthday dinner conversation.

"Who is E. G. Smythe? Why isn't he the king?" I asked.

"E. G. Smythe is not a person," King Tub explained. "E. G. Smythe's Salty Fire Land is an anagram for 'fairy tales, myths, legends.'"[15]

"Oh," I said. "That actually makes sense."

My parents smiled at each other, thrilled their 'Little Lily' was finally catching on.

"So, you're the king?" I poked at a cherry tomato.

"I'm not just the king, Lily." His tone was serious, and he lifted his chin. "I'm the Protector of the realm. Fairy tales, myths, and legends only survive for two reasons: The first is that they are loved and reread and retold. The second is that, since the very creation of E. G. Smythe's Salty Fire Land, someone from the Sparrow family has been their protector. I am the *only* protection against our enemies in Uppish Senna." He paused, "And, as my daughter, Lily, one day you will also be the Protector of the land."

The tomato I had been trying to stab skidded across the table. "I'm going to do pure mathematics research at a major university or be a code breaker for the National Security Agency." I'm not going to *not* be a brilliant mathematician so I can sit around in the world through the bathtub protecting stupid Rapunzel and her seven dwarfs.

"Lily," Mom began in a patient tone, "the day that you take over the Protectorate is still a long way off.

---

[15] Anagram = a word, phrase, or jumble of letters, that when rearranged make another word or phrase. An anagram of "pots" is "stop." "Mary" is "army." "Astronomer" is "Moon starer." Specifically, by rearranging the letters in "fairy tales, myths, legends," the name "E. G. Smythe's Salty Fire Land" is created.

It's not like you're moving to Smythe's SFL *tomorrow.*"
She laughed. I learned two key points from this motherly
speech:

    (A) Smythe's SFL must be a shorter way of saying
E. G. Smythe's Salty Fire Land. And
    (B) While I am sure that my mother meant to be
helpful in making this comment, she was not. It sparked
a new and scary thought in me: if I'm not moving to
Smythe's SFL *tomorrow,* when am I moving there?

    King Tub continued, "Exactly my thoughts,
darling." He smiled at my mother, who began serving
the next course: mashed potatoes, pork chops, green
beans, and biscuits.
    After taking a bite of pork, and wondering how
King Tub knew what my favorite meal was, I asked,
"Why haven't I seen you for fifteen years? Why did
Mom tell me you were dead?"
    He sipped his iced tea. "There is an ancient law in
the oldest records of Smythe's SFL concerning the heir
to the throne. It says:

> *'Marry from the Kingdom—*
> *All is well.*
> *Marry from the Outside—*
> *And you must fail.*
> *No contact, no letters*
> *Or the Outside, like fetters,*
> *Will bind you there.*
> *But, if both be Smythe, you can live with.*
> *If one be not, then you cannot—*
> *Until the time of fifteen years,*

Has passed away like drying tears.
Else the babe will never see
The salty land of Smythe's E. G.'

"Basically, the law says that if one of the parents
of the heir is not a Smythian, then the heir and the
Smythian parent must be separated for fifteen years.
Otherwise, the child will never be able to enter Smythe's
SFL and the parent (that's me) will never be able to
return. Since it was so vital that (a) I remain in the land
to protect the characters, and (b) you be able to come in
as heir later, we felt this was the only option."

What? What kind of law is that?

However, on the brighter, mathematical side of
things, I enjoyed the way King Tub delineated his
points–(a) and (b). That's a very mathematical approach
to arguing. But on the negative side, he did appear out of
nowhere in my bathtub.

"So, you had to live in the Salt Land—"

"Smythe's SFL," King Tub interrupted.

"Whatever," I continued, "you had to live there
and not see me until I was fifteen or else I wouldn't be
able to come later and you'd be stuck here?"

"Exactly," he said. "It's a very ancient law,
created to discourage royalty from marrying outsiders.
Plus, it sets up a very "fairy tale" scenario: a new parent,
forced to never see his child for fifteen years, a secret
princess, all the waiting and hoping. It's what good fairy
tales are made of. And all the background drama. My
parents weren't thrilled I chose Ginnie. But look how
well it's all worked out." He smiled at Mom again. "So
your mother lived in the castle with me until it was
almost time for you to be born. Then, when it was

unsafe for her to still be in the kingdom, she came back to this house."

"Oh," I said, resisting the urge to make an equation out of this. "Has the, uh, 'door' to Smythe's SFL always been through the upstairs tub?"

"No, it hasn't," King Tub answered. "It can be anywhere. We chose to have it from this house, because this is where you and your mother were going to be living. When my father was the King-Protector, the door was in the attic of his favorite theatre. My grandfather entered this world through the janitor's closet at a county courthouse. But the strangest entry of all was my great-great-great-grandmother's portal. She came in through the hold of a ship. She could never be certain where she was going to arrive. She would be off the coast of Jamaica one time and in the middle of the Pacific Ocean the next."

I interrupted. "You're saying that the hold of a ship is stranger than the upstairs tub?" I rapidly created an equation:

Regarding strangeness in arrival areas from E. G. Smythe's Salty Fire Land:
the hold of a ship > upstairs tub.

"You think the tub's stranger?" he asked.

I just looked at him. "What if I had been *going* to the bathroom instead of just brushing my teeth? What if someone was in the shower when you wanted to portal yourself to the real world?"

"Oh!" King Tub said suddenly, understanding what I was meaning. "On the Smythe's SFL side, there's a dial that tells you when the upstairs bathroom is occupied and what the person is doing."

"What the person is doing?"

"In general terms, Lily." My mother jumped in. "The settings on the dial are for shower, toilet, washing face, and brushing teeth."

"What if I was changing clothes?" I asked. I am sorry, but I do not think that a dial on a door explaining what I am doing in the bathroom is conducive to a happy home environment.

"Then the dial would just say *other.*" My mother said patiently, stacking our empty plates. "People in Smythe's SFL do not use the door without permission from the King, and never unless the door says *unoccupied.*"

"Or brushing teeth." I mumbled a little sarcastically.

"I was so excited about seeing you, that I portaled over anyway." His face crumbled like an unsound theorem. "I didn't think that—"

"Of course, you didn't," my mother said quickly. "I'll get dessert. Lily, Come help me."

I excused myself and went into the kitchen.

"Lily Elizabeth Sparrow," she began.

I sucked in my breath. By all mathematical laws, three names is bad news.

"I know that this has been a very stressful day and that you are confused, but you are not going to make your father feel bad because he came in through the tub while you were brushing your teeth." She said all this while furiously filling three bowls with cake and ice cream.

I made a huffing sound. "I'm in trouble because you lied to me all my life, and my father appeared magically in my bathtub, followed by seven rainbow dwarves carrying food, calling me princess, and—"

"Lily," my mother interrupted. "Try to understand. This has not been the ideal birthday or the ideal situation for you. We know that. We know that you are confused and that things seem very odd, very strange, and *very* unmathematical. But you can be confused *and* still have a good attitude. Now," she handed me a bowl of ice cream and cake, "Happy birthday." She carried the other two bowls into the dining room, leaving me in the kitchen.

I counted by squares to 484 before I had subtracted enough anger to keep myself from storming off.[16] "I can't gather data if I'm angry," I whispered to myself. "I can't notice patterns if I'm emotional." The only way to process all of this is to stay as logical and mathematical as possible.

Back in the dining room, my parents were smiling and eating ice cream. I sat down and noticed that everyone had a different kind of ice cream. I looked at my cherry vanilla. I looked at King Tub's chocolate. I looked at my mother's cookies and cream. There had only been one carton of ice cream in the kitchen that my mother dipped from.

"Why are there three types of ice cream and only one carton?" I asked.

King Tub smiled brightly. "It's Marvelous Midas Cream. Do you remember King Midas from the story?"

"Sort of." I have to confess that, although my mother is a writer of fiction stories, and my father is

---

[16] A square is a number multiplied by itself. 1 X 1 is 1. 2 X 2 is 4. To count by squares, you list just the answers: 1, 2, 9, 16, 25, etc. 484 is 22 X 22.

apparently the ruler of a magical fairy tale world, I know almost nothing about fairy tales. In my recollection, I think Midas could spin straw into gold or something. "Well," he continued, "Midas took the properties of his golden touch and made them marketable in ice cream." (Apparently, Midas was the one with the golden touch. At least I got the precious metal right.) "So when you buy a carton of Marvelous Midas Cream, you get in your bowl whatever kind of ice cream you want."

"That's convenient," I said, trying (for Mom) to have a good attitude and be positive.

"It really is. My grandfather, your great-grandfather, knighted Midas for creating such a useful invention." King Tub smiled, savoring his chocolate golden touch ice cream. "It was very handy when the delegation from Olympus came last month." He chuckled. "Can you imagine worrying about which god you will annoy because you didn't have their favorite ice cream?"

No, I could not. And do you know why? I can only think of one god from literature: Zeus. And here's another reason: I wouldn't be entertaining a delegation from Olympus—because they're not *real*.

I just smiled serenely and had a "good attitude" as I took another bite of my magical ice cream.

4

PRETZELS...AGAIN

Even though I am only allowed to have one math class, I was glad (for once) to be able to get to school. For me, school now equals normal.

School now = normal because of yesterday, because of my weekend plans, and because King Tub *stayed the night at our house.*

If I turn out seriously deranged, I will not be surprised at all.

On my walk to school, I thought about how I could not possibly tell anyone a shred of truth about my birthday.

Oh, wait.

I can tell them what we ate, right up until the magic ice cream.

Last year, my friend, Corrie, thought her life was ruined because her four-year-old brother ran through her birthday party–stark naked–screaming about poopy. Corrie is clearly clueless as to what ruins a birthday. Before yesterday, I planned to work on some equations from an old math book over the weekend. Now, I am going to E. G. Smythe's Salty Fire Land to be formally introduced to the populace. Great. When Corrie asks me what I'm doing this weekend, instead of saying, "Nothing really, just some math," I'll now be able to say, "Nothing really, just getting away with my formerly dead father and liar mother to the parallel kingdom in our bathtub to be introduced to a bunch of fairy tale princesses and talking animals."

I'm going to be very distracted in school today. Dwarves in berets keep coming down the stairs in my mind. I'm also distracted by the fact that my parents win the award for the World's Strangest Marriage. When Mom told me King Tub was staying the night, I thought, *Oh, well maybe the door only works once a day or something, so he can't get back tonight.* That was a false assumption. Any good mathematician knows that false assumptions can destroy an otherwise sound theory. It turns out they *wanted* to sleep in the same bed again. As I passed my mother in the upstairs hallway, I asked a very rational question about this.

"Don't you think having him sleep in your room will be weird, since you haven't seen him in fifteen years?"

Mom smiled. "*You* haven't seen him in fifteen years, Lil. I've seen him nearly every day since you were born."

Of course. This makes absolute perfect sense. Why shouldn't she have seen him? I mean, my goodness, the man rules a fairytale kingdom and travels through a bathtub. Why wouldn't he have time to see his wife?

Mom continued, "When you were a baby, he'd come over during your naps and later, when you started school, your father would come over while you were gone. We'd spend the mornings together. Or, sometimes I'd go to Smythe's SFL to see him. Then, he'd run the kingdom in the afternoons, and I'd get some writing done. The law only separated the two of you."

"Oh," I said. "It's nice that you not only lied to me, but had secret trysts with my father every day, too." I started to walk away.

"Lily," Mom called. "It wasn't like that. You know he couldn't see you until you turned fifteen."

I sighed. "I know that's what you're telling me now. You could be lying again." It was a little mean of me to accuse her of lying. I was 90% sure she wasn't lying about this, but all the brattiness I'd been pushing down was leaking out around me.

"Lily," Mom pleaded. "The law, Sweetie. Try to understand."

I turned around in the doorway of my room. "I understand, Mom." I said impatiently. "I'm going to go to bed now—or is there something weird about my bedroom you haven't told me? Do the three little pigs live in my closet?"

"Of course they don't, Lily. They live in the Fourth Wood." Mom sighed. "Look. Things are weird now. I know that. Will you just try to be understanding?" She moved a little closer to me. "You're lucky, Lily. You aren't stuck living a plain-old, normal life. You're going to get to experience so many things that people will never be able to imagine."

"Or believe." I closed the door to my room.

I cannot fathom why my mother thinks I'm lucky. And *what*, exactly, is wrong with being normal? In statistics, there is a whole equation devoted to the "normal" way data is distributed.[17] Speaking of statistics, my parents have obviously not seen any on teenagers. Otherwise, they would know that being normal (not being royal—or lied to!) is the single most important factor in the equation of high school.

When I got to school Friday morning, I waited by the east door for Corrie. Corrie always arrives at 7:40. *Always*. This is because Corrie's father is obsessed with punctuality and order. He leaves for work at the same time each day, and since he drops her off, she is always here at the same time. It's a simple equation.

Usually, I formulate some equations about the number of kids at the door before and after she arrives, but before the bell rings at 7:55. Sometimes I estimate how many will arrive before her or what percentage will be wearing a certain color. But today, I didn't really feel like doing math.

Not feeling like doing math = a clue that something is seriously wrong in my life.

---

[17]This is called standard normal distribution. It is especially useful in analyzing the data related to tests, battery life, and coin flipping.

"Happy birthday!" Corrie gave me a clumsily wrapped present. "I would have given it to you yesterday, but—"

"But you were busy faking sick to get out of your math placement test?"

"I really did have an upset stomach!"

"From freaking out about the test. I can't believe you missed the first day of school just to have an extra day of study."

Corrie is obsessed with history. She can't get enough of Henry VIII and Czarina Alexandra. Her history obsession has led to her being a tad deficient in the mathematical areas of the world. I think it's a little strange to be so captivated by dead people, but she thinks it's equally strange to spend your free time reading books about ratios and proportions.

"It's called test anxiety, Lily. It's an epidemic."

Corrie is in what I think is a very easy math class. If I were in her class, my only anxiety would come from knowing that I could teach the class in my sleep. But since dead people are her thing, I guess that's okay. To each her own.

I opened the present.

"Do you like it?" Corrie gets very excited by birthdays. The present was a biography of Isaac Newton. Mr. Laws of Motion, himself. "I think it is a nice compromise between history and math."

I smiled. Did I like it? I had only been hinting to my mother about this book for three months. And instead of mathy goodness in the form of the life of Sir Isaac Newton, my parents gave me a book of fairy tales. Yeah, I was thrilled by *that* gift.

The value of Corrie's present to me was incredibly > the book of little kid bedtime stories.

"I love it. Thank you very much, Corrie."

"So where did you go for dinner last night? Did you see any famous writers like you did last year?" Corrie flipped her dark hair behind her shoulder.

Last year, Mom was on tour for her latest book on my birthday. I joined her in New York City and when we went out for my birthday, Mom bumped into a group of famous writers. They all wrote poems and little story things for me about my birthday, right there in the restaurant.

"Well…." What am I supposed to say? "We didn't go out. We just had my favorite meal at home." There. My answer to Corrie = truth (sort of).

"You ate at home? You never eat at home for your birthday."

See? Corrie understood the mathematical quandary that yesterday threw me into. She understood the *normal* way of celebrating my birthday.

"I know." Was there any way I could change the subject? "My mom just wanted to celebrate quietly at home. She's been kind of busy since the last book tour." Also truth. Mom did finish a big promotional tour in July. *Of course*, she'd want to be alone with her only daughter for her daughter's fifteenth birthday–alone, with her living (non-deceased) husband and seven dwarves carrying food.

"Bummer." Corrie genuinely understood my birthday disappointment. I mean, she did have the naked, four-year-old poopy screamer last year. "Well, what did you get?"

Hmm. What did I get? Nothing much, just my father, access to another world, and a book of barely believable children's stories.

"A book." Truth again. Stats on truth-telling: Lily = 100%.

"Not the book I gave you?" Corrie was horrified that she might have accidentally made my birthday worse.

"No. I guess Mom was too distracted to notice all the hints I left about Newton."

I think Corrie would have asked what the title of the book was if the fight hadn't started then. Kelly Stewart and Trista Anderson started fighting over who was stealing whose boyfriend. Mr. Hatfield, our principal, and several other teachers ran over to stop the girls. I was blissfully swept away for the moment in a normal high school routine.[18]

My first class was Legendary Literature. I realize that it is only the second day of school, and I further realize that two days do not equal sufficient time to form an opinion of a class. Nevertheless, I do not like that class. And after today's assignment, I know I never will.

"We are going to analyze fairy tales this semester!" (Everything Mrs. Fox says seems to possess an exclamation mark.)

I rolled my eyes. Not more fairy tales. It's like I've made an error at the beginning of a long equation and now I can't get the answer to make sense. When did my life become so full of fairy tales?

---

[18] Fights at school = normal. Normal = well... normal.

"Who wrote fairy tales?! Why have they survived?! Why do we enjoy them so much?! These are some of the questions we are going to answer!" Mrs. Fox continued on and on. "Let's go around the room and share our favorite fairy tales!"

Panic. Let me again point out: I do not know any fairy tales. After quickly examining my options, I decided to just copy someone else's answer.

"Why don't we start with......" Mrs. Fox looked around the room for a victim, while her sentence hung there waiting for its exclamation mark. "Lily!"

I should have known. Was it mathematically possible for Smythe's SFL to be working its magic against me even at school?

Wait.

There could be no answer to that question because I had not yet proven that Smythe's SFL was mathematically possible. Therefore, the question of whether or not–

"Lily?!" (How is it possible to ask a question *and* make an exclamatory statement?)

"Uh....well....I...." I hate fairy tales. They have turned me into incoherent mush. I tried to recall anything King Tub might have said about a fairy tale last night. "Oh! I like that King Midian guy."

A few people in the class snickered.

Mrs. Fox looked puzzled for a moment, then, "Oh! You mean King Midas! An excellent tale!" She raced to the board to write *King Midas*. (The woman even moved like an exclamation.) "Becky! Tell us your favorite!"

Becky pulled Rapunzel out of the air. Isn't she the one that slept for a hundred years?

I stopped paying attention shortly after this, and was in a happy state of solving for x in my head, when Mrs. Fox exclaimed, "For your homework over the weekend, I want you to read *The Little Mermaid* and write a few sentences in your fairy tale journal about this wonderful tale! For extra credit, tell why you think this tale made Andersen so famous!"

Who is Andersen? Was the Little Mermaid the one with the evil stepmother and the poison apple? And what is a fairy tale journal? But, on the brighter side of things, I now have something to talk to King Tub about while we portal to worlds beyond the plumbing.

The rest of the day was an unmathematical event not worth remembering. The substitute in history never found the lesson plans to give us an assignment. She let us do whatever instead; I read about lovely Mr. Newton.

No one was home when I arrived. Normally, I would have thought this strange, since Mom works at home, but my ideas about strangeness have shifted somewhat since yesterday's festivities. Figuring Mom and King Tub were off gallivanting in the Salt World, I got my pretzels and decided to do my biology homework. I had just answered a question about DNA and its importance to all things living, when the brown dwarf from last night crashed onto the dining room table in front of me.

"Hi, Your Highness!" he said, as a voice from above started shouting:

"You weren't supposed to let her see you!"

I looked up. The woman in all purple was sitting on the chandelier, where I suppose the brown dwarf had just been.

"We're so sorry, Princess," she continued, though she didn't really sound sorry, as she started in on Mr.

Brown. "Geez, Peridiom, all you had to do was stay up here, and she would never have known we were here." She sighed, jumped and landed on the table, also.

"Um, why *were* you up there?" I asked, very logically.

"Her Majesty sent us through the tub to make sure you had an afternoon snack. After we put in your pretzels for today, Peridiom said," she paused here and looked hard at poor Mr. Brown, "that he wanted to climb up the light. Then, you came home, and we were stuck, and stupid Peridiom fell on your homework."

"Oh," I said, as if dwarves dressed in one color, falling from my ceiling were an everyday occurrence.

"Did you like the pretzels?" Peridiom asked.

I smiled, nodded, and helped Peridiom and Miss Purple off the table.

I don't know how much more of this "normal" life I can stand.

5

KEYS

After I finished my biology, I settled into the couch to enjoy Sir Isaac Newton and his first law of motion. Objects in motion were remaining in motion when my parents finally decided to come home to see if their only daughter had returned from school safely. They bounded down the stairs, holding hands and smiling.

"Are you all packed, Lil?" Mom asked, looking appalled by my biography of Newton. Mom, being a fiction writer and, apparently, the queen of a fairy tale kingdom, has an aversion to non-fiction.

"What exactly do I pack?" Questions about packing equal stalled time not spent in magical fairy tale kingdom. "Furthermore, why do I need to pack? It seems to me that if I need anything I can just zip back through the tub and get it."

"Go pack." Mom used her rare no-nonsense voice.

I took the tonal hint and went upstairs. In my room, I found my jeans from yesterday. Jeans are nearly mathematical all by themselves. I've created an equation regarding how many times you can wear them before you send them to the hamper. *And* the degree in which you wear them plays a part of the equation. For instance,

$$\text{if } x = \text{a wearing of jeans,}$$
$$2x = \text{two wearings of jeans,}$$
$$\text{but } x^2 = \text{dirty to the second degree,}$$
$$\text{a really dirty wearing of jeans.}$$

Math: Happiness and normality even when you are packing to go on a magical journey through your bathtub.

I stuck my hand in the pocket to clean it out and found the blue marble from *The Box*. Lovely. The blue marble equals a reminder of happier days when what I knew about my father could be contained in one small box. It's actually kind of sad, really. But which is sadder: losing *The Box* of what you know about your father, or being able to put everything you know about him into a box?

That was not a mathematical question at all, so I couldn't answer it. Without thinking, I put the marble into the pocket of today's jeans. (Today's jeans = 2x.) On to packing.

Ten minutes, a pair of pajamas, yesterday's jeans, two shirts, and an assortment of toiletries later, I returned downstairs to announce that I was packed.

"Where's your bag?" Mom asked, furiously scribbling something onto a post-it note in the kitchen. Several post-it notes, actually. She had quite a pile going. "It's in the bathroom." Where else do you put your bag for a trip to Smythe's SFL?

"Fine..." Mom trailed absent-mindedly.

"What are you doing?" I wanted to know what was so important it had to be written down at that exact moment. We were supposed to be embarking on our first trip as an entire "family."

King Tub came over, putting his hand on my shoulder. "Unfortunately, Lily," he sighed. "Your mother has been seized with an inspiration."

"Shall we sit down then?" I asked, slipping out of his grasp.

Mom ran to her office, calling, "I'll only be a minute!"

"I think so," King Tub chuckled, as we walked back into the living room. "Once she ignored me for two whole days." He smiled. "That was the Battle for the Magic of Andeer."

"I know what you mean. The week that she wrote the fall of Sir Wend, I only saw her at supper."

"That's one of her better villain downfalls, though."

"It is." We settled into a little silence; then our quiet was broken by Mom shouting from the office, "I've got you now, Tressa! Your plans to marry the prince are going to fail."

"Poor Tressa." King Tub sank back into the couch and sighed.

I should have been happy, really. I just had a "moment" of mutual understanding with my new-found father. Too bad the "moment" came from us waiting for my mom to come back from a world that exists only in her brain and computer, so that we can portal through our bathtub to a parallel world inhabited solely by fictional characters. And the awkward conversation we shared was about my mother's fictional worlds, instead of being a *normal* awkward conversation about school, the weather, or the new anchor on the six o'clock news.

And my mother wonders why I've found happiness in math.

Fifteen minutes later, Mom emerged from her office looking a little tired.

King Tub jumped up and said, "Did, uh, you get everything worked out with Tressa?" I think he was concerned we would never get to magic ourselves away into Smythe's SFL.

"Yes," Mom sighed. "It's just that…" She sighed again. "It's just that Tressa has found another way to get her clutches on the prince." Mom looked away, my father looked at me, and I looked down. I'm no good at consoling authors when the people they made up, and *therefore control*, do things that the author doesn't like. Honestly, that's about as unmathematical as the Easter Bunny.

King Tub, however, seemed to be a little better at this consolation. "You'll get her next time, dear. I'm sure of it. If you can bring down Sir Wend, how can little Tressa stop you?"

"Matt," my mother began impatiently. "*I* did not defeat Sir Wend. Driel did. And I'm not the one trying to stop Tressa. Laurel must do that."

"But—"

"Let's just go." She started up the stairs. "Are you packed, Lily?"

"Yes," I rolled my eyes, following her and trying very hard not to point out the redundancy of her asking me *again* if I was packed.

Before my entire family gets into the bathtub and showers away to a land where Sleeping Beauty's Wicked Stepmother really does exist, I would like to state the mathematical improbabilities I am about to face.

(1) Though Einstein and Schrödinger did some work on time gap theories, there is no mathematical evidence to support what we are about to do.

(2) It is a bathtub, not a door to a world unknown.

(3) I submit, as further evidence to Point 2, the fact that I have often taken a bath in the bathtub and have not seen any sort of thing likely to be a "secret lever" or "magic doorknob" or anything like that.

Mathematical improbability or not, we all got into the bathtub. I carried my bag. Mom had no luggage. But, I suppose, she already had everything she needed over there. You know, for her secret trysts and all. His Royal Highness, King Tub, pulled the shower curtain closed. It was rather tight. I had to hug the duffle bag to my chest.

Trying not to focus on the fact I was in the tub (fully clothed!) with my parents, I asked, "I don't want to sound critical or anything, but, um, how exactly do we get there? Do we just stand here and say, 'Open, thou door to Smythe,' or what?"

King Tub chuckled. "No. All we really need are our keys. Do you have yours, Lil?"

"What?" Generally, I prefer more exact questions. Questions full of exactness tend to result in answers full of equal proportions of exactness. But, in this case, surprise won over exactness. (surprise > exactness)

"Your key, Lily. Did you bring your key? Your mother and I have ours, but you'll have to use yours to get in. Everyone has to have their own key."

Rationally, I responded: "I don't have a key. I have a key to the house, and one to the—"

"Not a key like a *key*," Mom interrupted. "This key is the only key that will get you into Smythe's SFL."

"What?" I asked again. "What do you mean, 'not a key like a *key*'? That doesn't make any sense."

King Tub bumped his leg on the ceramic soap dish. Rubbing his knee, he elaborated, "For instance, Lily, my key is a paperweight made in the shape of a golden egg from the goose that lays the golden eggs." He pulled a miniature egg out of his pocket.

"Yes, and mine is the golf tee from the first time your father and I went golfing at Poseidon's Under Sea Adventures putt-putt course." And the golf tee was on display for me to see.

"So what's yours?" King Tub asked.

I just looked at him. "What?"

Both of my parents sighed, looking exasperated. Speaking slower than was probably necessary, King Tub said, "You've got to choose something to be your key. Once you choose it and use it with the intent to get you to Smythe's SFL, it will forever be your key."

"So I just pick something?"

"Yes." Mom inched a little closer to me to get out of the drip from the showerhead. "It should probably be something small, so it can fit into your pocket easily."

9

IS EVERYBODY HAPPY?

The next afternoon I sat in my wonderfully squishy chair reading more about Newton. It's amazing to me that the man who wrote the laws of motion and split the color spectrum was an absent-minded professor. I envision him being like my mother–distracted in all areas except the ones that really matter.

Distraction was on my mind as I read. Specifically, I was trying to create an equation that could make me forget about last night's tango with Levi. But it was like trying to find the beginning of a circle or the end of *pi*.[31] Trying to forget him was actually *not* forgetting him.

---

[31] *Pi* is a Greek letter. It looks like this: π. It is used in math to represent

97

Also, I was working very hard to justify not telling my royal parents about Levi's second greasy visit. My reasons for not telling them were simple. (1) They would freak out. (2) Mom would freak out and do something unmathematical like forbid me from going on balconies. (3) I think my father would freak out and kill Levi. (Assuming, of course, Levi didn't pull one of his disappearing tricks.) I would like to do my part to keep my father from committing homicide–no matter how justifiable. (4) I'm not sure about this, but I have a feeling that I shouldn't tell. Feelings are not definable, mathematical things. Ordinarily, I would not trust them. But…I don't know. This one's different. (5) If I tell my parents that Levi showed up on the balcony, I'm sure the story would get back to horrible "highly-classified" Calo, who doesn't like me.

---

the ratio of a circle's circumference to its diameter. (Circumference = the distance around the edge of the circle; Diameter = a straight line segment that passes through the center of the circle.) There is no end to *pi*. It is an irrational number and can't be expressed as a common fraction. When you write it as a decimal, the numbers never end, and there's never a clear pattern to them. It approximately equals 3.14159, but the first 100 digits are

3.1415926535897932384626433832795028841971693993751058209749445923078164062862089986280348253421170679 …. Also, some people (cool math people) celebrate *Pi* day on March 14th. March 14[th] =3/14, which is the beginning of *pi*, 3.14. And by celebrate, I mean make math jokes and eat pie with a π on it.

This would just be further proof that I'm a *liability* and a security risk. I don't want him to think he's right.[32]

Mom came in through the open door and flopped on my bed. "So, what do you think about E. G. Smythe's Salty Fire Land?" She said the name importantly.

"What do you mean?" I asked, being cautious. I didn't want to say anything to hurt my mom's feelings. It is a mathematical fact that mothers can have their feelings hurt very easily and very unintentionally.

"What do you think about it? Do you like it? Do you hate it? Do you love it? Are you glad you came? Is it wonderful? Is it everything you thought it would be?"

When she stopped for breath, I managed to say, "It's certainly *not* what I thought it would be. And I...do like it. Yes. I'm glad I came." And strangely, I wasn't lying. I did like it, a *little*. "I mean, I'm not saying I want to move here permanently, and it's still *completely* odd and weird, but I did have a good time. And that third little pig is practically a mathematician. He told me all about the calculations he made to build the brick house. And he has an income curve set up for his brothers so that their rent is based on a percentage of what they earn and not—"

"No math!" Mom buried her head in a pillow. "No more math." She sat up, took a deep breath, and said, in a more supportive tone, "I mean, Lil, I'm so glad you found someone here who enjoys math as much as you do."

---

[32] And, unmathematically, this reason is the most compelling of the five to me.

"Well, it was a key factor in my liking it here. Certainly one of the terms in the equation of—"

Mom groaned and threw the pillow at me. Unfortunately, she has terrible aim and hit Beryl in the head as she walked into the room.

Once Beryl had recovered from the shock of the Queen of E. G. Smythe's Salty Fire Land throwing a pillow at her, she announced, while replacing her beret, "Everything is ready for your return trip, Your Majesty."

"Thank you, Beryl," Mom giggled.

The return trip was = to the trip coming to Smythe's SFL minus thinking "E. G. Smythe's Salty Fire Land" + thinking my address (2317 Marshall Road) + flipping down a fold up water spigot in the wall next to our family portrait (so we had something to put our keys into).

When we came downstairs, Mom went immediately to her office to write, King Tub spread security briefs all over the dining room table, and after standing there alone for a few seconds, I went back upstairs to finish my homework.

That's approximately normal. Parents working; children doing homework. Except, of course, one parent is working on controlling fictional characters, and the other is reading about the security of his kingdom of fictional characters. But, other than *that*, it was a normal night for the Sparrow family.

After I finished my homework, I lay on my bed and began sorting data from the weekend. I hadn't been lying to Mom when I said that I liked Smythe's SFL. Could I like it even though I was mad at my parents? Could I like it and still be mad at them?

That was tricky. If I accepted that this magical world existed, then I had to accept that their laws were valid as well. That meant that Mom and Dad would have felt they had no choice but to set up the elaborate lie of his death.

I could accept that, but I was still a little mad about it. And unless I was planning to use a serious teen rebellion equation, I was going to have to cooperate on some level. I'm not really the rebellious type. (Math is a lot about following rules.) And I like my mom to be happy. If I want that answer, then my equation looks like this:

1 Lily, going to after-school job and Smythe's SFL on weekends + a moderately good attitude + general cooperation = a happy mom

I don't know what will make King Tub happy yet. Or even if I want to make him happy.

~~~

The next morning, as I left for school, King Tub stopped me. "Lily, I'm sure I don't have to tell you this, but, uh, it would be unwise to mention the kingdom to your friends."

I looked at him. Did he really think I was just dying to tell my friends all about my dance with Snow White's prince? Did he really think I wanted everyone to know that I had traded stories about uncomfortable beds with Sleeping Beauty? Instead of saying any of the four sarcastic replies that immediately came to my mind, I engaged my polite equation and said, "Okay. I won't tell anyone."

"Thanks Lily. Have a great day, and don't forget to portal over when you get home. Grimm is expecting you at his office at 3:30."

I groaned silently as I walked away. The after school job. I was looking forward to that about as much as my mother looks forward to doing geometry proofs.

I spent the walk to school thinking of primarily two things.

(1) Determining the probability of seeing Calo at work. I settled on 45%. He does work there, so I had to include a higher factor because of that, but I was able to take away most of that because he thinks I'm a security risk.

(2) Analyzing and sorting through the data of the weekend to combine facts so that I can *truthfully* tell Corrie what I did over the weekend.

Corrie arrived at 7:40, like she does every morning. There were twenty-two students waiting when she arrived. I had estimated twenty-four. Not bad.

"Did you have a good weekend?" I asked, as she dropped her book bag on the ground.

"Mostly," she sighed. "My dad made a schedule for bathroom time in the mornings." Corrie rolled her eyes. "We've got to get another bathroom."

"That would certainly balance the equation."

"How was your weekend, Lil? I bet *you* didn't have to spend it discussing with *your* mom whether or not you can brush your teeth *and* brush your hair at the same time. Because if you *could* do those two things at the same time, it would take off at least three minutes of your bathroom time." Corrie made a face.

"I had a good weekend." I chose my words carefully. "I spent some time reading that book on

Newton you gave me, and I met some of my mom's friends." There. All 100% truth.

"You are so normal." Corrie shook her head. "That is such a *normal* weekend. I spent forty-five minutes on Saturday watching my dad give a demonstration on the most efficient way to brush your teeth and still be cavity free."

I smiled sympathetically. And while I fully support Corrie in feeling that her family is not exactly normal, when did *mine* become normal? I think Corrie's time-managing father is closer to the mean of normal than my king-of-fairyland, used-to-be-dead, "Happy Birthday, Lily!" father.[33]

~~~

When I opened our front door after school, Peridiom was sliding down the banister. The dwarf dressed in purple (whose name, I discovered over the weekend, is Blaire) was standing at the top of the stairs, looking annoyed.

"Hey, Princess!" Peridiom smiled as he flew off the banister.

"Hey, Peridiom." I started upstairs. I wanted to change clothes before I portaled over for my first job.

"I apologize for Peridiom, Your Highness." Blaire blushed and curtsied as I passed.

"It's all right, Blaire," I answered, closing the door to my room. Apparently, I should be expecting the two of them every day after school.

---

[33] Mean is a math term that basically means (Ha! Punny!) "average."

I changed my clothes, grabbed the blue marble/key off my dresser, and headed for the tub.

My arrival in Arrivhall was quite different this time. No cheering populace awaited; only Macon Mind greeted me.

"Ahh, Your Highness. Right on time." He started walking away from the portal point, and I followed. "Their Majesties are occupied at present. Rumpelstiltskin got angry with the Farmer in the Dell this morning and stamped his foot. You can just imagine what happened. We've been dealing with that crisis all day."

"What happened?"

Macon stopped, confused. "Well–he–you really don't know?"

"Haven't got a clue, Macon."

"Right." Macon continued walking. "In that case, Your Highness, allow me to explain. When Rumpelstiltskin gets angry, he stamps his foot. When he stamps his foot, a huge crack in the earth opens up. So, when he stamped his foot this morning, he managed to have most of the Dell swallowed into the depths of the earth. Paul Bunyan and Hercules have been working all morning to dig the villagers out."

"Was anyone hurt or…"

"Killed?" Macon finished for me. "No, that's not possible. Only the people who survive their tales live Happily Ever After, so no one can die or be killed. The only thing they have to worry about is vanishing, which is what you're here to prevent." We had arrived at the main gate. "Alright Princess, some instructions about leaving the castle. As your key is needed to return you to your world, you must deposit it here at the door. We don't want them lost out in the woods." He pointed to a bowl on a small table. I dropped my marble in and we went outside. "Also, here is your bike." Macon pulled a blue bicycle from the rack in front of the castle.

"I have my own bike?"

Macon sighed. "We used to give horses out to everyone, but the talking ones made such a fuss about it. They got the enchanted horses to hoof a petition, then they unionized." Macon rolled his eyes. "And, of course, there is the whole mess about enchanted people. It's almost impossible to tell which is a real horse and which is a prince turned into a horse by Morgan Le Faye. So, what with all that, we just give out bikes now."

"That makes sense," I nodded to cover my confusion about talking horses and people being turned into horses.

"Do you know where you're going?"

"Nope."

"It isn't far. Just in the First Wood, but all the same, we don't what you to get lost." Macon reached into his back pocket and produced a wand.

"You have a magic wand?"

Macon looked confused by the question. "I'm in command of the entire castle, Your Highness. Of course I have a magic wand."

"Of course," I muttered.

He tapped the handlebars and bowed to me. "The bike is on auto-pilot and will take you to the office, Your Highness. But, please, do try to pay attention and learn the way. The bike will start to think for itself if we auto-pilot it too much."

"I'll remember." I decided to just ignore the bike thinking for itself bit. "Goodbye, Macon."

"Goodbye, Princess." Macon bowed again.

I got on the bike and pushed off. The bike immediately started pedaling on its own and I struggled to keep my balance and get my feet on the pedals. But like my dancing shoes, once I got the hang of it, it was as simple as basic arithmetic.

Exactly four and a half minutes later, I arrived at a tall, brick building. A large, flashing sign proclaimed it to be "The Office of Happily Ever After Affairs–Home of the Happiest Happiologists Around."

"What in the world is a Happiologist?" I muttered to myself, getting off the bike.

"You are, Princess Lily!" Grimm walked towards me. "And you're right on time. I haven't been waiting long. Wel—" Grimm stopped and looked from me to my bike, which, at that moment, moved of its own accord from my hands to the bike rack. Grimm raised an eyebrow. "Auto-pilot?"

"Macon set it up so I wouldn't get lost."

"Not a bad idea and easily fixed." Grimm tapped the bike with his own magic wand. "As I was saying, Princess, Welcome to the Office of Happily Ever After Affairs, but we all just call it HEA for short."[34] He spread his arms wide and looked around.

I looked around, too.

"We're very glad to have you. Training the new Protectors has always been a privilege, and I've no doubt your education will be a treat as well." He put his arm around me and guided me into the building. "Come in, come in. I'll give you the tour."

I was struck by the busy-ness of everything. People were rushing around, dropping off files, and

---

[34] HEA is pronounced [hee-ah].

furiously making notes at a wall covered with shelves full of different colored hourglasses.

"This is it, Your Highness." Grimm gestured grandly around the building. "In this one building, we monitor, record, observe, and analyze the Happiness levels of the entire kingdom. We make sure everyone stays Happy and if they don't, we make them Happy again. Watch this." Grimm turned toward a busy sector of the room and shouted, "IS EVERYBODY HAPPY?"

The entire room of busy people stopped what they were doing and shouted back: "H-A-P-P-Y!!" Then, just as bizarrely, they returned to what they were doing.

Grimm grinned mischievously. "I just love doing that. I think it reminds everyone of what we're here for. It renews perspective, and it's a great morale booster."

When I had sufficiently recovered from the office full of shouting people, I asked, "Why does everyone have to be happy?"

This is a logical question. Why *should* you always have to be happy? The pure mathematical facts are that there will be times in your life when you are not happy.

Grimm smiled at the question and motioned for me to follow him. We snaked through a series of cubicles. "I've often wondered that myself. But the fact is, Princess, these citizens only get to our kingdom because they are going to live Happily Ever After. When they stop being Happy, they run the risk of vanishing. If they don't stay Happy, if we don't maintain their Happy levels, they vanish, and if they stay vanished long enough, their tales cease to exist. Have you ever heard of *The Candlemaker's Daughter?*"

"No."

"Exactly. Many years ago, when my great-great-grandfather was running HEA, Celdan got so unhappy that she vanished. Several attempts were made to rescue her from Uppish Senna, but they were unsuccessful. She and her tale are gone forever."

"Two Questions: Your great-great-grandfather? And Uppish Senna? The kingdom in the South?"

"Yes, my great-great-grandfather. My name is Andersen Grimm. It combines the names of both the Brothers Grimm and Hans Christian Andersen. The Grimm Brothers were particularly skilled at collecting fairy tales; Andersen was a master at writing his own. I happen to be a descendent of *both* lines. Years and years ago, your great-great-great-grandfather tracked down one of my ancestors and recruited him for this job. We've been here ever since. Because of our ancestry, we have an important interest in keeping the tales alive, so we make great Happiologists."

So Grimm is distantly related to these fairy tale creator people. And that relationship results in a greater probability that he will successfully convince the characters of his ancestors to remain Happy.

We arrived at Grimm's office. "Sit, sit." He gestured at a chair. "To answer your second question: Uppish Senna is a kingdom in the corner of the Wildwood, although it isn't large, it's really just a fortress." He smiled at my look of confusion. "Let me begin at the beginning. Many, many years ago a writer named Louisa Austen wrote a fairy tale. Her main character was a sad, little man, and the tale was quite unpopular with her family and friends. She never published that story, but several years later, she revised it, cutting out the sad, little man and replacing him with a much happier character who has adventures, wins the princess and saves the kingdom.

"*But*, she didn't destroy that first draft completely. That sad, little man still existed and eventually he made his way here, to Smythe's SFL. He was the first first-draft character to ever do so. Most of our citizens came from oral tradition. His name was Tandem Tallis. The same Tandem Tallis whose gift to you caused all that trouble at your presentation.

"He was very difficult to live with. Jealousy burned in him against not only the character that had replaced him, but all true citizens." Grimm sighed and looked distant. "This was long before my family had come to live here. But something had to be done. This sad, little man was destroying the kingdom with his pettiness and jealousy, so he was banished to a corner of the Wildwood, where he still lives today."

"All alone?"

Grimm shook his head. "No. He has managed to attract other discontented people and even some other rogue first-drafters. And many years ago, tired of feeling second-best, they rebelled against our kingdom and formed their own country. It's a sad story; the people of Uppish Senna think they are Happy, but when they encounter the true Happiness here, they vanish back to their home. That's likely why Levi vanished after you opened your present. He was probably genuinely giddy with the thought of the anguish you would experience as a result of his gift, so he vanished."

"But our citizens vanish also?"

"Yes. It's one of Tallis' better assaults on our country. He has managed to gain control of all Unhappiness. If a person is Unhappy, they belong to him. So, if a citizen starts to become Unhappy, they are in danger of vanishing–being sucked right into the dungeons of Uppish Senna."

"But they can come back, can't they?"

"It's difficult. Very difficult. They have to become Happy enough that the power of Tallis' magic loses its hold on them. That's hard to do in a dank, dark dungeon, especially if they wound up there in the first place because they were Unhappy. It's simpler and far easier to maintain a Happy level here. And that is what you are going to be doing."

The door burst open. Calo stood scowling in the doorway. His curly brown hair fell across his forehead in a nice way.[35]

"Ah. Calo. You got my memo, I see?" Grimm motioned to him.

Calo walked swiftly into the room but didn't sit down. "Are you sure this is a good idea?"

Grimm sighed. "Princess Lily, Calo is here because I think it would be an *excellent* idea for the two of you to be partners."

Calo shook his head slightly.

Grimm ignored him and continued, "Calo is an exceptional Happiologist, Princess, and since you are the Future Protector, I want you trained by the best. Now, Calo, show the Princess to the cubicle you'll share, and get started. Go make some people Happy." Grimm beamed at us as we left.

My mind rapidly formulated equations as I followed Calo through a maze of cubicles. 45% chance of seeing Calo? Now, it was 100% *every* day. I redid my math from the earlier Calo equation. Conclusion: the math was right—the equation was wrong. I forgot a

---

[35] Wait. Why am I noticing that?

factor: that illogical, unmathematical magic of Smythe's SFL. It's out to get me.

When we finally arrived at our cubicle, I could see Grimm's office just off to the side. Calo had obviously taken a longer, more difficult route–probably for the purpose of confusing me. My probability of being happy at this job was declining rapidly, while my probability of being *annoyed* was increasing with each passing second.

"Okay. This is our cubicle. This is our in-box. Here we receive new cases. As you can see we already have one for today. These reports here are from the Observers. They give us updates on our client's levels every hour, on the hour. The binders on the bookshelf are organized by fairy godmother and the citizens under her care. They are color coded to match the godmother's particular color of sparks. Davin's is blue. Maggie's is green. Dori's is red. Glenni's is plaid. Pencil sharpener." He pointed to it. "Extra pencils are on the desk and the reference tales are in the Archive office. Any questions?"

I stared at him. He had delivered his entire speech quickly, in a monotone, and extremely mumbly. Oh yeah. It's going to be fun working with Calo.

I sighed and decided to ask a courtesy question. "So when I get here after school, I check the in-box and deal with the case?"

"Negative." Calo sat down in the swivel chair.

Who says negative?

He pulled himself up to his desk. "When you come in after school, you check with *me*, and do what I tell you to do."

"So, then the word *partner* has a different meaning in this world?"

Calo glared at me. "We are not partners. I'm just training you." He stood up. "Look. I'm very good at what I do, and I have an extremely successful record here. I don't need *or* want your help. And I'm sure *Your Highness* doesn't want to be working with a common miller's son."

"Believe me—who your father is has nothing to do with why I don't want to work with you!"

"Great." He smirked. "We can bond over our dislike of each other." He sighed and ran a hand through his curly hair. "Let's just work together for Grimm's sake until we can get out of this."

"Fine."

Calo took the file out of the in-box and sighed. "Arthur and Morgan Le Faye. I was hoping we'd get something easy for your first day, like the Gingerbread Boy." He punched the intercom button on the phone. "Hannah, couldn't you have given us something else for today? I've got the Princess now."

"Sorry, Calo." Hannah answered back. "Arthur will only see you."

Calo sighed again. "Fine. Have Holly pull the CD he likes from Audio."

"You got it, Calo. Good luck with Morgan."

"Thanks. We'll need it." Calo swiveled in his chair so he could face me. "Okay, Your Highness—"

"You can call me 'Lily.'"

He flashed an annoying smile. "Lily, take a seat over there, and let me run through what we're about to do."

I sat.

"Morgan Le Faye is getting close to vanishing. When she gets like this, she enjoys sending dangerous presents to her brother, King Arthur. This throws Arthur into a mood, and then we've got a potential double vanishing. Arthur is usually pretty easy. Play him some disco music, and he's content. Morgan will be a little trickier."

Someone (I assumed Holly) came in and placed a CD on the desk.

"Doesn't Morgan Le Faye turn people into horses?" Isn't that what Macon told me? The one fact I know about either of these people relates to the creation of enchanted horses. Promising.

"Not often." Calo picked up the CD and started weaving his way through the cubicles to the front door. After we got on our bikes, he said, "Just to be on the safe side, though, don't say anything stupid to Morgan." He paused, then added, "Better yet, don't say anything at all."

Great. Mathematically speaking: which is worse, being afraid of turning into a horse, or realizing that you actually believe it is *possible* to be turned into a horse?

The ride took seven and three-fourths minutes. Calo spent that entire time sighing and saying, "Oh. My. Goodness," every time I asked questions like: "So, King Arthur is the guy who married Cinderella?", "But I thought Merlin spun straw into gold for the shoemaker and his wife?", or "But if nobody else could pull the sword out of the stone, how could he do it, if he was much smaller? That doesn't make any kind of mathematical sense."

When we arrived at Morgan's castle, Calo said, "For pity's sake, do not let Morgan Le Faye know how little you know about her story. Just be quiet and don't say or do anything."

A little, hunched-back man with a pointed beard and squinty eyes opened the door. "Calo. Lady Morgan has been expecting you. And I see you've brought our new princess along."

"Yes, Kobold. Princess Lily is here to observe—only."

We followed Kobold into Morgan's parlor. She was sitting in an armchair on a raised platform, sighing deeply. Her long red hair trailed along the floor around her. Calo bowed, then stepped on my foot to remind me to curtsey.

Morgan looked at us. "I am sad." She sighed. "Calo, I feel that I *will* vanish this time. I feel...so cold and alone." Another sigh.

"My lady," Calo took a few steps toward her. "Think of what would happen if you did vanish. You would be gone from the legends. Arthur would rule unchallenged. The once and future king—forever."

"I have thought of that." She sighed again. (She's big on sighing.) "It isn't enough this time, Calo. Let Arthur have England."

"But, my lady—" Calo began again.

"Why are you sad?" I interrupted.

"What?" Calo and Morgan both said together. Calo looked at me, severely annoyed, his blue eyes flashing.

He turned back to Morgan. "My lady, Princess Lily, is here to observe and learn. Please ignore her outburst. She knows—"

Morgan interrupted Calo. "What did you ask, young lady?"

I took two steps forward. "I merely wondered, my lady, what it is you are sad about?"

"You could not possibly understand." Morgan lifted her head, proudly.

"Perhaps not." Two more steps. "But I do understand you could vanish, ruining your life and your

114

story. What could matter so much that you would risk vanishing?"

Morgan breathed in deeply. "If you must know," there was an edge to her voice, "my cook has had to return to her village for a few days to take care of her ailing mother."

"She's coming back, though?"

"Not until Thursday. My soup is all wrong."

"You're willing to vanish over soup?"

Morgan leaned forward, narrowed her eyes, and said, "How would you like to vanish?"

And, then, I did.

10

THE MIRROR AND THE MAIL

I found myself in my own room, back in the real world. I sat on my bed for a moment trying to mathematically figure out how I could have vanished to here. The only way to get from Smythe's SFL to this world is through our bathtub, and to do that, you must have a key. But I couldn't have come *that* way because I left my key at the castle.

Oh no.

I left my key at the castle.

I can't get back into Smythe's SFL. So, I can't go back to work. Although, as I explored the results of being vanished back home, I found myself more and more content.[36]

If I can't get back in (and I can't), then I won't have to go back to work with horrible Calo, at least not right away. Morgan Le Faye may be an extremely scary woman, but she sure comes in handy. I'm just glad she didn't turn me into a horse.

Since I was no longer able to make other people happy, I decided to make *myself* happy by doing some algebra homework. I had just finished the next to last problem,

$$x = 3x+3(x-5), \text{ solution: } x = 3^{37}$$

when Blaire came into my room with a stack of my laundry. (I noticed the jeans (2x) from the weekend. Clean jeans have no dirty-ness value (0x).) She looked like she had been crying and froze when she saw me.

"You're here." Her eyes were wide. "You're not languishing in a Sennish prison."

"What?" I asked, but Blaire dropped the stack of clothes and ran out of the room.

---

[36] Exploration of vanishing results = rising level of happiness.

[37] $x = 3x + 3(x - 5)$
$x = 3x + 3x - 15$
$x = 6x - 15$
$x + 15 = 6x$
$15 = 6x - x$
$15 = 5x$
$3 = x$

"Blaire!" I hopped over the clean clothes as I followed her to the bathroom.

She scrambled her little self onto the sink so that she could look into the mirror. Her purple beret was slightly askew. "Blai—" I started again, but was interrupted by her talking to the mirror.

"Mirror, Mirror on the wall, connect me, please. Place my call."

I took a step back, as a sleepy, elderly lady with her hair in a bun and a pencil behind her ear appeared in our bathroom mirror. She glanced up at Blaire. "What number, dearie?"

"Put me through to Macon Mind, please."

"One moment." Mirror Lady seemed to be pushing buttons, but I couldn't exactly see what her hands were doing.

So, apparently, our bathroom mirror is not *just* a medicine cabinet. It's also a communication device. Corrie should hope her dad never finds out. Imagine: brushing your teeth, brushing your hair, *and* placing calls–all at the same time.

"I'm sorry, dear." Mirror Lady looked at Blaire again. "All of Mr. Mind's calls are being held. He's involved in a crisis situation right now at the castle." She leaned forward and whispered. "They're saying that hoity-toity Morgan Le Faye went and vanished the Princess. The lines have been buzzing about it for an hour now."

"But that's why I've got to talk to Macon!" Blaire tried to gesture with both her hands, which led to her nearly falling off the sink. She caught herself and went on. "I know where the Princess is, Marie, so get Macon on the phone, now!" Her hands waved again, wildly.

I rushed forward to catch Blaire.

Marie gasped and said, "Good gracious! It's the Princess." She started pushing buttons again.

"I told you that's why I've got to talk to Macon!" Blaire nearly shouted. I moved my hand to rest on her back–preemptive spotting.

Marie, however, seemed to be ignoring Blaire. She turned around in her swivel chair.

"Frank!" She shouted. "We've got to get Macon Mind on the phone to Marshall Road."

An elderly man rolled into view, his chair bumping into Marie's.

"I told you, Marie," he said, grabbing the pencil from behind Marie's ear. "All of Macon's calls are being held, until such time as the crisis is called off." He tossed the pencil smugly like he had nothing better to do. He was a vision of what horrible Calo will be like when he is nearing retirement.

"Look." Marie caught her pencil and turned Frank's head towards us.

"Well, I'll be," Frank whistled. "Give me just a second." He rolled away.

Blaire looked at me. "They're Frank and Marie," she said, pointing to the mirror. "They run the switchboard for the kingdom."

"Really?" I said. I would have never guessed. And I never would have guessed that my bathroom mirror is a communication device that links my house to the hidden fairy tale kingdom. I'm just glad I haven't recited couplets beginning with "Mirror, mirror" while in front of it.

"I'm sure your parents will be glad to know you are safe," Blaire said, while wiping water spots off the mirror with her sleeve.

"Yeah."

I hadn't really thought about that. I assumed Morgan would tell them where I had gone. I further assumed they would realize I didn't have my key and couldn't come back. And, clearly, since I didn't know about the mirror, I couldn't communicate either.

But, therein lies the problem with thinking logically about Smythe's SFL. The moment you factor in an element from that world, the equation loses all sense of normal mathness. It is evident that you cannot say

what Morgan will do = x.

There will always be more variables that need to be considered. And to consider them fully—

"Patching a mirror to mirror call." Marie interrupted my thoughts. "Mr. Mind, are you on?"

"Yes, Marie," Macon's voice answered.

"Fine. Blaire, are you on?"

"Yes," Blaire chirped.

"And…" Marie pushed a few more buttons. "Patching complete."

Macon and his office appeared on the mirror.

"Your Highness?" Macon asked. "Are you alright? Are you hurt in any way?"

"No, Macon. I'm fine. I—" I was about to explain why I couldn't come back to the kingdom, when my mom suddenly appeared beside Macon in the mirror. She looked upset and her hair was falling out of its clip.

"Lily? Are you okay, sweetie? Why didn't you come back here after Morgan vanished you? We were so worried." She started crying.

"I couldn't, Mom. I didn't have my key. You know, you have to put them in the bowl when you leave the castle and—"

"Of course!" Mom interrupted me. "I'll be right there. Don't go anywhere." She ran off, presumably to Arrivhall.

Macon re-centered himself in the mirror. "We're all very glad you're safe and sound, Princess. I'll make sure your key is sent home with your father, and I'll alert HEA. They'll need to know you're fine so they can stop planning to rescue you from the Sennish dungeons. Your mother will be there any moment now, so if there is nothing else you need, Your Highness—" He paused, waiting for me to give him permission to hang up his mirror.

"No. Thank you, Macon. I'm fine."

"Excellent. I'll see you tomorrow, Princess." Then he added, "Mirror, Mirror, on the wall, thank you, thank you. That is all." The mirror went blank, or rather, returned to the business of *just* reflecting.

"So that's how you hang up?" I asked Blaire.

She nodded. "I'm glad you're safe, Your Highness." She hopped off the sink and left the bathroom, skipping. I turned to examine our mirrorphone more closely, but just then, Mom pushed back the shower curtain.

"Oh, Lily." She pulled me into a teary hug. "Were you scared? Was it awful? Oh, I always knew nothing good would come from giving that awful woman asylum. I wish there was a way to protect the stories and characters without protecting the villains that go with them." During this speech, she was hug-walking me back to my room, where we collapsed on my bed. "Tell me all about it."

So I told her about the visit to Morgan and how I had been shocked that Morgan would be willing to vanish over something unmathematical, like soup. ("Oh, but Lily, you've got to forget logic and math once you portal…") I told her about feeling stupid with Calo, because I didn't know the entire history of every fairy tale. ("Well, you'll learn…") And I told her about being relieved to find myself back at home ("Better than in a dungeon!") and about nearly finishing my algebra homework. ("Of course. Comfort math.")

"Well," she said, as I finished my story. "One good thing has come out of this: Morgan's happiness levels went through the roof. It was a complete turnaround."

"That makes sense. The next time her cook leaves, we'll just send her someone to vanish."

Mom laughed at my sarcasm.

"I suppose," I went on, "Calo ought to give me some credit. I did manage to increase a happiness rating my first day on the job."

Mom laughed again. "But Lily," she turned serious, "You may not know all the stories, you may not understand exactly what Smythe's SFL is all about, and you may be terrible at staying on Morgan Le Faye's good side, but," she smiled, "you *will* be good at being the Protector. It is in your blood. You were born to do this. Don't let today discourage you." She smoothed my hair. "So! I'm going to make your favorite cinnamon toast for supper. And you're going to do that last algebra problem I know your fingers have been itching to do."

"Algebra and cinnamon toast. And it's not even Christmas."

She smiled and stood up, kissing the top of my head. On her way out, she stopped at the door, turned, and said, "I'm really glad you're safe, Lily."

~~~

King Tub joined us for the cinnamon toast, which we ate in my room. I sat on the bed, with my parents on the floor leaning against my dresser. The whole story of my exciting afternoon had to be repeated for my father. He reacted differently than my mother.

He laughed.

Mom was not amused. "Why are you laughing, Matt? Our daughter could have been vanished away to a Sennish dungeon, and you are laughing. Why is that funny?"

"It's not *that* that's funny, Ginnie."

Actually, *he* looked funny as he gestured with his toast, spilling cinnamon and sugar on his lap.

"I just find it amusing that Lily actually stood up to Morgan." At Mom's shocked look, he continued, "Here we've got our best Happiologists catering to her every time her cook leaves or her hair gets tangled, and Lily, instead of staying quiet, says what everyone else is thinking. The look on Morgan's face must have been priceless. 'You're willing to vanish over soup?'" He chuckled, choked on some toast, and started coughing.

Mom whacked him on the back. "I don't see the humor in that."

"Well," my father managed, still coughing. "Unlike us, you've never been a Happiologist, and so you've never had the pleasure of working Morgan's case. Therefore," (more toast waving) "you've never wanted to say *exactly* what you think of her. It's a simple equation." He pointed to me. "Lily could delineate it for you, I'm sure."

Mom just shook her head at him.

THE CINDERELLA THEOREM

But I was struck by something other than the math in what he had said. "You were a Happiologist? Really?"

"Well, yes. That's what being the Protector is. Just once you get the throne, you tend to delegate more. Don't take as many cases–that sort of thing." He shrugged. "That's why we've got the HEA liaison office at the castle. Keeps me informed."

"So you've had Morgan's case before? Did you ever make her mad?"

"She was going to turn me into a horse."

"How did you avoid that?" I shifted my position on the bed, so I was closer to him.

"Well, Andersen Grimm was my partner, and he—"

"*Grimm* was your partner?"

"Yeah, but he went by Andy in those days. Anyway, Morgan was upset because she hadn't been invited to some banquet her brother was throwing–you know how Morgan and Arthur are."

Mom nodded and rolled her eyes.

He continued, "So I was trying to cheer her up by telling some jokes. Word to the wise, Lily: avoid knock-knock jokes with Morgan. They do not lead to the desired result. I should have seen it coming, though. Her face turned increasingly red with each joke. And Grimm was looking nervous, too. So, I, being the young and inexperienced Happiologist that I was, kept right on telling the knock-knock jokes. Knock-knock,"

"Who's there?" I answered.

"Horseshoe."

"Horseshoe who?"

"Horseshoe don't know who it is. Open Up!"

I groaned. "That's a terrible knock-knock joke." I felt the tension of the past few days lift some. It felt okay to be together—the three of us.

"Why, thank you." My father smiled. "Morgan didn't like it either. In fact, she looked angrier than she did before, if that was possible. Then her eyes got all narrow and dangerous, and she said," he put on his best Morgan voice. "'How would you like to be the horse to go with that horseshoe?'"

"Really?" I asked. Morgan is just not a friendly gal when she's unhappy. "Then what happened?"

"Well, Grimm pushed me down, sat on me, and pleaded with Morgan to not turn his partner into a horse. I think he cited lack of funds to buy feed as a reason."

"He sat on you?"

"Uh...yeah. He was trying to appeal to the part of her that enjoys pain and suffering. See, I was suffering by being sat upon, and Grimm was suffering because he was begging. It seemed to work. Morgan went up four levels of happiness."

"That is," I paused, "simultaneously, the most *and* the least mathematical thing I've experienced in Smythe."

"What do you mean?" Mom asked. "And please," she added, "explain it in such a way that I don't regret asking you a math related question."

I smiled. Mom hates math. "I just mean that an outside observer, like me, sees that

"Grimm pushing Dad = x.

"And the outsider can see that

"Morgan being happy = z.

"But the equation is

"$x + y = z$.

"The outsider can't fully solve because, he or she doesn't know y. It takes the insider's knowledge to give you that y. You had to have Grimm there to make the equation work, otherwise Dad would be eating oats and carrots instead of cinnamon toast."

Dad laughed.

"Let me check this problem with you in plain English." Mom began gathering our plates. "It's unmathematical to you because you can't see the y, right?"

"Right." I handed her my milk cup.

"But at the same time, it's also very mathematical to you because Grimm *can* see the y and so complete the equation?"

"Exactly."

Mom just shook her head, while she stood up. "Your dizzying math has made me tired. I'm going to do these dishes and go to bed."

Dad stood up too, cocking his ear. "Hey, Ginnie. I think I hear the mail. Will you check and see if it's here?"

Listening carefully, I could hear a whizzing/thumping sound coming from the bathroom. Mom put the plates and cups on my dresser, and went into the hallway.

"Yeah, you're right, Matt. Wow. We have a lot tonight."

"I didn't know the postal service delivered at night," I said.

Dad grinned. "The Smythian one does."

"To the bathroom?" I asked.

He nodded.

Why am I not surprised?

"It's delivered to the cabinet under the sink. It used to only come to the castle, you know, so you wouldn't suspect, but now that you know our little secret, I've had it sent here again."

Mom came in. "It looks like mostly security briefs for you, Matt, but Lily, you got several cards and letters. Probably well-wishers from this afternoon." Mom tossed some envelopes to me, handed my dad his mail, and gathered (for the second time) the dishes. "Sleep tight, Lily," she called over her shoulder.

Dad started out the door. "Don't worry about Morgan. Pull her case file and check out what happened to Calo on *his* first visit to her." He winked. "Good night, Lily."

"Night, Dad."

I stared after him, smiling slightly. I hope she turned Calo into a horse.

As I looked at the letters, I heard a mental echo of what I had just said.

Night, Dad.

Since when did I start calling my father "Dad"? I mean, he is my father, so

> if he = father
> and father = dad,
> then he = dad, as well.

But I don't think I can call him that. I've only known the man for four days and a birthday dinner.

> If c = calling my father "dad,"
> and a = my physical ability to say the word "dad,"

then I suppose m would = my mental ability to say it or to allow myself to say it.

However m also = k + t.

k = my level of knowledge about/comfort around my father. (I mean, I hardly know him.)

And t = time.

Therefore, c = a + m; m = k + t.

How much time has to pass before I can call him "dad"?

More than four days and a dinner.

I sat on my bed and sighed. Never did I imagine that I would be using math to create an equation for figuring out when I could call my father "dad." I'd pictured using math in pure mathematics research in the field of differential topology, sure, but never in "Night, Dad."

I pushed all math, pure or father related, out of my mind and turned my attention to the letters. There were five in all: one large manila one, two parchment colored ones, a yellow one, and a black one. I looked at the manila envelope. It was from Calo. I groaned as I opened it. A file folder slid out with a note clipped to it. Calo had written just two sentences on it.

I told you not to say anything.
Read this before work tomorrow.

I really don't like that boy.

I tossed the file folder on the floor, and grabbed one of the parchment colored envelopes. There was a royal seal on the back: red wax with an A pressed into it. The letter was from King Arthur, apologizing for his sister and saying he knew how difficult she could be.

The other parchment envelope was from
Cinderella, wishing me the best and assuring me she was
thrilled I was safe. She closed by inviting me to tea at her
castle some afternoon.

The yellow letter was sealed with an orange
smiley face and written on yellow paper with orange ink.
I had to squint at the brightness to read it. It was from
Grimm, and it was very happy. Grimm was glad I made
it home and thought it wonderful that I had such a
unique experience on my first day. He and Calo are very
different people.

There was just the black envelope left. The
address was written in grey ink. The letter was written in
black ink on grey paper.

Lily,
I heard you managed to vanish today. Pity you didn't
make it to the Sennish dungeons. We keep one ready just for
you. Do visit us soon, my dear–

Levi

I glanced down at the floor. A lily petal and a
sparrow feather had fallen out of the envelope. I looked
at my hands. They were greasy.

11

CHOCOLATE CHIP COOKIES

After washing my hands to remove the grease and brushing my teeth to remove the nagging Levi issue from my mind, I changed into my pajamas and rescued Calo's file folder from the floor.

The first page in the file was a schedule of events for the rest of my workweek at HEA. It seemed to be designed to keep me safe. Tomorrow, I would be learning about the "Happiness Monitors" and their relevance to HEA. Wednesday would be devoted to reviewing case histories, Thursday to examining hypothetical situations, to give me practice in making people happy, and on Friday, I would get to assist Calo in another case. However, to my mathematical eye, I saw that Friday's plan was dependent on Tuesday plus

Wednesday plus Thursday equaling success. I sighed and looked at the second sheet of paper.

A diagram of a Happiness Monitor was drawn on the page. All the levels were marked and labeled on the hour glass design. In the bottom half of the hour glass (under "Happy" in the exact middle), the level "Could be Happier" was marked in bold, and "Unhappy" was bolded, underlined, and circled in red. Calo had written across the top of the paper: *Memorize these levels for tomorrow. You will need to be able to fill in a blank diagram.*

Leave it to Calo to give me a test at work.

The rest of the pages in the folder were a survey about Fairy Tales and other Smythian characters. The instructions at the top of the sheet were: "Please complete this survey. Your answers on this will in no way affect your employment at The Office of Happily Ever After Affairs. So, please, remain calm and do not panic as you take this test. The questions are designed to assist your superiors in creating a plan to help you learn more about the citizens of our world. Again, do not panic. And, for pity's sake, don't get unhappy about it either. We can't afford to have our Happiologists vanishing on us. Enjoy!" The survey was five pages long (front and back; $5(2) = 10$ pages).

I groaned, found a pen on the floor, and started working.

Some of the questions were easy. (How do fairy tales usually begin? How do they usually end? What color is Little Red Riding Hood's cape? (*That* answer is in the question!) Name any two magical objects found in fairy tales.) Some of the questions I knew because of the time I had already spent in Smythe's SFL. (Who is King Arthur's sister? Who are the two main "writers" of fairy tales? What happens when Rumpelstiltskin stamps his

foot? What "mythological" creature speaks in riddles?)
Some of the questions I just had to guess on, usually
using mathelogical reasoning. For "How many step-
sisters did Cinderella have?" I knew she would have to
have more than one, as "sisters" is plural. Since that left
me with every other possible number (except zero), I put
two. It is plural, prime, and has the additional joy of
being the only even prime number. For this question, in
the fill-in-the-blank section, "_____ _____ and the
Seven Dwarves", I put "Six Gnomes". It makes sense. I
can easily see dwarves and gnomes being friends and
having adventures together; plus, six and seven make
thirteen, which is also prime. Then, there were some
questions that I had no hope of answering. (Name ten
ancient Egyptian gods. (Uh…) Why should King Arthur
never remove his scabbard? (What is a scabbard?)
Compare Achilles and Roland. Explain how their tales
shaped heroism. (Who are they?))

By the time I finished the survey, I understood
the need for the "don't panic" warning at the top. It's
not a survey likely to boost your self-esteem. I'm just
glad I can't vanish (from unhappiness) yet. I devoted the
last ten minutes before I fell asleep to studying the stupid
monitor diagram.

~~~

The next afternoon, Peridiom met me at the door
with a Ziploc bag of pretzels. I thanked him, climbed the
stairs, changed my clothes, grabbed my marble and
Calo's file folder of "fun," and headed for Smythe's SFL.

When I arrived, Carey, the dwarf dressed in all
yellow met me in Arrivhall. He gave me a note from
Macon.

Princess,

Things are a little hectic here today. (There was an upset in the kitchens when the Gingerbread Man came running through—with his entire story chasing him.) I'm sure you can find your way to HEA. Grimm returned your bike last night. Have a nice afternoon.

Macon Mind

I said goodbye to Carey and headed out of the castle, remembering to drop my marble into the key-deposit bowl. I enjoyed my bike ride to HEA until I got there. Calo was waiting outside, scowling as usual.[38]

"Grimm sent me out here to make sure you made it." He opened the door impatiently.

"Well, I did," I muttered shortly, pushing past him into the office.

As we made our way through the cubicles, Calo asked, "Did you get the file I sent?"

I scowled internally. "Yeah. Thanks for sending it. It was great." My tone must have conveyed some of the internal scowl, because Calo resumed his *external* scowl and said, when we entered our cubicle, "Do you know how embarrassing it is to have your trainee disappear on her first day? And do you know how that embarrassment is further compounded when your trainee also happens to be the Future Protector?"

"What?"

---

[38] ride to HEA = enjoyment
ride to HEA + Calo (in any form) = the opposite of enjoyment

"Seriously, I can't believe we haven't had ProFictionists storming our office, demanding you be removed. Do you realize how little you know about these people? How are you planning to protect them when you can't even tell them apart?"

"Hey. Aren't you supposed to be teaching me all that? Or are you too busy running around trying to have the best record?"

Calo scowled again.

I continued, "Yes, I am constantly aware, mostly thanks to you, that I know virtually nothing about this world, and I know that variable significantly subtracts from my success here. But, *I* am more than willing to learn. The question is, Mr. Perfect Happiologist, are *you* willing to teach me? Because I don't see any other way out of this situation."

"Did you complete the survey?" Calo sat down at his desk.

"What?" I asked, again–this time because I felt Calo's question was an inappropriate response to my rant.

"The survey I sent. Did you finish it?" Calo calmly pointed to the file folder in my hand, in case I still had no idea what he was talking about.

"Oh," I said, looking at the folder. "Yeah. Here." I gave the whole stupid file to him.

"Thank you," he said, handing me a blank diagram of the Happiness Monitor. "Fill this out." He turned back to his desk and began reading my survey answers.

I went to my desk and started filling in the diagram's blanks. Luckily, I have a good memory, especially if I can apply a mnemonic device. I finished the "quiz" in two minutes. Calo looked up when I handed it to him.

"You're finished already?" He looked skeptical.

I nodded, trying to look annoyingly sweet.

"Alright. Let's see." He grinned smugly as he grabbed a red pen from his desk and began grading. The pen was poised to point out any error, but he got to the end of the diagram without marking anything. He looked slightly puzzled; then he began checking the diagram again. I smiled with (at the very least) equal smugness. Score one for Lily.

After a few more minutes of checking and rechecking, Calo finally put the pen down. "So you've memorized the different levels of the Monitor."

"Just like you asked me to." I smiled.

"It's just too bad you didn't do what I asked yesterday at Morgan's."

I opened my mouth to argue.

"Anyway," Calo went on, ignoring me. "Today, we're going over the Happiness Monitor—its history, uses, what the levels mean, etc." He put an hourglass monitor on my desk. It was full of white liquid. "Now, you were given a monitor of your own at your presentation, correct?"

"Yes, but mine has plaid liquid in it."

"Right," Calo grabbed a three-ring binder and started flipping through it. "That's because your fairy godmother is Glenni. Her trademark is plaid. All of the godchildren in her care have plaid-filled monitors. I, like most of us, don't have a fairy godmother catering to my every whim, so I have white liquid in my monitor." He pointed to the one on my desk.

"Wait a minute," I interrupted. "Your monitor? You have one?"

"Yes, Lily," Calo said, exasperated. "*Everyone* has one. Section 4G of the Mandamus of Happiness." He put the binder away, got down on his hands and knees, and crawled under his desk. "And I quote: 'Every resident of E. G. Smythe's Salty Fire Land," (His voice was muffled, and he had completely disappeared under the desk.) "whether of fictional or natural creation, shall employ and retain a Happiness Monitor in the Office of Happily Ever After Affairs.' End quote." He came out from under the desk pushing a poster board in front of him.

"'Fictional or natural creation?'"

Calo pulled an easel out from behind his desk and placed the poster board on it. It was a giant diagram of a Happiness Monitor. "Right. 'Fictional creation' refers to the citizens from stories. Naturally created citizens are the ones like your family and Grimm—people who have been invited to live here."

"Oh." I mentally sorted fictional and natural citizens into a table. "Which are you?"

Calo looked at me for a moment. I thought he was about to say something typically rude and grumpy, but he just said, "Fictional. Fairy Tale, actually."

"Really? Which one?" I was a little interested, not because I'd know which story he would be talking about, but because it seemed like something you should know about one of your fictionally created friends. Corrie is a naturally created friend, and I know her parents and about her background. Her dad is Irish and her mom is Italian. (Although, it *is* possible that Calo doesn't satisfy the equation of "friend.")

"*Puss-in-Boots.*"

"Is that the one about the magic beans?"

"Uh...no. That's *Jack and the Beanstalk*. *Puss-in-Boots* is the talking cat. Kills the ogre for his master, you know."

I didn't know, but that wasn't the pressing point. "You're not a cat."

"Well, you *are* observant." Typical Calo. "No, I'm not a cat. But I am a second son."

"And?" Calo's hints are about as easy to figure out as trying to plot a line with only one set of coordinates.

He sighed. "How you can know so little is beyond me. In my story, my father dies. He left the mill— you do know what a mill is, right?"

"Yes." I'm not a moron.

"Good." He smiled and sighed in mock relief. "Anyway, Dad left the mill to my older brother, and he left the cat, which happened to be talking (though we didn't know it at the time) to my younger brother. And I, being the second son, was left my father's coat and hat. My older brother and I didn't get along so well, so I decided to make my way in the world."

"That doesn't seem very fair."

"Well, technically, the fairy tale is just about the youngest son. In the actual text, my older brother and I are only in the first paragraph. But since we were fictionally created—here we are." He pointed to the hourglass on my desk. "Citizens who must have their Happiness monitored."

I looked at Calo's monitor. All the measuring liquid was in the bottom half of the hourglass. *Under* the Happy line. "You're unhappy."

"No, I'm not Unhappy. You vanish when you're Unhappy, and yet I am still here. I'm Less Than Less Than Happy. There's a difference."

"Oh."

Calo pointed to the Less Than Less Than Happy line on the poster. "This is where I am. Less Than Less Than Happy is an acceptable state of happiness. People are not always going to be Happy from day to day. Fluctuations are expected. However," he pointed to the line below Less Than Less Than Happy, "at the Could be Happier Level, we, here at HEA, begin to be concerned."

"Why?" Could be Happier was still four lines away from Unhappy. "It seems a little far from the vanishing point."

"It is a safety measure. We send out Happiologists at Could be Happier, because a person who Could be Happier is easier to cheer than a person who's Been a Lot Happier," he pointed to that level on the diagram, "Or a person who's Not so Happy." The Not so Happy level was the one right above Unhappy.

That makes sense, oddly enough. Well, as much sense as measuring Happiness can. "So when a person's monitor shows that they Could be Happier, a Happiologist goes out and tries to cheer them back up to the Less Than Less Than Happy line?"

"Negative." Calo pointed to the Happy line in the exact middle of the hourglass. "When a person is being cheered, their level must go up to Happy before the case is closed. A Happiologist stays with that case until the person can maintain happiness for three days. I mean, people *are* supposed to be living Happily Ever After here, not Could be Happier Ever After. And they're less likely to have a relapse if we get them to Happy. Did you get all that?"

I nodded. The monitor is like a number line, with Happy where the zero would be. (I love finding math in random places!)

"Great." Calo took a sheet of paper off his desk and gave it to me. "This is the latest update–the three o'clock one. Doug'll be bringing the four o'clock pretty soon."

I looked at the clock: it was 3:53. "Doug?"

"He's Head Observer up in the Observatory. Observers make sure that Happiologists get hourly reports on Happiness levels." Calo pointed at the paper. "Glance over that and tell me who we should be concerned about."

I did not *glance* at it. Mathematicians rarely glance; the margin of error is greatly increased if you are only quickly looking at something. I *examined* the paper. The first thing I noticed was that it was only one page.

"This can't be everyone." I said, matter-of-factly. "There are only twenty-five names on here." I looked at Calo. I'm certainly not claiming to know everyone in this story world come true, but I think I could now name more than twenty-five.

"Oh, right." Calo sat on his desk. "Each Happiologist just gets one page of the list, just their clients. Some of the characters rotate around each month, and some stay with the same Happiologist. For instance, King Arthur and Morgan Le Faye are regulars for me."

"Who decides if they become a regular?"

"The characters themselves. They mail in a card at the end of the month indicating their choice for the next month. It's a pretty reliable system. That way they can find the Happiologist that works best with them.

You don't want to mess around with Unhappiness if things aren't working out between you and your client."

"So they just shop around?"

"Some do. Some don't. Some like the change, and some want a steady relationship."

I saw a lot of problems with this "reliable" system. What if a character, who liked to switch around, kept switching, but with each passing month the character's Happiness level dropped a little. How would the Happiologists be able to recognize the problem? Also, if a character got into a destructive pattern, it wouldn't be hard to—I stopped myself.

Why am I considering potential problems at HEA? I sighed. Against all mathematical reasoning, this place is becoming normal to me. And *that* is not normal.

I returned to examining Calo's portion of the list. On the left hand side, the names of the characters were listed and on the right, their corresponding levels of happiness. Calo had asked me to point out potential problems with citizens. That meant that I was looking for levels of Could be Happier and lower. I looked down the list.

The first name was Minerva (Goddess of Wisdom). She wasn't a problem at More Happy Than Usual. Both Hugo Wolf (The Big Bad Wolf) and King Arthur were Less Than Happy. Sirena (The Little Mermaid) was Averagely Happy, and Morgan Le Faye, at Rather Happy, still seemed to be delighting in the memory of vanishing me.

Near the middle of the page, I found my first Could be Happier—Baile (Third of The Twelve Dancing Princesses). I made a mental note and continued my examination. Two names below Baile, Amphi (The Frog Princess) had Been Happier, and Sula Gansa (The Goose

Girl) Could be Happier. The rest of the names on the list were Less Than Less Than Happy or happier.

I returned the list to Calo. "Baile, Amphi, and Sula Gansa are at risk. Amphi's risk is compounded by her being at the Been Happier level."

"Right." Calo handed me a green highlighter. "Your first job, when you come in to work, will be to take any hourly reports on your desk and highlight those we should be concerned about. I'll take care of the ones that come in while you're at school." Calo glanced at the clock; it was exactly four. "Ah," he said, turning to the bald man who appeared at the entrance of our cubicle, "right on time, as usual, Doug. Thank you." He took the four o'clock update from Doug and handed it to me. "Happy highlighting, Lily."

~ ~ ~

Wednesday and Thursday were spent at school (where there was not enough math), at work (where there was even less math), and at home (where there was plenty of math to be had–if I could get away from my parents to do it). Since Mom and King Tub both stopped working before supper, they wanted the "family" to spend the evening together in the living room. They also wanted the "family" to contribute to "family discussions" at "family dinners," which were all catered by Lubcker and company.

I discovered on Tuesday night another lie must be added to my mother's portfolio. It seems she can't cook at all. Apparently, Lubcker would bring supper over while I was still at school. Mom would heat it up, serve it to me, and claim it was hers. Mom was a little offended when I pointed out my whole childhood had been a lie.

"I don't see what the big deal is, Lily. It's not like you were malnourished."[39]

Work continued in its normal, Smythian way. Calo treated me like a child, making disbelieving noises when I asked questions he felt I should already know the answer to or openly mocking any ideas I had.

On Wednesday, during our review of case histories, I suggested that we make a chart to organize our data. Specifically, I was looking at Sirena's file. Since, as a mermaid, she lives in the ocean, I thought it would be to our advantage to examine tidal patterns and sea temperature trends and their effect on her Happiness. Calo did not agree.

"Because that would affect her Happiness *how* exactly?" He scowled. "She spends over half her time in her human form–on *land*."

"Suppose she likes to swim (as a mermaid *or* as a human) in a certain shallow area. She wouldn't be able to swim when the tide went back out, or—"

Calo interrupted. "That's stupid. Sirena likes things to do with humans. All you have to do is give her a fork or a sewing kit, and it raises her level. Once I gave her a set of water wing floaties and she went straight to Excessively Happy."

"But that doesn't fully address the problem, you need—"

---

[39] Mom now = mother + wife + (famous)writer + distracted – widow – cook.

"Yes, it does. The problem is that she is Unhappy. The solution is to make her Happy. Hammers and hand mixers will do that."

"But that doesn't tell us why she's unhappy. If we don't figure that out, we'll never be able to help her. The charts could—"

"Take up unnecessary time." He interrupted and annoyingly finished my sentence. "While we're out there measuring the sea's temperature and charting tidal fluctuations, she'd be getting unhappier and closer to vanishing. If we don't prevent her vanishing, then we'll lose her story. Which, to me, is far worse than never knowing the exact reason why she's unhappy in the first place." He stomped out of the cubicle, which was fine with me.

On Thursday afternoon, however, I had no extra time to consider revolutionizing HEA. Calo kept all parts of my mind occupied in solving hypothetical situations. They were basically cases in which you would figure out everything you would do to solve the case, without actually solving it.

Calo played the citizens and I, of course, was the Happiologist. He was especially entertaining as Potio Bane, pretending that his crop of apples had been sat upon by Jack's giant.[40] I think I did fairly well at making the fake people happy.

Solving cases involved looking at the case file, reading the story to brush up on familiarity (or, in my case, to learn anything at *all* about the story), and

---

[40] Calo was actually somewhat pleasant to be around when he subtracted the jerkishness from his equation and added a smile.

reviewing past cases to see what other Happiologists have found successful.

Calo seemed pleased with my progress. As I got on my bike after work, he said, "I think you're ready for some practice on an actual citizen. See you tomorrow, Lily."

There was some satisfaction in my smile as I rode back to the castle.

~~~

Kelly Stewart poked me in the back. "Pay attention!" she hissed.

"Lily?!" Mrs. Fox looked at me. "Did you hear my question?!"

"Uh...no, Mrs. Fox, I didn't." Once again, Legendary Literature had failed to hold my interest.

"Well! I'll ask it again!" Mrs. Fox bounced ever so slightly on the balls of her feet, completely the image of a living exclamation mark. "Will you read the handout please?!"

When did we get a handout? I looked at my desk. Not only did I have the handout, but I had already covered the margins with algebra problems.

I read, "'As a body of work, legendary tales are ignored by some students of literature. They feel that their oral beginnings lead to questionable, even laughable holes in the plot lines. These critics feel that the improbabilities of most of the plots in legendary literature reflect a simple culture, a time long passed, and a people inferior to modern man. But are they right?

"'You must decide. You may choose either argument: 'Legendary Literature is worthy of study' or 'Legendary Literature is not worthy of study.' You will write a three-page paper arguing your position with examples. For instance, if you feel that the oral nature of the tales makes them unreliable, then you will include examples of stories in your paper whose plots have suffered because they were not originally written down. Topics will be due on Monday and the papers on September 13th.'"

"Thank you, Lily! That means you'll have two weeks to write your papers! Don't put them off until the last minute!" The bell interrupted. "Have a good weekend! Don't forget to have your topic ready on Monday!"

A whole paper about fairy tales? Ugh. We do not do enough math-related work in this school.

~~~

I had just finished highlighting potentially unhappy citizens (there were five today), when Calo walked in and glanced over the list.

"Hmm. No change then." He dropped a file folder on my desk. "Okay, Lily," he said, cheerily. "King Arthur has kindly agreed to let you practice on him this afternoon."

"He's not in danger. He's only Less Than Happy."

Calo looked at me funny, looked at the update, looked at me again, and said, "How did you know that?"

I shrugged. "I've got a good memory."

"Clearly." Calo appeared for a moment to be about to say something else, but then he shook his head slightly. "Right. He's only Less Than Happy, which technically isn't in danger, but it also isn't Happy. I need you to have some practice with cases that uh…" He stopped and seemed to be trying to figure out the best way to say something.

"Cases that I'm not likely to mess up and cause someone to vanish?" I asked, helpfully.

"Exactly." He nodded. "Even if you do bring Arthur down a level or two, he won't be in serious danger, but he's still low enough that we'll be able to tell if you've made him happier. So, go over the file, make your plan, and let me know when you're ready to leave."

I opened Arthur's file and read the list of things proven to make him happier: disco music, chocolate chip cookies, Gwenivere, working with his hands, and cold, cold milk. I looked at past attempts to raise his level. Mostly Calo had just played disco music, while they both danced around in the throne room under Arthur's disco ball. Judging from the past reports, it seemed to be taking Calo longer and longer to bring about a Happy rating with this technique. Probably because he was doing the same thing every time.

I got a Happy Plan form out of my desk and completed it, outlining my plan for Arthur, along with a list of supplies I'd need. I showed it to Calo.

He smiled. "Creative." He pushed in his desk chair. "Let's go see if it'll work."

~~~

Arthur met us at the door of his castle. "I've been waiting for you all afternoon. Hello, Princess," he said, taking my hand. "Wonderful to see you." Turning to Calo he said, "And I've got my monitor here, so we can see how things are going. Should we go to the throne room?" He looked from Calo to me and then back to Calo, as if unsure of who exactly to ask.

"The kitchen, actually." I answered.

"The kitchen? How interesting." He gave his monitor to Calo and led the way.

The kitchen was large, warm, and oddly sunny for a room in the basement of a castle. I ignored the obvious flouting of mathematical laws like the refraction and reflection of light and took a CD player out of my bag. "Some music while we work," I said, as I pulled out the ingredients for chocolate chip cookies.

"Are those chocolate chips?" Arthur pointed.

I nodded. "I thought we'd make some cookies today."

Calo sat down on a stool in the corner with Arthur's monitor and a clipboard for taking notes.

"Excellent idea, Princess. I've never baked before." Arthur looked absolutely giddy. We had a good time baking and eating the dough before we made the cookies. Arthur was fond of scooping the dough out of the bowl and rolling it in his hands to make what he called "the perfect ball of cookie dough." And the music was entertaining. I know very little about disco music, but Arthur had an amazing wealth of knowledge on the subject. For instance, did you know that the soundtrack of *Saturday Night Fever* is generally considered to be more popular than the movie itself? And he knew the words to every song. When the first batch of cookies had cooled enough to eat, I reached into my bag and pulled out a thermos of milk. As we dunked our cookies into the cold, cold milk, a chime sounded from Calo's corner.

"Congratulations, Princess!" Arthur said while I tried to figure out what the noise was.

"What?" I asked.

"You made me Happy." He was smiling. "That's the noise the monitor makes when Happiness is achieved."

"Nice work, Lily," Calo called as he started packing his things.

Arthur and I had just started doing the dishes when two things happened all at once: Calo's back pocket started ringing, and a servant brought a letter in for Arthur, a black envelope addressed with gray writing.

I turned to see if Calo would know the envelope was from Levi, but he hadn't noticed. Strangely enough, he was talking into a make-up compact. Calo nodded and then closed the compact.

"It's a compact phone. Like the mirror phone at your house, but smaller. Doug from the Observatory called. It seems that Morgan heard about us coming here and is jealous; her levels are dropping pretty quickly. I'm going to head over there to see what I can do." He paused. "Uh...I don't think you should come, Lily. I mean, well, you know how she is. Can you make it back to HEA by yourself?"

"I don't think so." I hadn't paid much attention on the way over. I was busy thinking about what I was going to do with Arthur. "I remember something about a bridge."

"I'll put your bike on auto-pilot then, and Grimm can—" He stopped. "King Arthur? Is everything alright?"

Arthur was reading the letter with a look of growing disdain and anger. "That sycophant!" He spat out. "Implying that my kingdom can be–well!" He stopped and stalked out of the kitchen. "He'll receive a response back from me, he will!" He paused in the doorway. "You can see yourselves out, I suppose?"

"Certainly, sir." Calo answered. "But, are you sure you're alright?"

"I am fine. Forgive me, Princess, for losing my temper in your presence." He bowed and left.

"Is he going to be okay?" I asked Calo. "He was so happy before. Did that letter ruin—?"

Calo cut me off by pointing at the monitor on the counter. Arthur's level was still Happy. I stared at it, confused, for a moment. Then I followed Calo out of the castle.

It had started to rain. The drops were hard and angry. The wind was whipping around the castle, through the trees. Calo pulled a wand out of his pocket and looked worriedly at the sky. "Hopefully you'll get back before this gets too bad," he said loudly, tapping my bike. I could barely hear him over the wind and rain. "See you later," he called as he rode off.

My bike nudged my elbow.

"Alright," I muttered.

Lightning shot across the sky as I got on and started pedaling. The storm was getting worse; Rain came down in sheets. I was completely soaked and sure that HEA's CD player was ruined. Since I could barely see in front of me, I was glad to have the auto-pilot. Even if I had known how to get home, I would never have been able to find it.

I started to make an equation to figure out my percentage of visibility in the storm. I looked up to estimate how far I could see in feet, but I saw something much worse than minimal visibility.

The stream under the bridge had swollen well beyond its banks, and as I watched, the bridge tore apart and washed away.

I barely had time to begin mathematically determining how to get over the stream, when I realized there was a more pressing problem.

The bike would not slow down. I applied the brakes: nothing happened. And nothing I tried could keep the bike from heading right into the flooded stream.

12

OBJECTS IN MOTION

Newton's first law (objects in motion stay in motion unless acted on by an outside force) flitted through my mind briefly as I flung myself off the bike. Never before have I experienced one of his laws in such a dangerous way. I hit the ground, rolled onto my back, and looked to see what happened to my bike. It was being washed downstream.

"Stupid auto-pilot," I muttered. I stood up and mathematically analyzed my situation.

Torrential rains + auto-pilot bike + no knowledge of where I am = one lost, wet Lily, who will be walking wherever she goes.

I was also muddy, cold, and completely soaked. I began to walk along the flooded stream, in hopes of finding another (stronger) bridge. In a desperate attempt to keep my mind focused on anything but how wet I was, I recited the squares. "One squared is one. Two squared is four. Three squared is nine..."

At "fifteen squared is two hundred twenty-five," I saw a muddy path to my right. I headed straight for it.[41] I had no idea where the path was going. But being on it had to be better than wandering aimlessly by a swollen stream. It wasn't until "twenty-three squared is five hundred twenty-nine" that I realized my faith in the path was based on my knowledge of paths in the real world. In the real world, paths go somewhere. They move in a predictable manner. You travel for a while, then when you decide to take a turn, you take it. Steady. Predictable.

At "twenty-three squared is five hundred twenty-nine," I came to a fork in the path.

An actual fork.

The path ended. Trees were everywhere. I stood in the pouring rain and looked at the little, shiny fork that some picnicker had probably left behind. "This is in no way helpful. A path is supposed to go somewhere," I mumbled, turning around. "I wish I knew what to do."

"About time, too," said a voice behind me.

I turned back to the wall of trees. It was Glenni. Floating as usual, she wore a plaid rain slicker, complete with a plaid hat and plaid galoshes, and she carried a plaid umbrella. She snapped her fingers, and another

---

[41] The shortest distance between two points is a straight line.

umbrella materialized. She lazily shoed it to me with her wand.

"What is the point of having a fairy godmother if you never call on her?" She looked severely at me. "It *is* my job after all."

"Glenni! What are you doing here?" I quickly opened the umbrella.

Glenni sighed. "Did you or did you not just make the following wish: 'I wish I knew what to do'?"

What? "Uh...yes. I said that."

"A fairy godmother is summoned by her godchildren when they make wishes," she said tiredly, as if she had already explained this point to me–several times.

"Oh," I paused. "But I didn't mean to make a wish."

Glenni raised her eyebrows. "Do you mean that you *do not* wish to know what you are to do here, at the fork in the road?"

"No...I mean, yes, I do want to know what I should do. But I didn't mean to summon you. I was just wondering."

Glenni shook her hands in an impatient gesture. "Wishing, wondering–the point is you need help." She glanced at me. "And soon I'd say. You'll be growing gills to help you breathe in all this water if you don't get dry."

I started to laugh, but then I stopped myself. I realized that it was probably entirely possible in Smythe's SFL to grow gills when you're wet. Not wishing to delay, I asked, "So what am I supposed to do?"

Glenni pointed to the fork. "Pick it up."

Breathing deeply (in case I lost lung capability), I bent over and picked up the fork.

Six doors appeared around the path: two to the left, two to the right, and two in front of me, at the dead end of the path. Each door was a different color–red and orange to the left, yellow and green in front, and blue and purple to the right. "Well," I managed. "I guess it's not just a lost picnic fork."

Glenni floated over to me. "The blue door will take you to shelter." Then she disappeared.

Ignoring the fact that disappearing people no longer surprised me, I looked at the blue door. It was just a door; no wall connected it to anything. I could walk completely around it. There was no reason to believe that going through that door would take me anywhere than three feet off the muddy path. No reason, that is, other than the door was in Smythe's SFL, and was probably another portal device like my bathtub.

I kept standing in the rain, wishing Glenni had been more specific about where the door would take me. I didn't dare voice my wish out loud though; I would have to be more careful about what I said from now on. It seemed like Glenni had to drop whatever she was doing and whisk herself away every time one of her godchildren made a wish. That could get annoying fast. And I seem to recall something about not wanting to upset fairies. Didn't Rapunzel's hair just grow and grow because they didn't invite all the fairies to her christening or something?

I considered taking a different door, but the variability of what they could lead to was too great to logically consider actually using one. Glenni had said the blue one led to shelter; therefore, using the knowledge that is available, one can only determine that the others do or do not lead to shelter. Each non-blue door had a 50% chance of leading to shelter. The blue door had a

100% chance. But what did Glenni consider shelter? What if it was so completely fairy-godmothery that it lacked any kind of shelter aspect in a mathematical definition?

Finally, I remembered that Glenni had given me a calculus book, which showed enough mathematical sense for me. I opened the door.

There was no rain on the other side—only sunshine and clear skies. I quickly went through and shut the door behind me. As it closed, I realized I probably should have left it opened in case wherever I had come was dangerous. I looked around this bright land of sunshine; it was very clean. While folding my umbrella, I noticed there was no litter anywhere, and the sunshine made everything seem sparkly and new. There was another path through the woods to my left. I decided to take it.

Traveling this sunny path was such a completely different experience. I dried out a little and warmed up. Whoever lives in this area must always be happy. How could you be unhappy in sunshine like this? I was blissfully warm and happy and unaware of how far I had traveled when I saw a castle right in front of me. A sudden turn in the path had taken me out of the woods and into a clearing where it stood.

I did not recognize the castle. I considered that both good and bad. Good that it was not Morgan's castle, but bad that Glenni hadn't sent me back to my own castle. Who could live here? I mentally listed some possible characters. King Median or Midas or whatever and his golden touch ice cream would probably have a castle (kings usually do). Sleeping Beauty. That princess with the frog. But also, Potio Bane, the scary apple lady. She seemed like she had a castle, what with all of that clapping to summon her servants and her general attitude.

After several minutes of mathematical wondering (this time in much warmer, dryer conditions), I concluded that I could trust Glenni. The calculus book, the path of sunshine, and the floating math alarm clock were all things highly in her favor. I walked to the door, took a deep breath (happily noting that I still just had regular, *human* breathing), and knocked twice, using the shoe-shaped doorknocker.

A pretty and vaguely familiar lady answered the door. "Princess Lily? Come in," she was obviously surprised. I followed her into an entryway. "But whatever are you doing here?" Her dress was simple, but still elegant. "You're all wet!"

"There was a storm," I said, and noticing a delicate crown on her head, I added, "my lady."[42]

"A storm!" She looked outside.

"It was near King Arthur's," I helpfully supplied.

"Oh," she nodded knowingly, "that does explain it." I shivered involuntarily in my cold, wet clothes. "Stay here. I'll bring you something warm to put on."

As she left, I found myself wondering primarily two things.

(1) Who is she?

And (2) how does the fact that the storm was at King Arthur's explain anything?

---

[42] "My lady," I've noticed, is an excellent cover for all titles. If you're not sure if you are addressing a queen or a princess–throw on a "my lady." It's respectful, if a bit vague.

I looked around the room I was standing in.
Again, for a castle made of stone with few windows,
there seemed to be an awful lot of sunlight. It was
beginning to seem as if the Smythian architects knew a
way to magically suspend the laws about light refraction.
Which, I further reflected, they probably did.

On one wall, there hung a mirror (probably the
mirror phone). Under the mirror, sat a table with letters
piled on it. Next to the table was an umbrella stand. I
added mine to it and examined the pile of letters.

Looking through another person's mail generally
equals highly rude behavior, very bad manners, and
practically mail tampering, but it also equals way to find
out whose house you are in. I looked at few of the letters
in the stack. They were all addressed to Cinderella. Some
of them gave her additional titles. Princess Cinderella,
Her Royal Highness, or (my favorite) Cinderella, A
Charming Princess for a Charming Prince.

So I was at Cinderella's castle.

I immediately wished (again, not out loud) that I
knew more about her story. What *did* I know about her?
She gave me a pair of glass magic dancing shoes at my
presentation. I paused to consider how impossible glass
shoes are. Without the additional magic that *must* be in
them, I don't see how they could physically work. And
glass is see-through; why would you want to have
everyone see your feet? It's like being barefoot.

I shook my head to stop myself from thinking
about the shoes, and I racked my brain for anything else
I might know about Cinderella. I recalled she had sent
one of the letters I received after Morgan vanished me
on Monday. It was a nice letter. What else? Perhaps, she
had a stepmother? Although, that's just basic fairy tale
probability. Always guess a wicked stepmother.

Cinderella came back into the hall carrying some clothes and a comb. "These should fit you." She handed the stack to me. "They're one size fits all." She pointed to a little door. "You can change in the powder room."

I thanked her (using her name) and went into the powder room. Cinderella had given me a dress, undergarments, socks and shoes. Looking at them, however, I had some trouble figuring out what exactly was meant by "one size fits all." They were *much* too big for me. However, appearances do not mean the same thing in Smythe's SFL as they do in a normal (mathematical) setting, so I took off my own wet clothes, and began putting on the huge, dry ones. Oddly (or perhaps I should have expected it), the minute the clothes were in place they shrunk to my size. I can only assume, following this principle, that if I had been larger than the clothes that they would have grown once I got into them. But how would a larger person get in them? Perhaps that's why they were so big to begin with? I quickly combed through my hair, gathered my wet things, and went back out into the hall.

"Oh, here." Cinderella came toward me. "Let me have those wet clothes. We'll put them in the dryer." She pointed to another door off the hallway. "Go right through there. I've got all the tea things set up. Help yourself; I'll only be a minute." She left again.

I went through the door. The room was sunny, of course, and looked like a living room. Although, it was probably called a parlor or drawing room or something that sounds more like a fairy tale. "Living room" doesn't really convey a magical feeling. A tea tray sat on the coffee table: sugar, milk, little lemon wedges, several spoons, and a pot. There was also a tray of cookies.

I looked at the tea tray for a moment. "Yeah, I don't know what to do with that," I said softly as I sat down. I will just say I wanted to wait for her to start. After all, I am only a guest. Doesn't the hostess have to do a "hosting" thing with the tea?

In a few moments, Cinderella returned. "Your clothes will be dry in half an hour. In the meantime," she sat down, "you and I can have a nice visit. Wouldn't you like some tea?" She shifted in her seat so she could better serve.

"Of course."

"How do you take it?" She began pouring.

Uh... "With sugar," I said, glancing at the first thing on the table. Cinderella added the sugar cubes and passed the teacup to me.

"So," Cinderella began, "tell me, Princess, do you like our world?"

I surprised myself by saying, "I do, actually."[43]

"It must be very difficult to have your life change like this. Why," she paused, thinking, "you can't have known about all this for much more than a week, I imagine."

I nodded. "It is nine days, today."

Cinderella smiled, "I must say, Princess, I think you a have remarkably good attitude about everything. If my father were to come back to life after being dead, I don't know if I should be able to accept it as well as you."

---

[43] The hold this place has on me is certainly not mathematical. Maybe, like Mom says, it's in my blood.

"Thank you." I managed. During her last speech, I had burned my tongue on the tea. Shock from the fact she thought I had a good attitude led me to sip too much hot tea. I suppose I am trying, I can easily say that my attitude is infinitely greater than Calo's. "Please just call me Lily, though. I'm not used to all this 'Princess' business."

"And you must call me Ella." She passed the tray of cookies. "May I ask what were you doing at Arthur's? I hope his Happiness levels were not too low."

"No, nothing like that." I took a cookie. "He was within the normal range, only Less than Happy, but he volunteered to let me practice on him."

"How nice." She smiled and sipped her tea. "And what was the result?"

"It went very well; he became Happy, but—" I stopped. I wasn't sure if I should share my suspicions about Levi and the effect his letter had on Arthur.

"But?"

"But, well…I'm not sure it had a lasting effect." No one said it was a secret; there could be no wrong in telling. "He was so angry when I left."

Ella raised her eyebrows. "But angry is not the same as unhappy," she said slowly, then paused, "Why did he become angry?"

"I don't know exactly, but I think it was because of the letter he received."

"A letter," Ella repeated, thoughtfully. "Did he say who the letter was from?"

"No, he didn't. But," I went on in a rush, "I think it was from Levi."

"Levi? Levi, the sycophant?"

I nodded.

"But then," she smiled to herself, "yes, that would explain it all. Tell me, Lily: was it storming when you arrived at Arthur's?"

"No. It started as we were leaving."

"Exactly." She put down her teacup. "Come with me. I believe I can explain at least the anger and the storm to you."

I nodded and followed her out of the parlor. We went back into the hall and up the stairs. Ella led me into a room off the first landing.

"This is the map room," she said.

And I had to agree. Every inch of the walls (except for the small windows that let in copious and illogical amounts of sunshine) was covered with maps. A table in the center of the room was piled high with atlases.

"You have a lot of maps," I remarked, noticing detailed maps of my world, a wall devoted to maps of the moon, and a globe of a planet that I was not familiar with.

Ella looked around, "Oh, I suppose we do. Aven's a bit of a cartography nut, and he's Chief Cartographer for your father."

"Who's Aven? And what's a cartographer?"

Ella started moving the atlases off the table. They hit the stone floor with echoing thuds. "Aven is Prince Avenant–Prince Charming to you." Another atlas thud. She added as an afterthought, "And, he's my husband." (Atlas. Thud.) "Cartography is map-making, so a cartographer—"

"Is a map-maker," we finished together.

"Exactly." Ella dropped the last atlas to the floor. "But since he is out surveying Avalon for a new contour map the Weird Sisters have commissioned, we can use the map table."

There was a strange hint of bitterness as she spoke. I didn't know what a contour map was or who the Weird Sisters were, but I didn't think it was a good time to ask.

Ella felt along the side of the table and flipped a switch. Immediately, the map table lit up. A voice from somewhere in the table spoke:

> *"Many maps have I to show:*
> *of the Salt Land and Oslo.*
> *Make your pick.*
> *Speak it quick."*

"Good afternoon, Map Table," Ella said, clearly used to the demands of her furniture.

"Good afternoon, Ella," the voice answered back. "Good afternoon, Princess. You're a bit off your course, aren't you?"

"I got lost in a storm." Odd though it was, there was some unaccounted for excitement in talking to a table. I began to wonder if this was normal for Smythian furniture. Would the chalkboard in my room at the castle assist with math problems? Could my squishy chair tell me where I had left something I'd lost?

But I had to stop thinking about animated furniture and pay attention. The table was talking again.

"Ahh, a storm. Could have happened to anyone. It's easy to lose yourself that way. But you ought to be traveling with a map. I can't think why you haven't already been given one. I shall tell Aven to make you one. I say, it's dreadfully remiss, having your princess without a decent map."

"Map Table," Ella took advantage of a pause in his monologue on the evils of mapless travel. "Could you show us the weather map of the kingdom? And prepare the FK map as well. I want to explain the Fisher King myth to Lily."

"Quite right," the table answered, and a map of the kingdom appeared. I had not yet seen a map of Smythe, so I was interested to see my new world.

It was like a weather map on the six o'clock news, except in 3D. Clouds and suns dotted the map. I saw the Protector's castle right in the center, surrounded by its moat. Then, in beautiful, mathematically correct, concentric circles moving out from the castle were the woods. The First Wood was the first circle; the Second Wood was the second circle, and so on. There were seven in all. It looked like a giant had dropped my castle in the center of a pond and the woods were the ripples. A river flowed down from Mount Olympus to the north, joined the moat around my castle and flowed out again to the sea, in the west. In the northern waters off the coast were the island of Avalon and the city of Atlantis.[44] In the Southeast, there was a hilly area labeled "The Dell." And the Southwest was devoted to a large forest, different from the wood rings around the castle. The trees were clustered together, more like you would expect a forest to look. It was labeled "Sherwood." Directly south was a darker forest, almost black, labeled "The Wildwood." One corner of the Wildwood was

---

[44] Oddly, though, Atlantis seemed to be under the water, but I suppose that could just be a cartography mistake. How could a city be underwater?

completely black, labeled "Uppish Senna." The land of Unhappiness where Tandem Tallis lived and sent out dead lilies and sparrows, where greasy Levi came from, where citizens vanish to languish in dungeons. I shuddered.

"Okay, Lily," Ella began by pointing out King Arthur's castle in the Sixth Wood. "This is Arthur's, where you were when you got caught in the storm. What time did the storm hit?"

"Around five, I think," I answered, after doing some mental math.

"Great. Map Table, could you show us—"

"Now showing the Weather Map from five o'clock PM." The map changed slightly. Some of the clouds moved a few inches to the west.

"Thank you, Map Table. Now, Lily, looking at the map, tell me what the weather was like at Arthur's when you left."

I looked at Arthur's castle, expecting to see dark stormy clouds, with lightning bolts coming from them. What I saw was a sun over the castle.

"Well," I stalled, trying to mathematically figure it out. "The map says it was sunny."

"Yes, it does." Ella pointed to me as she spoke, emphasizing her point. "This is the map that shows the *actual* weather in the kingdom. Map Table, can we see the FK map now?"

"Now showing the Fisher King map from five o'clock PM." The map changed. It was still a map of Smythe's SFL, but some of the weather had changed. The most noticeable change was over Arthur's. It was hard to see the actual castle; thick, dark clouds covered it. Lightning flashed, and listening carefully, I could hear rolls of thunder.

"I don't understand," I admitted. "How can that storm not be the actual weather? How could I get drenched in a storm that wasn't real?"

Ella smiled. "Well, it was real, and it wasn't," she paused. "King Arthur is a king from the ancient days, and as such, he is subject to the Fisher King myth. In those ancient days, the people believed that the king was tied to the land, married to the land, even."

"Married to the land?" I asked, with a hint of sarcasm.

"Yes. If the king was healthy, the land would be productive and fruitful. If the king was ill, the land would become a wasteland," she paused again. "Of course, this is a very simple explanation of the FK myth. I'm sure there's a file at HEA that you could read for a more thorough explanation. Also, since there is so much magic loose here in Smythe's SFL, the effects of the myth are more pronounced."

I began processing this. "So that means Arthur would not have to be very ill to make his kingdom a wasteland."

"Right, and by extension, his other emotions are also bound up in the Fisher King myth."

"Like anger?"

"Exactly. When Arthur gets angry, storms come quickly."

"But his Fisher King weather isn't real?" That storm had seemed awfully real. My clothes are in the dryer; my hair is wet. And how hard would it be to live in a place where the weather changed with someone's emotions?

"It's real in the sense that you got wet and the rain was there. It's not real in the way the monsters you saw in the dark when you were little weren't real. You only 'saw' them because of the shadows or because you were afraid. You imagined them."

"I didn't imagine that storm."

"Of course not. And Arthur didn't either. The storm was only there because of his anger. When he calms down, the storm will cease. In fact," she turned back to the table, "Map Table, show us the current FK map."

"Now showing the Fisher King map for 5:43 PM." Once again, the table changed. The storm above Arthur's was different now. It was less—less dark, less clouds, less thunder, less rain, and only an occasional streak of lightning.

"You see?" Ella asked. "It's clearing off. He must be calming down. Probably, he wrote a strongly worded letter to Levi to release his anger."

Weather that's real and isn't. I am no longer surprised that these citizens have trouble staying Happy. Everything about their world is unmathematical and abnormal.

I asked a few more polite questions about maps and fake weather. Question: There are several kings in Smythe's SFL. Does this Fisher King thing apply to all of them? Answer: Not to the extent that it does for Arthur. His case is even more pronounced because of his ancientness. The others are only mildly affected by it. For instance, my father would have to be very, very sick or very, very angry before he could change the weather. One of my follow-up questions was interrupted when a maid came in to say my clothes were dry. Ella asked her to put them in the room I had changed in earlier. After I dressed, combed my hair again, and gathered my bag and Glenni's umbrella, I followed Ella out into the sunshine.

"I am very glad that the storm got you lost, Lily. I hope you will visit again."

"I'd like that."

"Good." She smiled. "After all, it's not like I'm ever not at home, like Aven. I don't have maps to be making or commissions to be filling. I'm always here." Again, I noticed that strange bitterness in her voice. We had reached the path back to the fork in the road. "You'll find that the orange door will take you back to HEA. You know your way back to the castle from there, I believe?"

"I do. Thanks for everything."

"Anytime. Goodbye, Lily."

"Goodbye," I called, starting down the path. When I got to the blue door, I went through it. The rain on the other side was not so bad now. I quickly splashed through the puddles to the orange door. Once through it, I knew where I was and would be at HEA in a few minutes. I also realized that Glenni could have sent me here in the first place. After all, HEA *is* shelter. I had (mistakenly) assumed all the other doors did not lead to places I knew or places that were safe. HEA was both known to me and safe.

So, why did Glenni send me to Ella's?

13

THE DREAM

Calo beat me back to HEA. He sat at his desk, filling out his case report on Morgan. "There you are," he said, as I came into the cubicle. "I thought you would have made it here before me. Did you have trouble getting back?"

"Well," I dropped my bag and sank into my chair. "The bridge washed away, and since the bike was on auto-pilot, it wouldn't stop, so I had to leap off at the last minute."

"By Excalibur," Calo looked at me. "Are you alright?"

I nodded. "Yeah, I'm fine. I wandered around in the rain for a while then ended up at Cinderella's."

"Cinderella's? But that's miles away from Arthur's and across the river. Unless...fork in the road?"

"Yeah. I ran into Glenni at the fork in the road and she sent me there."

"But, from that fork, she could have sent you back here."

"She didn't mention that. She only told me the blue door would lead to shelter."

"That's odd." We were both quiet for a moment, then Calo said, "Well, you just have to fill out the case report on Arthur, and you'll be free for the weekend."

"Great." I took the form from my desk. "Oh, what about my bike?"

"Hmm. Let me check the map room." He moved towards the door.

"You think my bike is in the map room? Aven's map room?"

"No, HEA's map room. And I don't think your bike will be in there, but I will be able to use the Enchanted Object Locator to find it." He grabbed the files from our outbox. "It's a good thing we put it on auto-pilot. You can't locate unenchanted objects using the map." He held up the files in his right hand. "Do you need anything delivered or put away?"

I shook my head. "No, thanks."

"Sure." Calo walked away.

I began filling out the case report, which would be filed with the citizen's other reports and case history. Everything was kept so the same mistake wouldn't be made twice (hopefully, no new Happiologists will ever ask Morgan why she's unhappy); the files also provide suggestions for things that *do* work.

Hannah, the secretary for our row of cubicles stuck her head around the corner. "Princess, you've got a mirror call." She continued walking.

"Wait, Hannah! I need directions to the mirrorphone."

Two minutes later, I entered a room off the main hallway full of mirrorbooths. Similar to photo booths found in malls and amusement parks, these booths have actual doors instead of curtains.

I sat on the seat, across from the mirror. Most of it functioned as an actual mirror. However, along the bottom two inches these words flashed: *TOUCH YOUR REFLECTED NOSE TO BEGIN.* I smiled and my reflected hand reached out to touch my nose.

The mirror went black, and green words appeared on it: *Thank you for choosing Mirage Mirrorbooths. Please state your full name and any titles you may hold.*

Full name = Lily Elizabeth Sparrow.

Titles?

Could they = Princess? Future Protector?

I decided to say "Princess Lily Elizabeth Sparrow, Future Protector of E. G. Smythe's Salty Fire Land."

The mirror changed again: *Welcome, Princess Lily. What would you like to do? Touch the green square next to your choice.*

Near the bottom of the mirror were two choices and two green squares. I could either *make a call* or *pick up a call.* I touched the square next to *pick up a call.* The mirror changed once again to show Blaire kneeling dangerously on our bathroom sink at home.

"Hello, Blaire."

"Hello, Princess." She waved. "Hold on." She hopped off the sink, disappearing from view. After a moment, my mother appeared in the bathroom.

"Hello, Lily."

"Hi, Mom. Did Blaire not need to talk to me?"

"No. She was holding the line for me. I didn't know how long it would take for you to get to the booths."

"Yeah, I've never used them before. I had to ask for directions."

Mom smiled. "Are you working late today? I've been wondering where you were."

"Yeah, I'll be home soon though. I've just got to fill out one case report and then I can go." *After I find my bike*, I added mentally.

"That's fine, dear. We're staying in Smythe's SFL for the weekend, so when you finish work, just portal back over here and grab whatever you need. Also, you should start leaving some things there for weekends. You know, an extra toothbrush and some pajamas, so you won't have to pack every week."

"Okay." I forced a smile, surprised and confused by this news. They were slowly moving me to Smythe's SFL. This week it was just a toothbrush. Next week, it would be some math books. Then, it would be "Hey, Lily, since most of your stuff is here anyway, why don't we just bring everything over?"

"Great, sweetie. We're eating dinner at the castle. I think I'll be able to be there, but I'm not sure. I'm waiting for a publisher on the West Coast to get back to me. And I can't exactly wait in Smythe." She smiled. "He can only call on non-mirror lines."

"Okay, Mom."

"Bye, Sweetie."

"Bye." I watched as Mom hung up and the mirror reverted to my reflection, with flashing words at the bottom asking me to touch my nose.

Nothing about my life is normal. Soon my house at 2317 Marshall Road will just be an address we use to get me registered in school, like those people who rent apartments in nicer neighborhoods so their kids can go to the school for that area. Assuming, of course, I am allowed to continue going to school. After all, I am a princess. Shouldn't I just have tutors and governesses? Then we'd never have to worry about portaling at all.

I sighed, counted backwards by sevens from one hundred five to calm myself down, and went to finish my report.

I had just signed it, affirming that everything I included in it was the whole and complete truth, when Calo came back from the map room. "Here." He put a warm mug in my hand.

"What's this?" I asked.

"Hot chocolate. You need to warm up from being in the cold rain."

"Oh. Thanks." I sipped and burned my tongue again while trying to figure out where in Calo's equation to put "being nice with hot chocolate."

Calo smiled. "Too hot? You should have used a formula to figure out when the temperature would be just right."

"Ha, ha."

"Oh, I found your bike."

"Really? Where?"

"Caught in a driftwood pile between the Fifth and Sixth Wood, near Hansel and Gretel's. I called and they're on their way here with it. Being washed down the river sort of messed up the auto-pilot, so they have to manually steer it back. Too bad; if the auto-pilot was working properly, it would have made its way back on its own." He looked at the report in my hand. "Did you finish?"

"Yes. What do I do with it now?"

"Give it to me." He took it. "When you're an actual Happiologist, you'll only need Grimm to sign off on it, but since you're still in training, you need both our signatures."

Calo skimmed my report, then we spent the next ten minutes arguing over a piece of data I included. Calo didn't think the letter from Levi should be in the report.

"It has no bearing on this case. He received the letter *after* you had made him Happy. Not only is the letter irrelevant to the case report, but, if you include it, you'll be invading his privacy."

"What?" I looked at Calo, in disbelief. "He got the letter while we were there. He made no attempt to keep us from knowing about the letter *or* how it affected him."

"Even if you choose to ignore the privacy issue, the letter still has no importance on the case. He was already Happy when he got it. Technically, we weren't even there. You can only include things that are relevant to his Happiness."

"But this is relevant! If he—"

"How, Lily? How is it relevant?" He snatched the Observatory's most recent report off his desk. "Look at this. What is Arthur's status?" He shoved the paper at me.

I looked down the list. "He's Happy, but that doesn't mean the letter isn't—"

"Yes it does!" Speaking slowly and emphasizing his words, he said, "The letter has had no effect on his State of Happiness. *He is Happy.* The letter is irrelevant."

I took a deep breath. "I think it needs to be on record that Levi is harassing him. Since Levi works for Uppish Senna, then I think it is *highly* relevant that Arthur has received a letter from him. We could start making random visits, or perhaps we could monitor his mail, or—"

"Lily, stop. Listen to yourself." Calo sighed and ran a hand through his hair. "If Arthur came to us and said he thought he was in danger of vanishing because of the letter, *then* we could do the things you suggested. But without his approval, they are invasive and illegal."

"But he could vanish—"

"Lily, we get a report every hour telling us his status. We'd catch anything before it happened."

"So that's just it? We watch him go lower and lower in his levels, not doing anything until he Could Be Happier?"

"Watching the levels is enough. They're entitled to have a life of their own. They're entitled to have changes in their moods without us rushing in to save them every time they're a little below Happy."

"But someone ought to know that Levi's going after Arthur."

"They probably already know." Calo started straightening the things on his desk.

"Who already knows?"

"Kara and the Agency," he paused. "Well, I assume they know. Kara almost always does. She usually knows before I do. But then, it's not really my job to—"

"Who is Kara?"

"She's one of the Twelve Dancing Princesses, and she's head of the Agency." Seeing I was about to ask another question, he went on, "What's the Agency? It's a top-secret group, started by your father and Grimm to monitor and eventually eliminate Sennish presence in Smythe's SFL."

"Like the CIA?"

Calo looked at me. "I don't know. What's the CIA?"

I shook my head. "Never mind. So they're working against Levi?"

He nodded. "And Tandem Tallis and his other agents of Unhappiness."

The conversation ended then, because Hannah popped in to say Hansel and Gretel had arrived with my bike. We said goodbye and I left.

I rode slowly back to the castle. I needed the time to sort out the persistent thoughts in my head. There were five of them.

(1) I was annoyed by the progressive moving of my stuff to the castle.

(2) I was worried that I might have made plans with Corrie over the weekend or even said, "Call me." What if Peridiom or Blaire answered the phone?

(3) Calo was driving me crazy. Why will he only look at the outcomes and not the causes of Unhappiness? It's like getting the right answer to an algebra problem, but not knowing how you did it. That is sloppy mathematics, and it will *always* cause trouble later, when you get into more difficult problems. And why is he sometimes randomly nice, bringing me hot chocolate and smiling his smile at me?

(4) The complexity of Smythe's SFL continues to astound me. And I am surprised to see order and logic in their world. Tandem Tallis is trying to make everyone vanish. Logically, there would be some kind of resistance group. When you examine it without magic, it makes excellent sense. (Of course, it's also easy to see the

illogical side of this place when you realize they measure Happiness, speak with talking animals, or ride on bikes that doesn't need steering.)

(5) If this Kara person usually knows about Levi's attempts to harass people, does she know about the tango? Does she know about the letter he sent to me? If she *does* know, has she told Calo?[45]

When I arrived at the castle, I picked up my key, and headed straight for Arrivhall. Mom was still waiting for her publisher to call when I got to the house. We chatted for a bit. She asked about school and work, and I told her about my successful afternoon with Arthur. When I asked about her day, she told me all about Tressa and Laurel and how she is afraid Tressa might get the prince after all. Luckily, I was saved from hearing

_____

[45] These questions can be answered with probability. Calo said that she *almost* always knows. That implies (at the very least) some failure. By setting her knowledge of Levi incidents at 90%, I can further determine the likelihood of her and Calo knowing about it. But for this equation, I must consider more data.

(a) Calo loves to make me feel inferior. If he knew about additional Levi incidents, I think he would let me know all about how I'm threatening security.

(b) The way my father reacted after the first Levi incident. If Kara and the Agency thought I was being threatened, they would have to tell the King his daughter was in danger. I think I would have noticed a rise in parental concern.

Since I have not observed a or b, I conclude that the Agency does not know about Levi harassing me, or if it does know, it hasn't told anyone.

Probability of Agency knowing: 10%
Probability of Calo knowing: 2%
Probability of my parents knowing, 1%

anymore about her imaginary world, because she realized I needed to pack and get to the castle for dinner.

Carey (the yellow dwarf) helped me get the luggage to my room. After I unpacked, I found my way to the dining room. My father was already there, speaking quietly with Macon Mind in a corner. They stopped talking when they saw me.

"Good evening, Princess," Macon bowed to me.

"Good evening, Macon," I said, curtseying. I turned to my father. "Good evening, D—" I broke off abruptly and tried to smile, absolutely uncertain about what to call my father. Instead of finishing or supplying some other name, I stupidly left the greeting hanging there. They both noticed and tried to cover it.

"Good evening, Lily," my father smiled awkwardly. "Macon, the Queen will be joining us later. However, the Princess and I will begin dinner now. Please ask Lubcker to bring it in."

"Certainly, Your Majesty." Macon answered, trying hard to look as if he had not noticed my unfinished greeting. He bowed and left.

"So," my father said, sitting down, "your mother is still waiting for the West Coast to call?"

"Yes," I nodded and sat also. I considered adding more to this answer, but just when I was about to say something like "I've never seen Mom wait for the West Coast past seven-thirty," an annoying thought flitted through my mind. When we do move here, it will be like this every time Mom has to wait for the West Coast to call: awkward and weird. It was so much easier when it was just Mom and me. We could be eating and talking while she waited for the call, and there was no awkwardness and no strange father person.

If King Tub noticed the lack of additional information, he did not show it. "I hear, Lily, that congratulations are in order."

I looked at him.

"Grimm says you were very successful at cheering King Arthur this afternoon."

"Yes, I was."

"He also said you were faster than even some of Calo's attempts."

"Really?" Beating Calo should be in my file as something known to cheer me.

"Yes. Grimm was rather pleased. He told me your creativity in making Happiness Plans was a sign of good things to come with you as the Protector."

I smiled, blushed, and was saved from answering by Lubcker and company bringing in the food. We continued to have awkward and halting conversation until Mom joined us thirteen minutes later. She was full of news about the West Coast publisher and the plans for her book. It was a relief to have her back. She was the middle of the Venn diagram of our family—the one thing that both circles have in common.[46]

------

[46] A Venn diagram is used to sort things into categories. In the math world, we call this elementary set theory. To make a Venn diagram, draw two circles. They should partially overlap each other. Now add your data. Let's say we are sorting fairy tales with evil step-mothers and fairy tales with fairy godmothers. Stories that only had an evil step-mother, would go in Circle A. Stories with only a fairy godmother would go in Circle B. But where would you put a story that had *both* an evil step-mother and a fairy godmother? That story would go in the overlapping middle part.

My mom belongs to both my circle and my father's circle. So having her overlap us keeps things from getting too awkward.

THE DREAM

My annoyed mood continued for the rest of the evening. I was annoyed during the apple pie made of non-poisonous apples from Hemlock, Lady Potio's estate. I was annoyed while we sipped hot chocolate and watched Shaherazhad's latest movie. (According to Mom, she is the premier Smythian filmmaker.) And I was annoyed when we all said good night, and the good night I gave to my father was the only one without a name attached to it.

After I closed the door to my room, I collapsed in my squishy chair. My family's lack of normality was one factor in my mood. The moving issue was a large factor, also. But, upon examination, I was surprised to find another factor. I was annoyed at myself for being annoyed. I created an equation for the annoyance:

abnormal family + 2(stealthily moving Lily to Smythe) + being annoyed = annoyance

I decided to sleep it off.

~~~

Saturday morning began in a better mood, but it was a lost cause after the dragon attack. Macon rushed in during breakfast to tell us Naga was in the Third Wood, breathing fire, and destroying things. She was also headed straight for our castle. My father jumped up, kissed my mother, hugged me, and ran out of the breakfast room shouting, "Get to the fireproof room!"

In the next instant, Mom grabbed my hand and took off running. A voice began to speak over a PA system (*We have a PA system?*), "Please do not panic. Make your way to the fireproof room, immediately. This is not a drill." The same message was repeated over and over again. After three full minutes of running, we came to an elevator. Mom pulled me on and pushed the button labeled *fireproof room.*

While breathing deeply, I managed to say, "I've never seen that button on the elevator before." I had traveled the elevators in the castle several times, and so far, I had only seen normal elevator buttons.

"It's the Enchanted Elevator," Mom said, between breaths. "Only takes you to magical rooms."

The doors opened to let on two guards and a very frightened maid. Mom smiled encouragingly to her. The elevator opened again this time to let on an ancient man. Mom whispered to me that he was the court wizard. (Shouldn't the wizard be fighting the dragon or something? What is his magic good for, if he can't fight the dragon?) Finally, the doors opened to the fireproof room.

I do not know how to mathematically define the fireproof room, but I do know that "room" is not sufficient. It was the largest "room" I had ever seen and was full of bunk beds and couches. Mom led me over to a corner couch. She took a book off the coffee table. "Here, Lily. This will keep you busy while I make sure everyone else is comfortable." She smiled and winked, "A queen's job is never done."

After she walked away, I looked at the book. It was Descartes' *Discourse on Method.* A nice, logical book to read while waiting for a dragon attack. I sighed and opened it.

~~~

Around midnight, we were finally able to leave the fireproof room. Mom woke me up and walked me back to my room. She said it had taken St. George and most of HEA to take care of the problem.

"So did they kill it or whatever?" I yawned.

"Kill it?" Mom looked scandalized. "Of course not! Dragons are also citizens of the realm. They deserve to have the same respect we would offer to any *human* citizens. Really, Lily."

I closed my eyes and sighed. Clearly we were having trouble with the values of the variables in my dragon equation. I thought taking care of the problem equaled killing the dragon. Mom had a different idea. I tried again, "So what do you mean by 'they took care of the problem'?"

"They talked to Naga, determined what had upset her, and helped her find a more constructive solution."

"Oh." Smythian logic is too tiring at midnight. I said good night and went to bed.

I woke early the next day. I hadn't done my homework yet, and evidently, I could never be sure a dragon wouldn't ruin my plans. It was a wonderful day for homework, too. My father and Macon were busy with some sort of paperwork dealing with Naga and her attack. Mom spent the day in the throne room listening to the citizens' claims for property damage. So while my royal parents dealt with the aftermath of Naga's tantrum, I finished all my homework without any magical interruptions and still had time to read about Newton. Reading about Newton helped me to break out a little from the annoyed mood I was in. (Newton = negative degrees of annoyance.)

Mom came by late in the afternoon to get me for tea. On our way, she said, "Lily, I don't think I've mentioned this to you, but as a gesture of goodwill and openness to our subjects, your father and I have decided to issue invitations each week for our Sunday tea. It really goes a long way towards building trust between the royal family and the citizens." She patted my shoulder. "So remember to be on your best behavior."

I managed to get through the tea with lots of fake smiles to cover my annoyance. For normal teenagers, it is annoying to spring guests on them at the last minute. For me, it is infinity annoying to expect me to entertain fairy tale guests when I haven't had a chance to review their stories or find out who they are.

I passed the cookies to Minerva, who was a goddesses from Olympus. I made small talk with Paul Bunyan, and avoided the Erlking, who, Paul told me, liked to steal children away from their parents. The other guests were three bears (mother, father, and cub) and a girl with curly blonde hair. I made several attempts to interact with them, but each try met with failure. Every time I got close to one of them, they all got up and changed chairs. I heard the little bear whining about wanting the chair the blonde girl had.

An hour and a half later, the guests had all gone home. There had been a bit of drama, when the Erlking nearly succeeded in enticing the bear cub to come home with him, but Paul stepped in and broke the spell. Mom and I made our way to Arrivhall (My father had to give Macon a few more instructions). Portaling home was made (annoyingly) easy by our lack of luggage. (Lack of luggage = constant reminder that my parents are slowly moving me and destroying my life.)

I went to bed on Sunday night with hopes that Monday would begin a new week, with less annoyance and more math. As I slept, I dreamed I was back at

Ella's, sipping a mug of hot chocolate from Calo in her sunny hallway. I went to the table under the mirror to look through her mail.

A black envelope was addressed to me.

I opened it.

Lily,
Don't get too comfortable, dear. You're just a step away from vanishing.

Levi

P.S. I'm airing out a dungeon just for you…

I dropped the letter and woke to the sound of myself screaming. Blaire was jumping on my bed, chanting, "Get up! Get up!" I lay there, breathing rapidly for a few seconds, before hurling my pillow at her. Both she and the pillow landed on the floor.

"You're late!" she yelled and ran out of my room. I looked at the alarm clock. I *was* late. Why hadn't my clock gone off? I checked the back. Somehow, the alarm had been turned off. I touched the alarm button to see if it was still functioning and I felt a sick sensation in my stomach.

I looked at the finger that had pushed the button. It was greasy.

14

EVERYONE VANISHES

In spite of my lateness, I sat on the edge of my bed for a few moments; I was tired of being a part of Levi's evil scheme and I didn't think I could handle much more of him and his grease. I got up and washed my finger in the bathroom.

I came back and rushed around, throwing on some clothes and grabbing my book bag. After checking the time, I calculated there was just enough left to brush my teeth and walk quickly to school. (Breakfast would have to be skipped.)

King Tub was already in the bathroom, but since he was only using the mirrorphone, he didn't bother to close the door. He should have. He was wearing no shirt; only the shorts he slept in and his hair was wild. He stood in front of the mirror, waving his hands and yelling at Macon Mind. It seemed Levi had messed with their alarm too.

I left my improperly clothed father and went to get my extra toothbrush from the hall closet. I could brush my teeth at the kitchen sink. However, when I opened the closet door, I remembered my extra toothbrush was in my bathroom at Smythe. I sighed, annoyed about fathers without shirts, toothbrushes in different worlds, and alarms that don't work because greasy sycophants turned them off. I went downstairs and grabbed some gum, not at all cheered by its dual role as breakfast and breath freshener.

Corrie did not help my annoyed mood. This was unfortunate, because as my best friend she has the greatest probability of solving that equation. Corrie was, in fact, annoyed herself, and she was annoyed at me. She tried to call me this weekend, apparently. Several times. No one ever answered the phone. (I wonder why.)

"I kept getting your machine. Did you go out of town?"

"Why didn't you leave a message?" I asked avoiding the out of town question. I needed time to think of an answer.

"You know I can't leave messages, Lily!"

"Oh. Right." I had forgotten, but it was true. In addition to being obsessed with punctuality and the effective use of time, Corrie's father is also extremely concerned with saving money. He says one of the secrets of the phone company tyrants (as he calls them) is that if you don't leave a message on an answering machine, then you won't be charged as much. Whether this is true or not, I don't know, but Corrie told me once she suspected him of listening on the other phone to make sure she didn't leave messages when she called people.

"So where were you?"

The bell rang, and we started walking to our lockers.

I panicked. I had hoped Corrie would never notice I was unavailable from three-thirty to five every day or that I was gone for entire weekends. I couldn't think of anything that I could twist around to make truth. "Mom and I were in and out a lot. We probably just kept missing each other."

"Yeah, I guess." Corrie picked up her bag and closed her locker door. "See you at lunch?"

"Yeah. See ya, Corrie." I sighed. Corrie (quite normally) walked to her first class, and I was left alone with an abnormal mess of half-truths and fairy tale people.

~~~

Mrs. Fox was in a terrific mood. She hopped around in her exclamatory way, asking about everyone's weekends. She would have loved mine. My mind strayed for a moment, thinking about Mrs. Fox planning a field trip to Smythe's SFL. "Make sure you bring your keys, everyone!" "Now, remember, don't upset Morgan le Faye!" "Who can tell me a story this handsome wolf is in?!"

"Alright, class! Let's begin!" The real Mrs. Fox called my attention away from the imaginary one. "Get out a sheet of paper! Put your name on it; then write the topic of your fairy tale paper!"

Fairy tale paper! Oh no. In response to the exasperated sighs from some of the class, Mrs. Fox said,

"Remember?! I gave the assignment on Friday! You are to turn in your topics today!"

I did not remember. A lot of things had happened since Friday. I ripped a sheet of paper out of my notebook, annoyed that I had let a massive storm, magical doors, tea with Cinderella, hot chocolate with Calo, a dragon attack, tea with bears, and greasy Levi make me forget a homework assignment.

Mrs. Fox circled the room, winding up her exclamation point. "Don't forget to start your topic with either 'Legendary Literature is worthy of study because' or 'Legendary Literature is *not* worthy of study because'!"

I stared at my paper, searching my brain for any kind of topic. My mind rebelled against the abnormality of writing about fairy tales. I couldn't think; it's not a normal thought process. In fact, since my birthday, nothing had been normal. A life filled with magic is *not* normal. My parents *are not* normal. Dragons *are not* normal. Practically lying to my best friend *is not* normal. Fairy tales *are not* normal!

I sat up. My mind turned that last thought over and over again. Fairy tales are not normal. They can never live completely Happily Ever After *because* they're not normal. They have poisoned apples and glass shoes and really long hair. No wonder HEA is so busy; the citizens don't stand a chance of being happy (Normality = happiness). Yet, their stories are still read to children night after night. And those children grow up thinking that to be Happily Ever After is some magical thing that can happen to them. I grabbed my pencil and started to write.

Legendary Literature is not worthy of study because it presents a false idea of happiness. Children, who read this kind of literature, associate "happily ever after" with these stories. Fairy

Tales, especially, should not be studied, since the children cannot relate to the characters. The magic and enchantment of the tales separate them from the reader. Fairy Tales can never present a normal picture of happiness, because they are not, in fact, normal.

~~~

Calo was out when I got to work. A note on my desk read:

I had to take an emergency case. Not sure when I'll be back. Use the afternoon to brush up on some stories—you definitely need it.

Calo

I crumpled his note into a ball and threw it away.

I had just finished highlighting the citizens who were in danger on the latest report when Lane (the dwarf in blue) entered the cubicle.

"Got a letter for you, Princess." He handed it to me.

I opened the envelope, relieved it was not black; it was from Cinderella. She thanked me for a pleasant afternoon last week, and hoped I would visit again. She was available at any time, she said, because, unlike Aven (who probably couldn't join us, because he was so busy), she had nothing occupying her at present.

Again, that hint of something that was always in her tone. Bitterness?

I grabbed the three o'clock report. Ella was only Less than Happy, just below Happy. I mentally processed the past reports I had highlighted. I could not remember a time when Ella had been above Less than Happy. I found the other reports for the day on Calo's desk and looked through them. She'd been Less than Happy all day.

I felt close to making a hypothesis or even a conclusion, but I stopped myself; I needed more data. (Hypothesizing with insufficient data is really unacceptable.) I grabbed the inter-office phone and called Hannah.

"How can I help you, Princess?"

"Can you connect me to the Observatory?"

"Of course."

I heard a clicking on the line; then; "This is the Observatory, Doug speaking."

"Hi, Doug. This is Lily…uh, Princess Lily," I added, stupidly.

"Certainly, Princess. How can I be of service to you?"

"I'm processing some past Happiness data for a report. Could you tell me when Cinderella's levels were last over Less than Happy?"

"Sure. One moment."

I could hear Doug typing in the background. "Uh, Princess?"

"Yes?"

"We only keep observation records in our files for three months, and I have no record of Cinderella being over Less than Happy in that time. She dipped a couple of times but never to Could be Happier."

"Oh," I paused. "So, there's no way to know when she was last Happy?"

"No. Well, after three months, we transfer our files to the Archive. They'll be able to help you, and you'll have the advantage of looking at the whole file— you know, Happiologists visits and notes, things like that. Ask for Kikika. She'll help you."

"Kikika?"

"She runs the Archive. She's Sirena's oldest sister."

"Who's Sirena?" The name sounded familiar.

"The Little Mermaid," Doug said slowly, like he wasn't sure why I didn't already know that Sirena was the Little Mermaid.

"The Little Mermaid has sisters?"

"Yes. Five to be exact."

I decided to end the conversation before Doug found out I truly know nothing about this world. "So, I should ask Kikika for the Cinderella File?"

"Yeah. She organized the entire Archive when it opened. She'll be able to find whatever you need."

I thanked him and said goodbye.

I sat back in my chair to think. If I was right about Ella, her file would show she hadn't been Happy in a while. In every encounter with her, I've felt that odd bitterness. She's not Happy. And if that was true, I could use her for my paper. I could use her to prove fairy tale characters aren't happy because they aren't normal.

~~~

Kikika, for all her organization, was not in the Archive. She was not even in the building, her replacement, Debra, told me.

"She's on vacation."

I was a little disappointed. Even though I didn't know that The Little Mermaid had five sisters, I knew Sirena would be the only one to have legs. I was curious to see how Kikika managed to be working in an office. A rolling tub of water? A controlled flood? Some magical apparatus that defies all logic and math?

I smiled at Debra. "Perhaps you can help. I need to see Cinderella's complete file."

"Certainly," Debra came out from behind the counter. "The C file cabinet is over here."

"Thanks." I wondered what story Debra was from, but didn't think I knew her well enough to ask. Debra went back to the counter, and I turned my attention to the first drawer, Ca–Cm. Cinderella (Ci) would be in there. I found Ella's file without any problem; I was about to close the drawer when something caught my attention. Every file had a round yellow sticker on it, right after the name. Every file, except one: the Candlemaker's Daughter (Ca). It had an orange sticker. I took both files to the desk.

"Did you find what you wanted?" Debra asked.

"Yes. I want to check out Cinderella's, and I have a question about this one." I held up the Candlemaker's Daughter. "Why does it have an orange sticker? All the other files have yellow ones."

"Hmm. I don't know." Debra took the file from me and looked at the sticker. "Yellow stickers mean the story is active, but I'm not sure what an orange sticker means."

"Do you know how to find out?"

"I guess I could look in the notes Kikika left. It might be there." Debra flipped through a well-organized three-ring binder. Her finger jabbed at something in the middle of a page. "Orange stickers mean the story is inactive."

"What does inactive mean?"

"It means the story's been vanished."

~~~

I decided to take both files. The orange-stickered one intrigued me. Logically, of course, my interest was a natural and mathematical result of the sensation of seeing *only one* orange sticker in the row of yellow ones. Besides, something about a story that had vanished was intriguing.

Calo still wasn't there when I returned to our cubicle. I was glad; I wanted to ask some questions about orange stickers and vanishing stories and was relieved I didn't have to ask him. Grimm was never condescending when I asked questions.

Grimm waved me into his office when he saw me at the door; he was on the phone. "Absolutely, Kara. I totally agree.... But.... No, but if he hasn't broken international law, then we'll have no case.... No. I don't think so. I think Tallis will argue that Marshall Road is an extension of Smythe's SFL, because it's a portal point."

Apparently, Grimm and Kara (from the Agency) were discussing Levi and his alarm clock trick.

"I realize the King is calling for action, but we both know the law is unclear on this point. If we pursue this, Tallis will have the excuse he needs for a full assault.... What excuse? The unlawful detainment of one of his operatives.... Okay.... Sure.... Alright. I'll be there. Thanks again, Kara. Goodbye." Grimm placed the phone on its cradle and turned to me. "Well, Lily, Levi's latest stunt is causing an international uproar."

"What do you mean?" International like the UN and Uganda and China?

"By law, Levi and the other agents of Uppish Senna are not allowed to enter your world." Grimm straightened a few things on his desk.

"Oh. So, this morning was illegal?"

Grimm sighed. "Not exactly. Tandem Tallis will argue that, because your house has a mirrorphone, is on the magical mail network, and is the portal point to our world, it is an extension of Smythe's SFL. Therefore, Levi *was* technically within the law."

Nice. It could be completely legal for Levi to come to my house. "What do you think?"

Grimm shook his head. "I think we have to concede that Tallis has a point. Our best plan is to work on clarifying exactly what your house is in the International Council. Then, the next time this happens, we'll know exactly what to do."

"Who, exactly, meets in the International Council? Do you meet with France and New Zealand?"

"No." Grimm smiled. "The International Council is made up of just E. G. Smythe's Salty Fire Land, Wonderland, and Uppish Senna. But," Grimm clapped his hands together, "I doubt that you came in here to discuss international law. What can I do for you?"

"I have some questions about vanishing."

Grimm raised his eyebrows. "Interesting. Any particular reason this subject came up today?"

I hurried on, "Calo's out, and I was studying the notes he left and thought of some questions."

Grimm looked at me for a moment and smiled. "Well, ask away, then."

"Okay. First, when one person vanishes in a story, does everyone else vanish also?"

"Not at the same moment, but they will. Unless they have significant ties to another story."

"What does that mean?"

"Our citizens often have siblings who aren't the main character of the story. They're just there." Grimm shifted in his seat. "For instance, Prince Harry, the prince who rescued Rapunzel, is also the second son of the king in *The Golden Bird*."

"I don't understand. How can he be in two stories?"

Grimm smiled. "You may have noticed, Lily, that there are often three sons in fairy tales. The story almost always involves only the youngest. The other two leave home to seek fortune or fail to achieve the quest. But the youngest succeeds, and there we have the story. The others are only included to make it seem more heroic when the youngest does win. It's standard underdog philosophy. You want the little guy to prove that might isn't always right, that you don't have to be the first born to have good things happen to you, and that *you* can do it too."

A philosophy that completely ignores the principles of probability. The simple odds are that the bigger person will win in a fight, that older children have more experience, and that there will be things in life you *cannot* do.

Grimm went on. "Anyway. The older two princes in *The Golden Bird* do not succeed in the quest. The youngest son, we are told in the story, does succeed and everyone lives Happily Ever After—but what do his brothers do? The second son took a walk in the woods one day and found Rapunzel's tower."

"Oh. So, let's say Rapunzel has vanished, would this second son vanish also?"

"Anyone *only* in Rapunzel's story will vanish within the week of her vanishing. Harry, the second son and prince, still has a connection to an active story. He won't vanish, but his levels will be visibly affected."

"In what way?"

"He'll drop faster. It won't take as long for him to fall to Could Be Happier, and it will be harder to raise him back to Happy."

"That makes sense. And would Rapunzel's tale vanish as well?"

"From the records in your world, yes. But, because Harry's still around, our copies and files on those citizens in Rapunzel's story would also still be around, which is nice because we can use our files to try to rescue them."

Time for the big question. "If everyone in a tale vanishes, then the tale is gone—even from us?"

"Exactly. And all the files and notes made by our Happiologists vanish too; it's one of the reasons it's so hard to get someone back if the entire tale vanishes. We don't have any history or records. That's why *The Candlemaker's Daughter* is still missing. We have no files on them."

Missing? I looked up, careful to catch all of this. "Where do the records and stories go, when they vanish?"

"We don't know. Best (and most logical) guess?" Grimm suddenly looked tired. "They go to Uppish Senna, where Tallis and his cohorts use the information to torture their captives." He sighed. "Imagine being faced with the things that make you unhappy forever and ever."[47]

---

[47] Imagine an eternity where my pencil always broke just before I solved a complex algebra problem or being forced to write wrong answers to simple calculations or listening to children chanting incorrect multiplication tables.

"And all the characters in *The Candlemaker's Daughter* vanished?"

Grimm nodded. "We've been trying to rescue Celdan and her story for over a century, but we're no nearer to it than we were just hours after it happened."

I asked Grimm a few more questions about vanishing; then I walked back to my cubicle. I was confused and intrigued by the file on my desk. I looked at the orange sticker.

If the story completely vanished, why was the file on my desk?

15

THE IMPORTANCE OF
LAMPLIGHT

I had a lot of work to do, so I turned down my
parents' invitation to join them in listening to the new
Bremen Town Musicians CD. But I could still hear
the music; it floated up the stairs and made me wonder
again how four animals could make music of any kind.

I really wanted to examine the Candlemaker's
Daughter file, but I knew that I should at least do *some*
work on my Cinderella research. Technically, the Ella
work counted as homework (Ella = research for that
stupid paper) and, therefore, took precedence over the
mystery of *The Candlemaker's Daughter*.

I opened Ella's file and began organizing the papers into three main categories: Happiologists' reports, monitor history, and copies of the story. Additionally, I made a miscellaneous category for the leftovers, things like memos, correspondence, and a list of related stories. The list surprised me. There seemed to be a Cinderella story for every country: Korea, Persia, Ireland. I paused for a moment. If all of these cultures have a Cinderella story, which is the original? Is there an original? Are all of these Cinderellas living in Smythe? I made a note to ask someone (not Calo) about that. It might not have any relevance to my research or to my paper, but it seemed like one of those things that if I didn't already know about it whenever it came up, I'd get surprised our-princess-knows-nothing looks.

I read the story first. Several things caught my attention.

(1) Ella spent the whole story crying. She cried about her mother dying, she cried all over her mother's grave (watering the branch she'd planted there; her tears made it grow), and she cried when her step-mother said she couldn't go to the ball.

(2) She talked to birds. Regularly. The girl needed some human friends. *That* might have helped with the crying problem in number one.

(3) Contrary to popular belief, her slippers (in this version) are made of *solid gold* not *glass*.

(3a) Although, I *do* consider gold to be sturdier than glass, gold slippers do not make any more mathematical sense than glass ones. If you were wearing gold on your feet, they'd be too heavy to lift.

(3b) What is the deal with gold in fairy tales? That King Midas guy turned everything to gold when he touched it, someone could spin hay into gold or something like that, and that girl that married the frog dropped her golden ball into the well.

(4) Aven, for all of his cartography, seemed to be a bit of an idiot.

(4a) He decided that whoever fit the shoe would be his wife, not considering the fact that people can have the same size feet.

Then (4b), he blindly assumed (because of his faith in the shoe) that each of the step-sisters must be his mystery girl, even though neither of them looked anything like the woman he danced with.

And just when I thought I couldn't be more annoyed by the story, (5) there was the violence. Cinderella's scary bird friends peck out the step-sisters' eyes at the wedding. Eww. According to the story, the birds pecked out one eye of each girl on the way into the church, and one eye of each girl on the way out of the church. Apparently, no one sought medical attention for them, and the pain and shock of losing the first eye in no way lessened their ability to attend the wedding. How mathematical.

I can totally understand how Ella stays Less than Happy; her life is completely abnormal. If she had grown up in a normal way, if she had talked to people instead of birds, if she had worn leather footwear instead of golden, she would be more normal and able to be happy. But that is not reality. The reality is that she was this weird crying slave who talked to birds and put glass (or gold) on her feet.

I looked at the Happiologists' reports. There were only seven. Ella hadn't dropped low enough to need a visit often. Calo had only been to see her twice in his time. His reports were typical and very Calo: he got her happy, then left her alone. I compared the dates of his visits to the printouts of her monitor history. A week was the longest she'd maintained Happy after a visit from him.

My father, who was her Happiologist before Calo, also visited her twice. His methods showed more creativity than Calo's. Calo gave her a bird the first time he visited and paintbrushes the second time. My father combined her love of cleaning with her need to be useful; he asked her to come clean his office, saying his usual maid was too busy. Another time, they painted pictures of her friendly, eye-pecking birds. She stayed Happy two weeks after my father's visits.

Her first Happiologist, however, was the most successful. (Additionally, she must have also been fictionally created, because two hundred twenty-three years separated her second and third visit.) Miranda (the Happiologist) just went over to Cinderella's castle and talked to her. The report said they talked about all kinds of things: birds, the weather, cleaning supplies, Aven, Ella's disdain of the need for maids in the castle (apparently, she preferred to do the cleaning herself). Miranda wrote, "Ella seems lonely. She probably just needs a friend. Her levels even went up a little when I mentioned I might drop by again. Also, I think Ella needs to be doing something. Anything." Ella was Happy for a month after Miranda suggested that she take up painting as a career.

Questions:

(1) If Miranda was fictionally created, and, really, living that long can only be explained by being fictional, was she still a Happiologist? Why did Ella stop being her client? Citizens get to choose their Happiologists. Ella seemed very content with Miranda. What had changed?

(2) Why were my father and Calo satisfied with only a few weeks of Happiness, if a whole month was possible?

(3) What happened to the painting career?

I flipped to the front of the file folder. (Essential facts were typed on a sheet stapled to the cover.)

Name: Cinderella/Ella
Marital Status: married to Prince Avenant
Children: none
Creator/Collector: Brothers Grimm
Address: #35, Fourth Wood
Favorite Color: Blue
Fairy Godmother: Glenni
Things proven to raise Happiness: birds, painting, cleaning, fruit salad, sleeping by the fireplace, being useful.

There was no listing for career or profession. I was surprised, however, to find her fairy Godmother was Glenni.

Next, I looked through the monitor history printouts. Ella was very consistent. She was almost always at Less than Happy. And only rarely, did she get Happy without the help of a Happiologist.

I looked at my notes about her abnormal life. I looked at the Happiologists' reports. I looked at the line graph I had quickly made to chart her happiness. After thinking about all of these things, I got out a new sheet of paper and made an equation.

$H = ln$.

Where $H =$ her Happiness, and more especially, being Happy,

l = her actual Happiness level, which is dependent upon n, and

n = her normalness.

So, when you multiply l and n you get H. But the product, H, is made up of both the monitor level *and* being normal. Raising the amount of normal in Ella's life could only result in her becoming more Happy.

I would help Ella become normal. Then, she would be happier, and I could prove for my paper that fairy tales don't live Happily Ever After. I could prove to Calo that the best way to raise Happiness is to help the citizens become normal. I could prove to my parents the vital necessity of normality, and they will stop making me do abnormal things, and everything will be like it was before. Normal.

I decided to call my efforts *The Cinderella Theorem*. One day, when my mathematical brilliance is recognized all over the world, and I win the Fields Medal, my biography will say something like "Sparrow began her career with *The Cinderella Theorem*, a unique study into the importance of normality."[48]

I smiled. Everything was going to be perfect and perfectly normal now.

Discovering my mathematical genius made me hungry, so I went downstairs to get some pretzels.[49] As I

---

[48] The Fields Medal is a prestigious math award given every four years by the International Math Union (IMU). It is basically the highest math award there is, like a Nobel Prize. There's a cash award with it, and you have to be under 40 to be eligible.

[49] Pretzels are a great mathematical snack. You can estimate how many you'll grab out of the bag, use the mini ones as counters, or the sticks to form numbers and equations.

poured the pretzels into a teacup (teacup = an easy way
to transport the salty sticks), I became aware of the
music my parents were listening to. More accurately, I
became aware that my name was in the song. I stood
there, listening for a moment.

We'll be seeing that Levi less and less,
Because of the return of our Princess…
Lily, oh yeah, Princess Lily, Lily.

I went into the living room. My parents had
moved the furniture and were dancing together in the
middle of the room.

"I'm in a song?" I asked, disbelieving, even when
faced with the chorus repeating my name.

My mother stopped spinning. "Yeah, isn't it
great? The BTM wrote a special tribute for you."

"The BTM?"

"The Bremen Town Musicians. The cat has some
killer vocals on the second verse. Do you want us to start
the song over?" My father moved toward the stereo.

"No, thanks," I said, quickly. "I'll listen another
time; I've got a lot of work to do." I took my pretzels
and escaped upstairs, trying to forget the sound of my
father singing along. I consoled myself by thinking that
when *The Cinderella Theorem* is finished, abnormalness like
being memorialized in song will no longer happen.

I sat at my desk again and looked over the
Cinderella stuff I had spread out. As a reward for
discovering the secret of Happiness, I decided to spend
some time examining *The Candlemaker's Daughter*. I
gathered up the contents of Cinderella's file and (with
the notes I had made) put them back into the folder.

This file was much thicker than Ella's (Regarding file thickness: *The Candlemaker's Daughter > Cinderella*). I started organizing the contents, like I had done with Cinderella's and immediately discovered the reason for the thickness. Cinderella's file only held the paperwork related to *Ella*. None of the other characters were represented. The Candlemaker's Daughter file held the paperwork for everyone in the story. In addition to copies of the story, Happiologist notes, and monitor printouts for all the characters, there were also vanishing reports for each of them, and the essential facts sheets for everyone were stapled to the inside of the folder.

I decided the best place to start was with the story, so I took out a clean sheet of paper for making notes.

Once upon a time, a poor candlemaker lived alone with his daughter. His wife had died when the girl was young, but the candlemaker tried to be both mother and father to his little girl.

The daughter, whose name was Celdan, was pleasant and cheerful, never happier than when she helped her father in his shop. In the fall and winter, she kept their cottage warm and cozy. In the spring and summer, she picked flowers and herbs to scent and color her father's candles.

One sunny, spring day, when Celdan was 18, she went to a hilltop to find daffodils to dye the candle wax yellow. As she gathered the flowers and sang softly to herself, a young man, leading a white horse, came over the hill, singing the same song. Celdan and the young man looked at each other, smiled, and continued singing. When the song was finished, he sat next to Celdan and introduced himself.

His name was Colin, he told her, and though he was a prince, he was not proud or boastful. They talked for hours, occasionally moving to different spots on the hill to gather more flowers. Celdan told him about life as a candlemaker's daughter, and Colin told her about life as a prince. When the sun began to set, Colin helped her onto his horse and led her home. In that one afternoon, they had quite fallen in love with each other.

Colin stayed for supper with Celdan and her father. Since Colin was a prince, Celdan had been a little afraid he would find the meal too simple; it was only bread and cheese, but Colin thought it was wonderful—the best bread and cheese he'd ever had. He wanted to stay with Celdan forever but knew he must return home before his mother worried.

At the door, Colin said goodnight to Celdan; her father followed him outside. The candlemaker wanted to say something to this prince who loved his daughter, but he couldn't find the right words.

Colin spoke first: "I love Celdan, sir. May I come again tomorrow and ask her to marry me?" The candlemaker readily agreed. He had never seen his daughter so happy, and her happiness was all that mattered to him.

Colin returned to his castle slowly. He wanted to savor the memories of Celdan, and he wondered what he should tell his parents. His mother was a proud and haughty woman. She wanted Colin to marry a princess, or, at the very least, a high born lady. But Colin could only listen to his heart. He decided not to tell them yet.

The next evening, he returned to the candlemaker's cottage. After another simple supper, Colin and Celdan sat together under the window, and he asked her to be his wife. Without hesitation, she said yes.

Colin wished to be married right away, and since he knew his mother would never agree, he made arrangements to return the next day and be married in the village church.

After the ceremony, Celdan packed her belongings and said goodbye to the cottage and her father. The castle was not far away; she would see her father often, but it was still sad to think of him alone in the cottage.

When Colin introduced Celdan as his wife, the king was surprised, but pleased his son had chosen a clever, industrious girl. The queen, however, was outraged, but she hid her anger and laid plans to destroy Celdan later.

In time, Celdan gave birth to her first child. The queen had offered to assist Celdan during the delivery, and no one else was present in the birthing room. After the baby, a boy, was born, Celdan slept deeply, tired and exhausted. While she was sleeping, the queen took the child and hid him in her room.

Later, Celdan awoke and asked to see her son, but since no one else had witnessed the birth, the whole castle had believed what the queen told them: the child had lived for but a few minutes, then died. The queen also said she had him buried quickly, so as not to upset Celdan.

The entire kingdom went into mourning. Celdan and Colin were very sad. The candlemaker came to the castle daily to try to cheer his daughter.

The queen had planned to kill the baby herself, but found that she couldn't when the time came; he looked too much like Colin. So she took the baby boy out to a distant hillside and left him there to die. She returned the next week to see what had happened. Bloody clothes and tiny entrails were strewn about. He was dead, mauled by wild animals. No one suspected the queen because she seemed just as sad as the others.

But one night, a magical fairy, who was both wise and good, sent a dream to Colin. The dream revealed to him the truth of what had happened to his son. When he awoke the next morning, Colin was disturbed by the dream, but he did not believe it; he did not believe his mother could do such a thing. The fairy sent the dream twice more, and on the third morning, Colin knew that the dream was true.

*Colin convinced his father and Celdan of the truth, and
they confronted the evil queen. She did not deny what she had done,
and she told them angrily that she was glad the child had died
alone on the hill. While everyone was still shocked and surprised,
the queen fled from the castle and was never seen again.*

*Colin and Celdan held another funeral on the hill for their
baby, and in time, the pain lessened and they began to heal.
Eventually, they had more children, and though they were
occasionally sad about their first son, they still lived*
HAPPILY EVER AFTER.

Typical. The "happily ever after" stood out like it
was the all important thing. Never mind only Colin and
Celdan have names, never mind the queen had some
serious issues regarding her son, and never mind the
candlemaker let a total stranger marry his daughter. They
lived "happily ever after" so everything's fine.

I sighed. I wasn't surprised these characters had
dropped low enough to vanish. After the early happiness
on the daffodil-covered hill, things only got worse and
worse.

Next, I read the vanishing reports. Celdan went
first. She told Colin that she was going to the hill where
their son had died. The Ugly Duckling, who was flying
overhead, testified that he saw her vanish while she
stood beside the grave. The monitor printouts confirmed
the times. Colin, the candlemaker, and the king followed
soon after. They were sad about Celdan, and with so
much grief already in their lives, it didn't take long for
them disappear. The queen, according to her report, held
out as long as she could. Her final despondency was
fueled by the thought of Colin in a dungeon.

I didn't get it. Everyone was either dead or
vanished from this story. The candlemaker vanished. His

wife died before the story. Celdan vanished. Colin vanished. The king vanished. The queen vanished. The baby was killed by wild animals. Everyone was accounted for, so why was the file still in the Archive?

The probability of the file being in the Archive for the entire time they had been vanished was low. Kikika seemed too organized to let years and years pass by without going through the files. Besides, other Happiologists would have been in and out of the drawer during that time. One orange sticker in a row of yellow ones sticks out.

Conclusion: someone had been holding on to the file for a while and had only recently put it back.

I realized this conclusion wasn't entirely backed by evidence, but it made sense. And yes, there were a few holes in my theory. For instance why didn't the file vanish like it was supposed to? And who in the kingdom would be evil enough to want to prevent a whole story from being rescued? I considered Colin's psychotic mother, but that wasn't probable. She'd already vanished, and not being rescued would only hurt *her* as well. Morgan Le Faye was pretty evil, or that Lady Potio with her death apples. But their evilness seemed to be focused only on their own stories. (Morgan seemed exclusively the enemy of Arthur, and as far as I knew, Lady Potio had only tried to poison her own step-daughter.)

I sighed and turned on my desk lamp. Good lighting has not yet been proven to help you work and think better, but I don't think it can hurt.

I stared at the manila file folder, astonished.

The extra lamplight exposed something I hadn't seen before around the edges of the folder: grease stains.

16

DON'T EAT DULCITA'S MIRROR

Not Levi. *Again.* Will we never be free of that grease ball? I sighed and began to examine the evidence. Levi clearly touched the file; his greasy hands are forever betraying him.

But when had he touched it? When I went downstairs for pretzels? At HEA, when I left the file on my desk while I talked to Grimm? Or had he been the one who put the file back into the Archive? If that was the case, how did he get in there? He seems like the kind of person who would be banned from the HEA office.[50]

---

[50] I considered asking King Tub which solution he thought most likely,

There was no evidence Levi had touched anything inside the folder. Perhaps he wore gloves? Perhaps he never opened it? (But that seemed unlikely. How could he have the folder for all these years and never once open it? I only had it a few hours, and I couldn't help opening it.) Perhaps he...?

I stopped myself from thinking any more about it. The greasy fingerprints would have to wait until tomorrow; I was too tired. I shoved the folder in my Smythe's SFL bag and returned it to the top shelf of my closet.

I brushed my teeth and went downstairs to say good night to my parents. They were still dancing, but managed to stop briefly for hugs (the one with King Tub was awkward) without losing too much of their rhythm. The lyrics of the song followed me up the stairs:

> *Oh, we live in a magic land.*
> *Protected by the Sparrow hand.*
> *There are fictional and natural—*
> *Citizens all are we! Yeah!*

As I closed my door, the rooster began crowing a verse about fairy godmothers. Those animal singers would forever be a mystery to me.

---

but decided that wouldn't be smart. This is another example of what is wrong and abnormal about my life. A daughter, should be able to tell her father that she thinks an intruder may have entered her room. But I am not so fortunate. I am afraid King Tub will:

(1) finally make good on his threat to kill Levi,
(2) declare war on Uppish Senna,
and/or (3) take the file folder away from me.

I didn't sleep well. I dreamt of eye-pecking birds and baby entrails. Glenni wielded a fork and chased me around the Archive shouting, "Eventually, they had more children, and though they were occasionally sad about their first son, they still lived HAPPILY EVER AFTER! HAPPILY EVER AFTER! HAPPILY EVER AFTER!"

I woke at two AM, breathing hard and a little frightened of Glenni. I couldn't get the sound of her voice out of my head. "Eventually, they had more children...eventually, they had more children...eventually, they had more children." I sat up. Colin and Celdan had more children! If those children didn't vanish when everyone else in the story did, that would explain why the file hadn't vanished.

I jumped out of bed and turned on my desk lamp. Hurriedly, I looked through the Candlemaker's Daughter file again. There were no vanishing records for the extra children. In fact, there was no record of the mystery children at all. It was as if they never existed.

My mouth had that gross middle-of-the-night feel to it, so I went to the bathroom to brush my teeth. (Getting rid of gross feeling = joy; getting rid of gross feeling + getting to brush my teeth = immense joy.) As I started on my bottom teeth, I glanced into the mirror. My reflection had vanished, and Levi was staring back at me through the mirror. I spewed all my toothpaste at the mirror.

"Not very far along in our etiquette classes are we, Princess?" He was sitting in Marie's chair, twirling a pencil through his fingers. One leg was draped over the arm of the chair. His leather pants glistened with grease.

I continued staring at him, mouth open, chin covered in toothpaste dribble.

"Didn't you hear me? You ought to clean up." He snapped his fingers. Automatically, I began to wash my mouth and chin. My hand moved on its own, controlled by Levi's magic. I rinsed my toothbrush and dried myself with the hand towel, then wiped the mirror clean.

"Much better," he said. "Now, we can have a nice little chat, just you and I." He cocked his head and looked at me. "But I daresay you'd be more comfortable sitting." Another snap and a stool appeared behind me. The padded seat was covered in black leather; the legs were made of dark, dark wood, and the whole thing looked greasy. I grabbed a towel and threw it over the seat.

"How resourceful. I assume you, like the other disgustingly happy Smythians, dislike grease?"

I gave him a shaky smile. "That's a fair assessment of the situation."

Levi flashed a greasy grin. "So, Princess," he began in his slippery voice, "I wondered if you might have some questions for me—some questions related to say *The Candlemaker's Daughter*, perhaps?"

"How did you—" I began, but stopped myself.

"How did I know you had the file?" he asked, smirking. "My dear Lily, I have been working Celdan's case for a very long time; I know the file well, and I make it my business to know who has it."

I ignored his arrogance. "What exactly do you do when you 'work' a case?"

He shrugged. "Different things for different people. Lots of observations and reconnaissance in the beginning." He began examining his fingernails. "Mostly, I just cause trouble until I find a way to make the person genuinely unhappy."

"Did you find a way to make Celdan unhappy?"

He smiled. "I didn't find it. It found me. Besides, any junior ranked Dark Mesa could have found out what would push her over into Sadly Ever After. She was a mess." He shook his head. "I did her a favor by getting it over with."

I shuddered, disgusted at the callous way he talked about ruining a person's life. "Dark Mesa?"

"Like a Happiologist, but working for my Lord Tallis at SEA."[51]

"So, a Dark Mesa is an *un*happiologist? And SEA is like HEA, but you make people sad?"

"Something like that. But SEA is different from your nasty little HEA; we only exist to make *your* citizens sad; we don't care at all about our own."

Logical. Uppish Senna was just as organized at unhappiness as Smythe's SFL was at happiness. "Does Tandem Tallis get out like the Dark Mesas and make people unhappy?"

Levi made a scoffing noise. "He's the counterpart of your dear father. He was, of course, once a Dark Mesa himself, but now he coordinates the efforts of the rest of us. He doesn't have the time to be flitting around coaxing people into unhappiness."

Grease ball. "So, you're the Dark Mesa assigned to me?"

"Well," Levi ran a greasy hand over his greasy hair. "I *am* the top Dark Mesa and, probably, the only one qualified to vanish you, excepting my Lord Tallis, of course."

---

[51] Pronounced [see-ah] not [see]. I know it doesn't make logical sense, but it's supposed to rhyme with HEA [hee-ah].

"Well, qualified or not, you're wasting your time. I can't vanish yet, since I haven't reached Happily Ever After." Levi flinched a little at the words "Happily Ever After." "Besides, you've only annoyed me. Feathers and flowers aren't exactly depressing." That was true. I wasn't saddened by the Levi letters; just annoyed and disturbed.

Levi smiled. "Delightful as your criticisms are, especially since you know *nothing* of how saddening works, I suggest we move on; I doubt you brought me here to talk about dead birds and dead flowers. We still have the matter of Celdan to finish discussing."

"I didn't bring you here," I protested.

The scoffing noise again. "Lily, Lily, Lily. Your ignorant innocence is refreshing." He flashed a smile full of pity. "I'll let you ask three questions, but after that, I simply must go. I've got dry cleaning to pick up. You can't clean pants like these at home." He pointed to the greasy leather on his legs.

I organized my thoughts quickly; I certainly didn't want to keep Levi from his *precious* dry cleaning. "Alright," I nodded. "Question one: How did you get the File? Question two: What happened to Celdan and Colin's other children? Question three: Why didn't the file vanish?"

Levi smirked and raised his eyebrows. "Excellent questions. Answer one: I stole the file from the Archive. Answer two: Colin and Celdan had three more sons. They all died in infancy. Answer three: Files only vanish when every character has either vanished or died; therefore," he paused, looking meaningfully at me, "someone from the story is still in your nauseatingly happy land." He stood up to leave.

"But, wait," I argued, "that doesn't explain it. Everyone is dead or vanished already!"

Levi held up a finger. "I did say only three questions. Until next time, dear Princess. You can keep the stool." He bowed and disappeared.

"Wait!" I yelled pointlessly, but only my reflection stared back at me. I sighed, "That sycophant."

I sat on the edge of the tub and thought of about seven possibilities to explain why the file hadn't vanished, and none of them were remotely mathematical.

I dragged the stool to my bedroom and tried to sleep.

~~~

The morning found me staring, once again, at my face in the mirror as I brushed my teeth. I left a note for Mom (who was doing an early news show interview about her latest book), telling her that I would be home late from work. I wanted to stop by Ella's; it was time to implement phase one of the Cinderella Theorem: that girl needs to get out of the house and get a job.

School flew by in a whirl of exclamations, notebook paper, half-truths to Corrie, and beautifully balanced equations. And I had a whole page of algebra for homework. I almost hated to leave it, but Calo would probably be thrilled to write me up for being tardy. He was working on a Happiness plan for Okera (Sleeping Beauty) when I arrived, and was not in the mood to hear any of my suggestions.

"The soothing sounds CD from the Sandman worked last time, Lily. It's not as if..."

"But that doesn't tell you why she can't sleep. If you knew *that*, then you could be treating the *actual* problem instead of just..."

Calo kept thumbing through his files, ignoring me. "I could try a sleeping pill, maybe."

"A sleeping pill? Calo, that's crazy!" I tried to move into his line of vision. "She's probably stressed or worried about something or maybe her insomnia is caused by some other magical variable, but you can't just—"

He held his hand up to stop me. "Kara told me Okera's visits from Baldric have been increasing, so that's probably the reason for her insomnia. But it is vital that we—"

"Who's Baldric?"

"Her Dark Mesa. But that's not the point. If we don't get her sleeping again, she's only Beauty, and we've already got one of those."

I stared dumbly at him.

"From Beauty and the Beast," he added.

"Oh yeah. Right," I responded, faking understanding.

Calo sighed and closed his eyes. "Perhaps, Lily, while I'm taking my nap, you could review some *more* of the stories. You seem to have forgotten a few."

"While you're taking a *nap*?" I asked indignantly. "What about all this running around trying to get Okera to fall asleep?"

Calo closed his eyes again and breathed deeply. "Since I want to help her with her sleeping, it's got to be a *night* visit, doesn't it?"

"Oh yeah. Right." Calo: 2. Lily: 0.

Calo shook his head. "I'll be in the nap room."

~~~

I was working my way through *Beauty and the Beast* when Lane came in.

"Package for you, Princess." He left the box on my desk.

For a moment, I was torn. Was I more interested in the package or in the ending of the story? I shook my head. What was I thinking? Was I actually interested in this story? Reluctantly, I began to examine the data.

(1) The story, apart from the magic, had made sense.

(2) I really admired the daughter (Beauty) for taking her dad's punishment and sacrificing herself so he could be free. It was almost mathematical; the illegal rose picking happened (x), so then someone staying (y) must happen. Beauty just put herself in for y. (If x occurs, then y must also occur.)

(3) I also liked that the Beast and Beauty actually spent time together and fell in love. It wasn't love because of a kiss or magic shoes or frogs turning into princes. They actually got to know each other and *then* fell in love.

The data indicated that I was clearly interested in the story, but I decided I would open the package first. It's one thing to be interested in a fairy tale but quite another to let it control what I'm doing. I opened the box and read the included note.

Princess Lily,
My map table told me you don't have your own map of our exciting country. How unfortunate! I've enclosed a miniature map table for your own use. It is a copy of my own.
Best Wishes,

DON'T EAT DULCITA'S MIRROR

Aven
Prince Charming and Chief Cartographer

A small table, about the size of a jewelry box was under some tissue paper. I quickly found the switch. The table lit up and a female voice said:

> *"How can you get there if you haven't tried?*
> *How can you get there without a map-guide?*
> *What map would you like to see?*
> *Salt Land? Greenland? Italy?"*

"Good afternoon, Map Table," I said, trying to remember what Ella and I had done in her map room.

"Good afternoon, Princess. What map would you like to see?"

I'd really only turned the thing on to see if it worked. "Um..." I stalled, buying time to think. "Oh!" I realized, suddenly. "Show me the best way to get from HEA to Ella's." The only way I knew was a trek to Arthur's, followed by a massive storm and a fork.

"Now giving directions to Cinderella's castle," the table announced.

The map changed and zoomed in on itself, showing a closer view of the first four Woods, south of HEA. "Now showing the fastest route to the residence of Ella and Aven. Please observe the arrows, Princess." I blinked and looked at the map; arrows were appearing along the route as the table spoke the directions. "Travel west to Pele Fork. Take the orange door to Ella's; follow the usual path to her castle." The arrows reached Ella's castle. "Estimated travel time: 10 minutes." The arrows disappeared. "Now showing the scenic route to the residence of Ella and Aven. Once again, please observe the arrows."

I grinned. The table was very efficient.

"Take South Road to the town of Bremen. Follow the Fourth Wood west to Ella's. Estimated travel time: 40 minutes."

Evidently traveling by forks made quite a difference.

"Is there anything else, Princess?"

"No, thank you, Map Table."

"Very well, Princess. May all your travels be well-guided."

The table went dim, and I turned the switch to *off.* I carefully put the table in my bottom desk drawer, deciding I liked using map tables. They were very useful, and based on their calculation of traveling time, quite mathematical.

I finished reading *Beauty and the Beast,* then went on to *The Wild Swans,* making plenty of notes. Finally, it was time to go to Cinderella's. I packed my things back into my work book bag.[52] A sheet of paper fell on the floor. It was my list of questions about Cinderella. My eyes fell on the name "Miranda," that mysterious Happiologist of Ella's. Miranda, who had done so well with Ella's levels, but wasn't Ella's Happiologist anymore. I wondered if Grimm was in his office. Perhaps he would remember Miranda.

---

[52] I had found a plastic one at my house. Plastic book bags equal more protection for your belongings against random, emotionally charged, fairy-tale-land rain. I certainly didn't want the Candlemaker's Daughter file to get wet.

Grimm was on the phone when I arrived. "Frank and Marie are certain?" He waved me in. "Grease stains on the switchboard." He scribbled notes on a pad.

It sounded like Levi's phone visit had been discovered. "And they have no way of knowing who he called?"

I deliberately avoided Grimm's eyes.

"Hmm...Erased the phone records." Grimm wrote and spoke at the same time. "Okay, Daniel, thanks for the information. Write up a report and get copies to me and the king." Grimm hung up the phone, capped his pen, and looked at me. "What can I do for you, Lily?"

"Why don't you have a mirrorphone?" I asked, suddenly realizing that Grimm always used a normal phone.

He smiled. "I ate part of Dulcita's mirrorphone and she cursed me."

I opened my mouth and then closed it. Grimm's reply was not at all what I had expected. I had expected something like *I think mirrorphones are impractical*, or *I think traditional phones are more private*.

I sighed, preparing myself for another illogical revelation. "Who's Dulcita?"

"The witch from Hansel and Gretel."

I racked my brain for a reference. "They returned my bike after the storm," I said, surprised at my recollection. "And," I added, slowly, remembering something else from Calo's assigned readings, "don't they have an evil stepmother?"

"They do," Grimm confirmed.

I smiled, proud of myself for remembering a fairy tale. "So you ate Dulcita's mirrorphone, and now you can't have one?"

"I was a beginning Happiologist, and at the time, there were no forks to allow for rapid travel. I had biked nearly around the entire Seventh Wood, and I was starving. I came upon a little cottage made of candy and gingerbread." Grimm licked his lips. "Anyway," he shook his head, "in the yard were all kinds of things: tables, chairs, dishes–you name it. At first I thought it was a yard sale, but everything was really food, so I assumed it was a bake sale.

"I decided I would buy the mirrorphone cake. I was so hungry I started eating while I waited at the pretzel table to pay." He sighed, sadly. "Little did I know that Dulcita was really just brushing crumbs off her walls. She had moved the furniture outside, so it wouldn't get crumby."

"Oh," I interrupted. "Let me guess; she came outside, saw you, and angrily cursed you."

Grimm nodded. "Exactly. Now, whenever I look in a mirrorphone, I turn into a statue."

My eyes went wide. "Wow. That's horrible!"

Grimm started laughing. "It's not so bad, really. The curse wears off in a week, and the stone does wonders for your skin. It's just an annoying hazard mostly." He grinned. "But you didn't come in here to ask about mirrorphones, did you?"

I stopped calculating Grimm's total mass in stone and paid attention. "Right," I nodded. "I'm doing some in-depth research on Ella for Calo." Not exactly truth, not exactly lie. "And as I was going through the file, the name of a Happiologist I didn't know came up: Miranda. Do you know her?"

Grimm half-smiled and nodded. "Yes, I'm acquainted with Miranda."

"Well, do you know why Ella switched Happiologists from Miranda to my father? All the reports indicated they had an excellent relationship. Miranda was making real progress in maintaining Ella's levels."

Grimm shifted in his chair. "Miranda married and was considering cutting back on her case load, so she could have more time with her husband. She usually carried well above the normal number of clients and decided to scale down to an average load. Miranda never intended to drop Ella from her client list, but Levi heard about it and twisted it to serve his own purposes."

I looked up. "Levi?"

Grimm nodded and continued. "He told Ella that Miranda was going to drop her because Miranda was too happily married to spend time with her anymore. And if you are studying Ella's file, you know her own marriage is a source of her unhappiness. Ella was jealous of Miranda's marriage and, I think, her job. So she dropped her."

"Miranda dropped Ella?"

Grimm shook his head. "No. Ella dropped Miranda. She changed Happiologists, citing irreconcilable differences. Miranda tried to explain things, tried to make her see, but Levi's words were stuck in her mind." Grimm sighed. "It's too bad. He's entirely too good at what he does."

I smiled uncomfortably. "Really?"

"Yes, from a SEA standpoint, he's brilliant. He doesn't just make a person sad. He thinks fifteen steps ahead, but, more importantly, he understands that a person's depression never impacts only them; it touches everyone close to them."

I thought of Celdan and her four dead children. Watching her suffer must have impacted Colin and her father, slowly destroying them.

"Ella's firing of Miranda had an effect on Miranda as well. She felt responsible, and her levels reflected that for a time." Grimm sipped some coffee.

"Is Miranda still a Happiologist?"

"Yes. Her office is upstairs." Grimm pointed to the ceiling.

"Who did she marry?"

Grimm smiled and raised his eyebrows, "Me."

~~~

I didn't use either of the map-table's routes to Ella's. Instead I made a detour to Once Upon a Tine, to speak with Puss, the talking-cat owner. His tail swished around behind him, and he stroked his whiskers often, but I suppose he washes his paws before he returns to work. Puss agreed to my proposal, only on a trial basis, but that's still something.

I biked back around to Pele Fork and went to Ella's. Everything near her castle was still impeccably neat. The grass was amazingly green and perfect, as if it were daring you to litter and destroy the happy picture.

I used the glass (or gold) slipper doorknocker to announce myself. Nothing happened. I knocked again and waited. Ella was breathless when she finally came to the door.

"Lily!" She rested her hand on her chest while she breathed deeply. "What a wonderful surprise. Do come in."

I followed her into the parlor.

"I apologize for keeping you waiting, Lily. I gave the maid the day off and I was up in the attic cleaning and didn't hear the door. Then, when I *did*, I had to run to answer it."

"Oh, that's fine." I wondered if the other princesses cleaned out their own attics. I pictured Okera finally finishing hers and being able to sleep again, her mind cleared of the nagging disorganized attic.

"I'll bring some tea." Ella and her deep breathing went out of the room.

I looked around the room and noticed that the furniture was positioned differently from the last time I was here. The entire room had been rearranged and now the furniture faced the window instead of the door.

"You've moved the furniture," I commented as Ella returned.

She looked around at her room. "Oh, yes, I did." She shrugged her shoulders. "I was bored over the weekend, so I decided to make a little change."

"That's nice." I blinked as I realized the walls had been painted also. Ella has a very loose definition of *little*. "Did Aven help you?"

Ella smiled and raised her eyebrows. "No, Aven was on Olympus all weekend."

"Mount Olympus? Where all the gods live?" I surprised myself again. My fairy tale retention level was rising.

Ella nodded. "Neptune's map of the sea floor got dry, so it was completely ruined." She sipped her tea. "He went over there after finishing the map of Avalon. I'm not sure when he'll be back. It takes ages to map out the sea floor."

"I can imagine," I agreed, calculating the square mileage of the ocean floor. I sipped my tea and decided to change the subject. "Oh, by the way," I began, wanting my precious Cinderella Theorem to seem as unplanned as possible, "do you happen to know anyone who paints? Pictures, I mean, not rooms." I glanced at the lavender walls.

Ella smiled at my clarification and looked thoughtful. "Well, I…um…yes, I might possibly know someone who paints." Her words were slow and halting.

"Wonderful. I'm working Puss-in-Boots' case. He's distraught about a recent downturn in business at the restaurant," I lied. (There was no way to half-truth this story. Although, Puss *had* agreed to comply with my story if asked. I just hoped Calo didn't find out.) "Puss thinks that if he had art displayed for people to look at and maybe even purchase, he'd attract more business."

"That's odd." Ella added some milk to her tea. "I was in Once Upon A Tine the other day, and there was quite a crowd for dinner."

"It's the lunch crowd he's worried about," I lied again, hoping there was no magical curse lurking in the atmosphere, waiting to pounce on liars.

"Oh." Ella stirred her tea, thoughtfully. "I wonder," she went on. "I used to paint." Her eyes glazed as she remembered.

"Really?" I faked surprise. "You painted?"

"Yes." Ella smiled. "I really enjoyed it. There's just something about holding a brush. It makes you feel completely different. You can say things you can't normally say."

I smiled. "Well, if you've got some paintings lying around or if you want to make some for Puss, you should talk to him. He's very anxious to boost that lunch crowd."

I changed the subject after that, but I could tell Ella was still thinking about the paintings. She was probably going through them in her mind, picking out the best ones. I thanked her for the tea and made plans to come back sometime soon for another "friendly" visit.

On the ride home, my conscience raised a few doubts about the Cinderella Theorem. It might technically be wrong to trick Ella like this, but Puss *was* open to displaying the work. He just wasn't having any trouble with his business. And given Ella's touchy history when it came to her Happiologists, it might not have been a good idea to take advantage of her and "be friends" just to prove she can be happy by being normal.

But it was all for a good cause: the ends justify the means. Having Ella reach Happy by being normal was considerably greater than any conscience pricking.

I decided to stop back by HEA to grab a few more tales to read. Once I finished making Cinderella normal, I'd need a new subject. Who would be next?

~~~

I was quiet as I went through the cubicles. I didn't know where Calo's nap room was, and I didn't want to wake him up. I didn't need (or want) any Calo questions about where I had been or what I'd been up to.

But I canceled out all of my previous quietness by shouting, "Sweet Pythagoras!" at the stranger sitting at Calo's desk. "Who are you?"

"I apologize for frightening you, Princess." He stood up. "I'm Thomas, the miller. Calo's older brother," he went on, when it was clear that *Thomas, the miller* hadn't cleared things up for me.

"Oh," I said, breathing more slowly.

He smiled. "When do you expect Calo to return?"

"I don't know. He's taking a nap."

Thomas raised his eyebrows, "Taking a nap?"

I nodded, "He's got to make a night visit. Sleeping Beauty can't sleep."

"Of course." Thomas nodded in understanding. "I'll leave a message for him, then." He looked around, "Do you have a pad of paper or—"

I grabbed a pencil and pad off my desk, "Here."

"Thank you." He sat down at Calo's desk to write.

I sat at my own desk and pretended to be reading some of my files. Thomas finished, said goodbye, and left. I counted by threes to ninety-nine, then got up to read the note.

Calo,
Swing by the mill when you get a chance. I found something that I think you should see. It's important.
Thomas

I wondered what could be so important. I mentally searched my Calo data and remembered that Calo was the second of the three miller's sons in *Puss-in-Boots*. Thomas got the mill, the younger brother got the talking cat, and Calo got an old coat and hat and made his way in the world.

DON'T EAT DULCITA'S MIRROR

Mills don't exactly equal places of great mystery and intrigue. What, other than grain, could you find at a mill? And why should Calo see it?

17

A BIG MESS OF WORRY

Calo never directly mentioned the mill mystery, but I caught him reading the note a few times on Wednesday while we processed the outcome of his visit with Okera. Calo managed to raise her one level, but that was all. She was sleeping, but still Less than Less than Happy.

"Maybe," I suggested quietly, "her insomnia wasn't the cause of her unhappiness."

"Maybe," Calo shocked me by agreeing.

Then I noticed he was reading the note again. He wasn't paying attention to our debate.

"Maybe," I tried again, "you only treated a symptom of the unhappiness, and not the *actual* cause of the unhappiness." There. That was practically a blatant accusation. That would get the usual Calo response.

"Maybe." Calo stared blankly at the wall behind me.

Wow. I'd never seen him like this. The mill thing was obviously a big deal. He looked so worried. I wasn't balancing my equation properly. I'd left out a huge factor.

"Oh, by the way, your brother, Thomas, stopped in yesterday. He couldn't wait, so he just left you a note. Did you find it?"

Calo's head turned sharply. He shoved the note into his pocket. "Yes, I found it." He looked down at his desk. "What were we talking about?"

I just looked at him. The mill issue was becoming a larger factor by the minute. "Okera."

Calo nodded and began to shuffle papers around his desk.

I took a deep breath. (Deep breaths = the extra courage and strength needed to do something that you wouldn't ordinarily, normally do or that you would ordinarily, normally realize was a mistake.) "Calo, is there anything wrong? You seem a little…off today. You didn't even argue with me when I suggested you should have considered a more long-term goal with Okera."

"For the love of Rumpelstiltskin's beard, Lily!" Calo jumped up; his anger towered over me. "Okera's case is mine and *I* will manage it."

I moved my head back an inch.

"And for your information, nothing is wrong. Oh wait, could I possibly be tired after staying up to help Okera sleep? Could I be wondering how I will get my nap before going to Okera's *and* get to the mill to talk to Thomas about whatever it is he has found?"

I didn't answer Calo. I was 85% confident he didn't really want an answer. Rhetorical questions are completely unmathematical. In a nice, orderly mathematical world, one asked question leads to one answered question. When a person goes around throwing out rhetorical questions, all you have is one asked question leads to nothing. And people who ask questions, to which they do not in fact expect answers, are often annoyed when you (quite mathematically and normally) answer them. Judging from Calo's exaggerated hand motions and red face, I placed him on the *Doesn't Really Want an Answer* side of my rhetorical question chart. I kept my eyes on my own desk and sat quietly.

"I'm taking the rest of the day off," Calo stomped out of the cubicle.

~ ~ ~

He wasn't himself on Thursday either. When I came in, he was on the floor, staring at the ceiling with his arms folded behind his head.

"Calo?" I asked, cautiously. "What're you doing?"

He turned his head–the better to see me with, I guess. "I'm lying here wondering."

When he didn't offer any more data, I asked a clarifying question. "Wondering about anything in particular?"

"Sure," he smiled oddly. "About everything, about nothing."

I just looked at him. "Okay," I whispered slowly. "Are we going to work today, or just keep on wondering?"

"Work, of course," Calo sprang up, surprised I would even suggest otherwise.

I noticed the levels in Calo's monitor had dropped slightly. Perhaps only a millimeter, but enough for a mathematician to notice. I looked at Calo. He seemed to be busy, but a far off look was in his eyes. Probability of him actually comprehending anything he was reading: 15%. Those are not good odds.

"Calo, listen. I, uh, want to apologize for everything that happened yesterday. I didn't realize you were so upset."

He looked up. "That's alright, Lily. I have rather low expectations regarding your people skills, so I didn't take offense." He smiled.

I scowled back at him, already regretting my reluctant apology.

"I do apologize for yelling though. Thomas and I so rarely talk that I was concerned about the seriousness of his situation."

"Oh," I subtracted the warnings in my head and asked anyway: "Did you visit him, then? Is everything okay at the mill?"

Calo looked like he was thinking very hard for a moment, or focusing all of his energy on something. It's the way Corrie looks when she's trying to understand math. "Let's look at the briefing I wrote up about Okera, shall we?" He pointed with his pencil to a manila folder on my desk. "I made a copy for you." This time his eyes were clearly there, daring me to ask another question about Thomas.

"Sure." I sat down and opened the folder. Worry about Calo clouded my equation.

~ ~ ~

On Thursday night, my father showed me how to mail a letter using the magical mail network. It was pretty simple. You just place the letter in the cabinet under the bathroom sink. ("Of course, Lily, this only goes for our mailbox. Everyone's got a different one: Jack uses a leaf of his beanstalk, so does the giant, for that matter; Robin Hood and the Merry Men have a hollowed out oak tree that they use–you get the picture.") Once you have closed the door, you say:

Magical Mailbox, under my sink,
Please mail my letter before I blink.

Then you blink, and check to make sure the letter is gone.

I had two logical questions about that. "Okay, number one. Why do you have to blink if the rhyme asks for the letter to be gone *before* you blink?"

King Tub considered the question. "I don't know, Lily. I haven't really thought about it." He sat on the edge of the tub. "I guess if you don't blink, the magic will know you aren't being serious."

"'The magic will know you aren't being serious?'" I repeated.

"Yep," he stood up. "Now, what's your second question?"

I blinked in surprise. "How did you know I had a second question?"

He smiled. "You said number one. Why point out your first question without having a second one? If you only had one question, you would have just said, 'I have a question.'" He bounced happily on his heels ever so slightly.

He might not have been able to satisfy the mathematical equation of *Father*, but he surprised me with his logic sometimes. He was refreshing after Mom for fifteen years. Mom would never have thought to ask what my second question was; Mom could only be counted on to answer the first question about 50% of the time.

I smiled. "Two: does everyone have the same rhyme? It doesn't make a lot of sense for the bird and the happy friends to be rhyming about sinks when they drop their letters into the oak tree."

He looked puzzled for a moment. "The bird and the happy friends," he repeated. "The bird and the happy friends," he tilted his head, "Oh! You mean *Robin Hood.*"

"Right. Isn't that what I said?"

My father stood there for a moment, then shrugged, "Exactly. To answer your second question: no, everyone does not have the same rhyme. Whenever you set up your mailbox you have to create and register your rhyme. Your mother wrote ours, because she's a—"

"Writer," we finished together, laughing.

Before I went to bed that night, I wrote a letter and carried it to the bathroom. After I had said the rhyme (and *then* blinked),[53] I sat on the edge of the tub, with my chin resting on my hand.

I had no doubt my letter would get to Cinderella and that she would say it was indeed fine for me to come over for a visit on Saturday. I had no doubt she would be happier, because she had something to occupy her time

---

[53] I hope no one has ever tried to make a mailbox out of a difficult word to rhyme–like orange or month.

and was surely closer to being normal. So why did I feel guilty?

~~~

When I arrived at HEA on Friday, Calo was spinning around in his desk chair, muttering something that sounded like, "I'm a hot head."

"No argument here, Spinning Boy," I muttered as I sat down.

Calo grabbed the edge of his desk to stop the spinning. "Lily, I have a brilliant idea."

He seemed much happier than he had previously. I checked his monitor, expecting it to be higher. It wasn't. He'd dropped another millimeter and was just under Could Be Happier–the point at which HEA becomes concerned. The point at which Happiologists are sent out. Do Happiologists even *have* Happiologists?

Calo went on, without waiting for me to be curious about his brilliant idea, "Ice cream! We should have ice cream. Go see Tybalt at Once Upon a Tine and get some."

"Tybalt?"

"It's Puss' real name." Calo started spinning again. "No one wants to go through life with a generic name like Puss or Prince Charming."

"Huh. I've been calling him Puss all this time," I said to myself. "Calo, have you seen your monitor today?" I decided to employ a very mathematical technique– appearing incapable. Appearing incapable will often bring about a desired result if the person you're dealing with is like Calo who likes to be a bossy know-it-all. "I might not be reading it right, but it looks like you're at Could be Happier."

"Why do you think I need the ice cream?" He stopped spinning. "A dish of cherry vanilla will make everything better."

I stared at him. I did not, for one microsecond, believe that ice cream would fix this. But that was the Calo method: give them something they want and ignore the actual problem. "Fine, one dish of cherry vanilla coming up."

I went to get the ice cream, because I needed to make sure Calo stayed unvanished long enough to deal with the actual problem.

As I left the maze of cubicles, pure mathematical genius struck me. Grimm. I would tell Grimm about Calo's strange behavior. Grimm would be able to fix it. I smiled and maneuvered back through the maze to his office.

I stopped at his door, or rather, his door stopped me. It was closed. Grimm very rarely closed his office door. It was usually open, a literal "my door is always open" kind of thing. A *Do Not Disturb* sign now hung from the knob. I flipped the sign over to see if there was any additional information: a time that he would be available, the cause of this closed door, etc. But nothing was written on the back, and the sign accidentally fell off from my flipping. I picked it up, hung it back on the knob and gasped.

The doorknob was greasy–*Levi* greasy.

~~~

I quickly put my ear to the door. I couldn't hear what was being said, but I could tell that Grimm was nearly shouting and that Levi was laughing. That sycophant.

Frustrated with the results of my eavesdropping, I decided I'd better go get Calo's ice cream. I biked around to Once Upon a Tine, analyzing the reasons I was glad to get out of HEA–if only a few minutes.

(1) Calo. His behavior was really worrying me, but I didn't know what to do about it. Talking to Grimm was still an option. Could I go to the mill and ask Thomas? That might work, if I could come up with a plausible story for why I needed to know what he showed Calo, and if Calo never found out I'd gone behind his back. But what if I did nothing and Calo vanished?

(2) Levi. Why was Levi here? Was he trying to vanish Grimm? Was Grimm arresting him? *Could* Grimm arrest him?

I had no answers there, either.

(3) Ella. I was particularly glad to get to Once Upon a Tine to talk to Tybalt (whose name is not Puss) about the Cinderella Theorem. Had Ella shown him any of her paintings? Had she seemed happier?

When I went inside, the lyrics of yet another Bremen Town Musician Song assaulted me. This time, however, they were live and in person, rehearsing on the stage at the left end of the restaurant. The rooster moved the mike stand around a lot, bouncing it between his wings.

Mirror, Mirror
On the wall,
Who's the evilest
Of them all?
She poisoned that apple–oh yeah.
She poisoned that apple–oh yeah.
Just one juicy bite, my dear.
Just one, there's nothing to fear.

She poisoned that apple–oh yeah.
She poisoned that apple–oh yeah.

"Do you like the new song?" Tybalt came out of his office, stealthily, like a cat. (But, I suppose since he *is* a cat, I cannot use "like a cat" to describe him.)

"Yes." I nodded. "It's got a nice beat."

Tybalt swished his tail along with that nice beat. "What can I do for you, Princess?" He smiled slyly. "Do I need to participate in another lie for you?"

I ignored his lying reference. "I need a dish of cherry vanilla ice cream to go, please."

"Coming right up." Tybalt wrote the order down and passed it back into the kitchen. I looked around while I waited. There were several new paintings on the walls. Were they Ella's? I examined them closely. One of them was of a bird. Ella *had done* several paintings of birds with Miranda. Another painting was a still life, featuring cleaning supplies: a broom, a mop, and a bucket. Ella *did* like to clean. There was a series of three landscapes depicting what could only be Ella's pristine estate.

Tybalt noticed my interest in the art. "Yes, yes," he said, coming from behind the counter with the container of ice cream. "Ella came by on Wednesday to show me her paintings. She has some quite nice ones. They ought to be in a museum."

"Really?" I turned away from the painting called *Alone, I Clean.* "Did she seem happy to you?"

"How should I know?" Tybalt threw up his paws. "*You're* the Happiologist." He shoved the container into my hands. "Now here's the ice cream. I'll put it on Calo's tab."

"How did you know it's for Calo?" I took the bag.

"Oh, please," Tybalt sighed. "Calo's the only person who ever orders that flavor."

"I like cherry vanilla, too," I said, somewhat hotly, defending my favorite flavor.

His cat-eyes widened slightly. "How nice." His voice was a soothing purr. "What a perfect match you are." He glided away.

I frowned. What does that mean?

~ ~ ~

Calo *did* seem to be happy to have the ice cream. He stopped the spinning and muttering and snatched a spoon out of his desk drawer.

"There's nothing like cherry vanilla!" he cried happily. I slyly peeked at his monitor. It was rising slightly.

"Enjoy your ice cream, Calo. I'll be right back."

"Where are you going?" Calo's words were garbled by a mouth full of ice cream.

"Oh," I loosened my tongue for the lie I had practiced on the ride back. "Doug stopped me on the way in, and asked me to come up to the Observatory. A chart I wanted is ready to be picked up."

Calo rolled his eyes. "You and your charts." He shoved another spoonful in his mouth. "Hurry back. We need to go over Okera's case again."

I nodded and left.

Did all Happiologists lie this much? Did the great Miranda have to lie to her clients? Did my father? At least, I *was* going to the Observatory, so it wasn't a total lie.

On the way, I tried to visit Grimm, but the *Do Not Disturb* sign still hung on the closed door. I reluctantly went on to the Observatory.

When I entered, Doug was staring at a wall of hourglass monitors, making notes on a clipboard.

"Wow," I breathed. "That is a lot of monitors."

All of the wall space in the huge room was filled with monitors. Along a different wall another Observer worked from a rolling ladder.

Doug turned around. "Yeah, it is a lot." He looked up at them. "And this isn't even all. I guess you've seen the monitors in the entrance way."

I nodded. "Your job must be huge."

Doug shrugged. "It's not so bad, better than accounting."

"You were an accountant? What fairy tale has an accountant?"

Doug laughed. "None of them, actually. I'm naturally created. I went to college with your dad, and a few years after graduation, he recruited me for this job. He said he wanted someone with attention to detail."

"So you just moved here? What about your family, your parents?"

"Well, we didn't move right away. I commuted for a while, through your tub, but after we had kids, my wife and I decided to move here permanently. It's a great place to raise a family, very safe."

"Except for witches and curses and possible vanishing."

"Sure, sure. There are risks everywhere. We worry less here though, and we actually rent an apartment in your world, so we'll have an address for mail and a place for the grandparents to visit when they come to town."

"Right," I said, trying to focus. My mind created equations about the probability of these grandparents phoning when no one was there or dropping by for a surprise visit only to find their children's apartment abandoned and dusty. Then my analytical mind jumped ahead to my future. Would I live a double life as well? Would I have a real world apartment to invite my friends to, while I portaled through my tub to my job and other life?

I also started to wonder what my mother told her parents about my father. They'd died while she was in college. And did my dad have parents? I suppose he had to inherit the throne from someone, so maybe his parents were dead also. I was balancing my equation for grandparental death probability, when I realized that Doug was speaking.

"What?" I asked stupidly.

Doug smiled. "I didn't think you were hearing me. I asked what could I do for you?"

"Oh, right." I ran a hand over my hair and collected my thoughts. "I wanted to know if there was a way to make a special update list." Tybalt made a good point. I was the Happiologist. *I* needed to know how Ella was doing.

"A different one from Calo's?"

I nodded. "I just want to be updated on one person, and is there any way I can get the update delivered directly to me, no matter where I am, this world, my world, wherever?"

Doug must have been used to odd requests from Happiologists, because he just said, "No problem." He studied me, starting at my head and moving down to my feet. "Do you always wear those shoes? Or could you always wear them for as long as you want the special updates?"

"Yeah, sure," I looked at my sneakers.

"Great," Doug pulled a magic wand from his back pocket and tapped my left sneaker. "Okay." He stood up. "You'll start getting your updates there, folded into eighths, every hour. Who do you want on the list?"

"Ella," I answered, and then, without thinking, I added "And Calo."

~~~

"Are you sure you don't want to come?" Mom spooned strawberries into her cereal.

"Yes, I'm sure. Ella's expecting me." I took a bite of my waffle.

"Oh, but Lily, you'll miss all the best parts of the fair. The ribbon dance, the parade of vegetables, the yodeling contest."

I opened my mouth to say something sarcastic, but King Tub spoke first.

"I think it's nice that Lily has made a friend here in Smythe," he smiled. "Maybe, after she and Ella visit, they'll both walk over to the fair."

"Oh, I suppose you're right." Mom was still disappointed I would miss the ribbon dance. I ranked the importance of attending the Bremen Town Annual Fair fairly low: above reading fiction and just below studying for a non-math class.

Several things were bothering me, and they all added up to one big equation of worry. I was telling lies left and right (a), and while they were *all* for a good cause and had *only* the best motives behind them, it still felt wrong. The lying guilt was no doubt intensified by the moral tone in several of the fairy tales I had recently studied. Liars always get punished, and nothing good happens to them.

Hearing my father call me Ella's friend was also pricking to my conscience (b). I *did* like Ella, but I knew I was only spending all this time with her to prove my school paper. I had to make Ella normal. (Manipulation is another one of those things that isn't rewarded in fairy tales.)

Calo was still a source of worry (c). What was going on with him? Should I tell someone?

(a), (b), and (c) were compounded by (d): the nagging thought that Levi was up to something. Throw in an (e) lack of time for Corrie and an (f) the continual issue about the vanished-but-still-here Candlemaker's Daughter file and you've got a big mess of worry. (a + b + c + d + e + f = a big mess of worry.)

I sat up suddenly. Another update had arrived in my shoe. They still surprised me. I should have asked Doug how long it took to get used to them. I wondered if Doug and his family would be in the kingdom today, or if they were commuting back to the real world. I looked at my mother.

"Did your parents ever know about the kingdom?"

Mom choked on a spoonful of cereal. She coughed, took a sip of juice, and said, "You know they're dead, sweetie." She looked at King Tub.

"But how did they react when you told them about the kingdom?"

"They died before I met your father, Lily."

I closed my eyes, thinking. I can say with 97% accuracy that my mother has never told me a single thing about my grandparents–other than they were dead. They were never mentioned, and I grew up thinking that I shouldn't mention them, either.[54]

"How did they die?"

Mom swallowed more cereal. "In a train wreck."

"That's how you said Dad died!"

Mom's eyes darted to King Tub's. "Well, that's where I got the idea for your father's death. You know, art imitating life." Mom looked at her watch. "I've got to hurry. I'll meet you on the terrace, Matt." She kissed the top of my head. "Have a nice day, Lily."

I added (g) to my equation of worry.

(g) = my mother may be lying about her parents.[55]

Why would she need to lie about her parents? (a + b + c + d + e + f + g = a big mess of worry.)

I took my bike out of the rack and looked around; no one was watching. I quickly stooped down and pulled the latest update out of my shoe. Studying it, I was surprised. Ella was Happy. Actually Happy. Everything was moving according to my plan. My worries were momentarily relieved, except for the fact that Calo's levels had fallen to Been Happier. He was now just three levels away from vanishing. I wondered

---

[54] Strange, I know. But after about 24 conversations with my mom had ended with her in tears, saying, "They're just dead, Lily! Let's not talk about it," I realized there was no more forthcoming information. A good mathematician knows when something has become futile, like trying to make 2 and 2 equal 5.

[55] And the probability is pretty high since she is a proven liar. Of course, a strict examination of the facts proves me to be a liar also. Like mother, like daughter. But let's not follow that line of thinking...

again who his Happiologist was. Shouldn't someone be doing something? What if he vanished?

~ ~ ~

Ella's maid answered the door. "Her ladyship is expecting you, Your Highness." She curtsied. "Allow me to lead you to the studio." I followed the maid upstairs. She stopped on the first landing, opened the door to Aven's map room, and announced, "Princess Lily." She held the door open as I walked in.

My jaw dropped. All of Aven's maps were gone. The floor was covered in a drop cloth, the map table was shoved to one corner and covered with paints and brushes, and eight of Ella's paintings hung on the walls. Ella sat on a pile of atlases facing the easel with a smock tied over her dress. She turned around. "Lily, I'm so glad to see you!"

"You took over the map room," I said.

Ella looked around. "Yes, it's got the best light."

I doubted that. All the houses and rooms in Smythe's SFL seemed to let in a plethora of light. Ella motioned to the painting on the easel. "What do you think?" I looked at the painting and saw the Bremen Town Musicians singing. "The BTM saw my work at Once Upon A Tine and asked me to do some album art for them. Isn't it wonderful?" she gushed. "And look at this:" she pulled something out of her smock pocket—her plaid-filled monitor. "I'm Happy! Really Happy! Oh, it's just amazing!" She smiled and looked around the room. "Let's go have some tea, shall we?" She took off her smock and twirled out the door. "I'm so happy!"

Ella kept talking while we waited for the tea. "The studio is just the perfect place to work. Besides the lighting, it's spacious, and cheery. It's got such good energy."

"Yes," I nodded. "It was nice of Aven to let you have that room."

"Oh." Ella looked down. "Um, Aven doesn't actually know I'm using it." She shrugged. "He still hasn't been home. I half expect him to tell me that he's just going to rent an apartment in Atlantis while he's working on the sea floor map. I don't even know if he'll make it in for your tea tomorrow."

"My tea tomorrow?"

"Yes, your parents invited us for Sunday tea."

"Oh, right." I had forgotten about that gesture of good will and openness.

"But I don't think Aven will mind that I'm using the room. He hardly has a chance to use it himself." She smiled. "And I suppose it's sort of my payment for forever dusting all those atlases."

I rode home later confused and thoughtful. Ella was Happy, but her marriage was in trouble. Shouldn't that make her *less* happy? Or since she was becoming normal (according to schedule for my paper), was she realizing that because she married a guy who loved her for her shoe size, she didn't have a normal marriage? What would her new "normal" do about this? Was she Happy because she knew she could be free of the shoe marriage? She had a career now (painting album art = career); did she even need Aven anymore?

I smiled. If Ella's levels were any indication, I would be a *brilliant* Happiologist, converting all my citizens to normality. Instead of poisoning apples, I imagined Potio Bane and her stepdaughter going to therapy. Talking animals would be gone–they'd be happier as normal animals anyway. After all, normality equals happiness. Dulcita would stop building houses of candy and start a dentistry. I sighed contentedly, because with everyone normal and happy, I would have unlimited time for math.

I was so swept away in my future world of normal that I forgot all about the Bremen Town Fair. Mom was still upset about it while we waited for the Sunday tea guests to arrive.

"And there won't be another one until next year, Lily," she sighed. "The ribbon dancers were particularly good, too."

"Mom," I groaned. "I'm sorry. I'm *infinitely* sorry. I forgot, okay, I just forgot."

King Tub looked uncomfortable. "Who did you say was coming to tea, Ginnie?"

Mom sighed again. "Cerise, her mother and grandmother—Granny's cold is much better, and Hugo Wolf. We'll have to watch him." She ticked the guests off with her fingers. "Aven and Ella and Odin."

"Who's Odin?" I asked, glad King Tub had changed the subject.

"High god of the Norse," he answered.

"He gave an eye away," Mom added.

"What?" I asked, but no one answered.

Macon Mind ushered someone in. It was clearly the one-eyed Odin. His other eye socket was empty. A girl in a red coat, a middle-aged lady, and an old woman came in soon after. They were followed by a talking wolf. He cast hungry glances at the girl. Odin and the old woman—who wanted to be called "Granny," swapped optometry stories. (Apparently, Granny had cataracts.) Cerise, the girl in the red coat, kept looking at the tray of cookies. Her mother and my mother were deep in conversation. And predictably, King Tub and the wolf had a lot to talk about.

I stood stupidly off to the side like an extra piece of information in a word problem. (Sarah has three marbles and seven pencils. Danette has two pencils. How many pencils do Sarah and Danette have together? Answer = nine pencils.) I was the three marbles that no one needed.

Macon Mind walked over and bowed. "Princess, I wonder, as you happened to see Lady Ella yesterday, do you know if she and Aven are planning to attend the tea? We can't start pouring without all the guests."

"I know Ella's planning to come. But she did say Aven might not make it. He's working on a map of the sea floor. Apparently—" But I was unable to finish explaining to Macon why the sea floor project took so much time. Loud shouting was heard in the hallway.

"I cannot believe you, Aven!" Everyone already in the tearoom stopped talking to listen to Ella. "I am Happy, truly Happy, for the first time in ages and all you can say is 'Where are my maps?'"

"Ella, you're not listening." Aven wasn't shouting. He actually spoke quite patiently. "I am glad for you. I'm willing to let you keep the map room, and I think it's terrific that you're starting your career again, but I need my maps. Tuna migrations are preventing us from getting to a particular part of the sea floor. I need the map of that area so I can finish the job."

"Maps! Maps! Maps! That's all you care about. You were perfectly willing to just keep me at home dusting those blasted maps. Now, you just want me to quit painting and go back to being your maid."

"Ella," Aven pleaded. "I didn't say any of that." There was a pause. "Alright, let's just go in and have some tea."

Everyone in the tearoom immediately re-engaged in conversation, so it wouldn't look like we'd been listening. I turned to Macon, "I guess Aven came after all."

He bowed again. "I'll alert the servers that all the guests have arrived."

Aven and Ella came in, and everything was a little subdued after that. Ella made her way over to me with a cup of tea. "Aven and I just had the worst fight," she confided. "I suppose everyone heard us?"

"Oh," I stalled. "I don't think everyone heard; it was probably just the people near the door."

Ella looked relieved. "Good. Did you hear us?"

"I–uh–yes, I–I did."

Ella shook her head. "Aven is *so* selfish."

I nodded, not sure I really wanted to continue this conversation. But curiosity is a dangerous, unmathematical thing, and I couldn't help but ask, "What *did* you do with his maps?"

Ella rolled her eyes. "I burned them."

~~~

By the time I got to work on Monday, neither Ella's nor Calo's levels had changed any. Calo, however, was excited that Ella had reached Happy. He went on and on about it for seven minutes, acting like he had been the cause of her happiness. Since I didn't want to tell him exactly how I'd been involved in Ella's sudden happiness, I ignored Calo and focused instead on the opening sentences of my Legendary Literature paper. So far, I had:

Fairy Tales have had an extraordinary influence on our society. Our children grow up expecting Fairy Tale happiness. I wanted to add something about how no one can live happily ever after, but every time I picked up the pencil to add *But is this happiness achievable?* or *But this happiness comes connected to a world unlike ours, so Fairy Tale expectations are not realistic,* I saw the look in Aven's eyes. I think he had been (however bizarrely and unmathematically) living Happily Ever After with Ella. I think he loved her. He *loved* her, and she burned his maps.

~~~

Hannah nearly knocked me down when I entered the lobby at HEA on Tuesday. "Sorry, Princess," she yelled, racing away. "No time."

"That's alright," I called after her, but she was gone. I looked around me. There was an air of panic in the office. Everyone rushed around, busy. I headed straight for our cubicle. Calo was on the floor again. He looked depressed.

"Oh, forget it," I muttered, stepping over him. I dropped my bag on the floor and went to Grimm's office. I was determined to:

(1) find out about the panic feeling and
(2) to tell him about Calo's depression, which was putting a lot of worry into my equation.

But Grimm wasn't in his office. A woman sat in his chair, reading reports. Her feet tapped on the floor every so often, like she was unintentionally tapping dance steps.

"Where's Grimm?" I asked, skipping introductions.

The woman looked up and smiled. "Princess Lily, I'm pleased to meet you." She rose and extended her hand to me. I shook it, annoyed that she wasn't answering my question. "I'm Miranda, Grimm's—"

"Wife, I know," I finished for her. "Is Grimm sick?"

Miranda raised her eyebrows and sat back down. "No, I'm sure he feels fine."

"Then where is he?" I was exasperated. "I don't mean to be rude, but I really need to talk to him."

"Oh, I am sorry, but you'll have to wait a week to see Grimm. Unfortunately, he's been turned—"

"Been turned into a statue?" I sat down, flabbergasted by the news. "But he's so careful! We have to go to a separate room to use the mirrorphones and everything. You don't have any at home, do you?"

"No," Miranda shook her head. "We don't. Kara's still investigating, but we're almost certain Levi turned our hall mirror into a mirrorphone last night. Grimm always puts his tie on in front of that mirror. When I got out of the shower, there he was, a statue."

Miranda was handling this very well. My own mother would probably be hysterical if my father was suddenly stone. "You're not very upset." I couldn't seem to stop being rude.

Miranda smiled. "Well, it's bothersome and annoying, of course, but it's happened quite a lot. I know he'll be back in a week, and I can content myself with the knowledge that I have full control of the remote while he's a statue. All the other Happiologists have kindly divided up my cases for this week, so I can do Grimm's job." Her feet suddenly stopped tapping. "There is one thing that's odd, though."

"What?" I asked the woman who was mildly glad her husband was stone.

"Usually this happens when Grimm's not careful on a case, when he stumbles on a mirrorphone accidentally. Levi's never turned a mirror into a mirrorphone. And that's another thing–Levi isn't even Grimm's Dark Mesa. Why would he want Grimm to be a statue for a week?"

Since I could empirically determine that this was *yet another* rhetorical, unanswerable question, I ignored it. Her ponderings about Levi hadn't helped my mess of worry. But maybe I could get rid of the Calo issue? Surely Miranda would know who his Happiologist was.

I took a deep breath and said matter of factly, "Calo's been out of sorts for six days. He's dropped to Been Happier. I'm concerned that nothing is being done about this."

Miranda nodded and sipped her coffee. "You're absolutely right. I'm Calo's Happiologist, but he's taken this adoption thing a lot harder than I thought he would."

"What adoption thing?"

Miranda looked at me, surprised. "You know, Thomas found his father's journal in the rafters of the mill. And their father wrote about how his wife found Calo on their doorstep one morning." Miranda wasn't encouraged by my continued look of astonishment. "Didn't Calo tell you? I told him to tell you, that you would, as his partner and friend, be understanding."

I just shook my head.

"I can't believe he didn't tell you," she went on. "You need to know, because I want you to take over Calo's case for me this week."

"Me?"

Miranda nodded again. "Of course. You're particularly qualified since you are around him so much, and you've shown real concern for his welfare by bringing it up."

"Calo hates me!" I pointed out the obvious. "He didn't even tell me he was adopted; how am I supposed to make him Happy?"

"Oh, Lily, I know he's hard on you, but that's just because he wants—" Miranda began, but she didn't finish. A piercing alarm interrupted her. Miranda paled. "Oh, no," she whispered.

I jumped up. "Is it the fire alarm? Where's the nearest exit?"

Miranda shook her head. "It's not the fire alarm."

"Then what? Tornado?"

Miranda shook her head again. "No. It's the vanishing alarm. Someone's vanished."

18

EVERYONE VANISHES²

"Calo," I whispered to myself. Calo had vanished; I knew it. I knew it as surely as I knew the sum of two complimentary angles was ninety degrees.

Miranda reached for her phone, and I ran back to our cubicle. My heart raced, and an uneasiness settled into my stomach. I felt the way I had in seventh grade when I finished half of a math worksheet and realized I had done all of those problems without considering My Dear Aunt Sally.[56]

---

[56] Please Excuse My Dear Aunt Sally = PEMDAS = order of operations = Parenthesis, Exponents, Multiplication, Division, Addition, Subtraction.

My eyes went straight to the floor–to the spot where Calo had been. He wasn't there now. I began forming an equation about Calo languishing in a dungeon in Uppish Senna.

"Why are you staring at the floor, Lily?"

I looked up. Calo was at his desk on the phone. "You're not vanished."

Calo rolled his eyes. "Of course I'm not."

"But—"

"If you want to do something useful, instead of standing there like a *dolt*, you could get on your phone and call the Observatory. Maybe you can get through." He pointed to my phone. "I've been on hold since the siren started going off."

I picked up the receiver and pushed the numbers. "Why are we calling the Observatory?"

Calo sighed and shook his head. "It's like you have no deductive abilities." Ignoring my noise of protest, he went on: "Someone at the Observatory will be able to tell us who vanished."

I was about to show off my *deductive abilities* by saying that we would need to quickly formulate a plan to protect the other characters in the vanished person's story, when I heard a voice on the line. "We are experiencing high call volumes at the moment. Please stay on the line; your call is very important to us. A representative from the Observatory will be with you shortly." This same message repeated itself every forty-five seconds. In between the recorded messages, upbeat music played. I think I recognized a BTM tune.

To pass the seconds, I estimated how many times I would hear the message before I spoke to an actual person (estimate: seventeen). I was up to eight when

Calo slammed his phone down. "Forget it," he said. "Let's just go up there ourselves."

I hung up my own phone and followed him into the hall. As we went through the cubicles, I noticed everyone was on the phone, and everyone looked like they were on hold. "There ought to be some sort of PA system when things like this happen."

Calo snorted. "The names of the vanished can't be released until the appropriate people have been notified."

"Then why were you calling?"

"Because at some point, the Observatory will finish notifying your father, Grimm, or in this case Miranda, and the other members of the vanished person's story. Then, *clearly*, I want to be the next person they tell."

"Why?"

Calo pushed the up arrow and sighed as we waited for an elevator to come to our floor. "Because, the sooner I know, the sooner I can research. The sooner I can research, the sooner I can present the data to the rescue team. The sooner the data has been presented, the sooner the team can form a plan. The sooner—"

"I get it!"

"You asked," he shrugged.

I made a frustrated noise. "What rescue team?"

Calo opened his mouth to speak, but at the same time the elevator doors opened. An official looking person stood on the elevator, holding a clipboard. "Security clearance?" He asked, looking at us.

"Three," Calo answered.

The official raised his eyebrows. "Both of you are Level Three?"

"The Princess is covered under my clearance, Gavin, you know that."

"Policy is policy, Calo, you know *that*." Gavin marked something off on his clipboard and then the elevator doors shut. They opened back up immediately when Calo pushed the button. "Prince Avenant, or Prince Charming, as he is often called, has vanished. Thank you." Gavin pushed a button, and the elevator doors closed again.

The uneasiness returned to my stomach. *Aven* had vanished. The cartographer who just wanted to make his maps and live Happily Ever After with his wife. Then she got a new job and burned his maps. I stopped my thought process just short of analyzing my part in all of this.

"So what's the plan?" I asked Calo.

He didn't answer.

"Calo?" I asked again. "Calo? Did you hear me?"

He was very pale and taking deep breaths to calm himself. "We have to get him back. The ramifications of this are astronomical." He let out a breath of air. "I mean, this is *Cinderella* we're talking about. If her story vanishes, there will be some serious repercussions in your world. Have you seen the popularity ratings for *Cinderella*? It's got to be in the ninety-eighth percentile. It's one of the all-time favorites. And do you have any idea how many cultures have a Cinderella tale?"

Actually, I did. I remembered the number (345) from my Ella research. But I didn't think Calo really wanted an answer. (Another rhetorical question.)

"So what's the plan?" I asked again, hoping to focus Calo away from useless panicking.

He sighed. "I need to meet with Miranda." He
ran a hand over his hair. "I hope Aven's Happiologist is
on duty. We'll need his notes, files, and personal insight."
"Right," I began, "you head straight for Miranda.
I'll grab some notepads and pens, and meet you there."
"Meet me where?" Calo looked confused.
"In Grimm's office, for the meeting with
Miranda."
Calo made a half laugh, half snort sort of noise.
"You're not going to the meeting. You don't have that
much clearance." He headed for our cubicle.
I followed him. "You just told Gavin that I was
covered under your clearance. I should be able to go
where you go, Calo. I may have insights on this situation
that—"
Calo held up his hand to stop me. "Lily, your
actual security clearance is *T*. Do you know what *T*
stands for?" He rushed on, clearly not wanting an answer
to his (rhetorical) question. "It stands for Trainee. Do
you know what the clearance of Trainee means?" Again,
no pause. "It means that the *Trainer*–that's me–has full
discretion about what you–the *Trainee*–are allowed to
know."
"But—"
Calo went on. "You're doing well in your
training–actually quite better than I'd expected, but you
don't have enough knowledge to be a part of this
meeting. You'd only be in the way." He grabbed a
notepad and some pencils and left.
I might not be the most successful Happiologist
ever, but I did know one thing that Calo, the *trainer*,
didn't. I knew why Aven had vanished. I considered the
variables, calculated the outcomes, and decided to march
right into Miranda/Grimm's office and tell them what I

knew. I would just come out and say, "He's upset because I tried to make his wife normal and she burned his maps." Unfortunately, I was too busy polishing my calculations that I didn't watch where I was going, and ran right into a group of people.

"Security has been breached. I repeat, security has been breached. Secure the perimeter."

I looked up. Each person in the group was dressed in a dark trench coat. They wore dark glasses and had walky-talky radios. One of them seized my arms and pinned them behind me. "I've got her!" He shouted as he lowered me to the ground. "Get Kara to safety!" He whispered in my ear, "Thought you could take out Kara, didn't you? Hmm? Well, your little Uppish Senna plans are going to fail, girlie!" He planted a knee in my back.

Rapidly, I created an equation for this incident. Trench coat person (a) had mistaken me (L) for a Dark Mesa (d).

(a) intended to cancel out (d), but would actually mistakenly eliminate (L).

A different trench coater came over to us. I rolled my eyes up and strained my neck so I could see her. She removed her glasses and looked patiently at us. "Release her, Daniel."

"But, Kara, she tried to—" Daniel still held my arms, his knee crushing my spine.

"You're mistaken, I believe. Don't you recognize our own Princess Lily?"

Daniel hastily pulled me to my feet and bowed. "My apologies, Your Highness."

"Okay," I muttered, unsure of the precise princessly thing to say at the moment. I stepped away from him.

With a gesture, Kara shooed her entourage on down the hallway. "You must excuse Daniel." She smiled. "He takes his job as head of my security very seriously. He's an excellent Agent, though a little enthusiastic. You're not injured, I hope?"

I shook my head. "No." After a pause, I added, "ma'am."

Kara smiled again. "Excellent. Do excuse me, Princess." She turned to leave. "Miranda's waiting for me."

I watched her walk down the hall. I rolled my shoulders and swayed from side to side to work out the pain from Daniel's grip. Security is a serious business in Smythe's SFL. I carefully reconsidered my plan to burst into the office with my information. I had no evidence that Daniel and the trenchies carried weapons, but I had no evidence they didn't carry them either. Conclusion: the risk was too great.

desire for safety > desire to help

I retreated to my cubicle. (In this equation, retreated = ran as fast as I could.)

I sat down and drummed my fingers on my desk for a moment or two before standing up again. I looked out into the hall. Everyone was busy. Every few minutes, one of the trenchies would come out of Grimm's office and whisper something to a waiting Happiologist. The Happiologist would run off, I assumed, to do whatever the trenchie asked. Everyone seemed to be following preset guidelines about what to do when someone vanishes. As a *trainee*, I hadn't been trained by my trainer on this procedure. I stood stupidly in my cubicle.

I jumped slightly; the hourly report had arrived. I didn't think Doug and the others at the Observatory would have the time to continue giving me the special updates. Perhaps magic kept the updates coming? Or perhaps the Observers weren't involved in rescuing? After all, their job title does seem to imply that all they do is observe.

I pulled the paper out of my shoe, and rolled my eyes when I saw Calo had risen a level. That made sense. He loved to be commanding and condescending. "Using condescension" should be on his list of things proven to make him Happy.

But while Calo was getting happier, Ella was not. Her levels were dropping quickly. She was already at Could Be Happier. Her Happiologist should be going out to cheer her, but I didn't think Calo would want to be interrupted for this. I was sort of her Happiologist, wasn't I? And I was mostly the reason her husband vanished, probably contributing to her unhappiness now.

I balanced the equation and realized I was the only person likely to know that Ella was about to vanish. As far as I knew, none of the other Happiologists got Ella on their update list.

I grabbed my bag and left.

On the ride over, I thought of several points to emphasize to Ella.

1. The truth. I could tell her I had been trying to make her Happy, so I could prove that a person had to be normal to be Happy.

2. Her career. The way I saw it, Ella had to stay and finish her paintings. Her clients deserved that.

3. The fans. I could always resort to the illogical appeal of fairy tales throughout ages and cultures. Ella

wouldn't want all those little girls to grow up without a Cinderella, would she?

No one answered my knock, so after several moments of debate, I opened the door and went in. A painting flew from the studio door and bounced down the stairs, breaking the frame on impact. The canvas looked like it had been shredded.

I closed the door and went upstairs, narrowly avoiding decapitation from a bird painting.

"Ella?" I asked nervously as I went into the room.

Ella wiped her wet, red eyes and blew her nose on her smock. Her face was red and blotchy.

"Lily," she breathed in rapidly, several times. "What a pleasant surprise." She nodded to the floor where strips of canvas were strewn everywhere. "I'm just ripping up my paintings before I burn them."

"Burn them?" I whispered.

"Yes, I'm afraid they have to go, Lily. I let my pride and selfish desire to paint ruin my marriage." She sobbed and slumped on the pile of atlases. "Aven hated to be away from me on his trips, did you know that?"

I shook my head slowly and inched further into the room.

"It's true. He always wanted me to go with him. He'd ask *every* time, but I'd always say no. After all, a *princess* just doesn't run around the countryside like that. She's supposed to stay at home and be proper and embroider something." Fresh tears started; they ran down her face and fell on her dress. "I vanished him. I burnt his maps and made him miserable." Ella started sobbing again, and the only words I could make out were "….fault…why…shoe."

Ella looked at me, waiting. She had apparently asked a question.

Since "fault" plus "why" plus "shoe" do not in any way equal a question, I said, "I don't know, Ella." I walked over and hugged her. "I don't know how we can fix it." I adjusted our hug so I could look at her. "But I do know that we have to keep you from vanishing. Little girls all over the world look up to you. They dream of *being* you. What will their lives be like if you vanish?"

Ella pushed away from me, sobbing harder. "That's the worst of it." She was crying, breathing, and talking all at once—not a coherent mixture. "I'm a horrible princess. I let my selfishness ruin my story. I let my husband vanish. I'm an awful role model. No one should want to be *me*."

"Ella." I started moving towards her.

She sobbed again and vanished.

I stood there for an entire minute, counting and thinking. I came to two separate conclusions each with similar outcomes.

1. I could not bring Ella back, so I shouldn't stay.

And 2. I didn't know if people (possibly Daniel and the trenchies) would swoop down on the castle like police officers and CSIs to a crime scene. I could not imagine a situation in which it would be advantageous to be hanging around when they arrived, so I shouldn't stay.

I ran out of the castle, hopped on my bike (peddling at a velocity greater than usual) and jumped off at our castle. I grabbed my marble out of the bowl, headed for Arrivhall, and portaled to the safety of my bathroom. I immediately snatched up my toothbrush and started brushing. Then, when I was finished, I went to my room, closed my door, and tried to lose myself in algebra.

It didn't work. For the first time in my fifteen years, I wasn't able to focus on math. Tears kept dripping onto my paper. I couldn't remember any of my square roots, and my nose was running. I pushed the book away in frustration and threw myself on my bed, sobbing.

I had calmed down some when I heard Mom knock on my door. "Lil?" she asked. Her voice sounded tentative. "Can I come in?"

I said nothing for a moment, wiping my eyes and smoothing my hair. "Yeah, come in, Mom."

She looked tired. Mom's hair is often a gauge of how hard she has worked. When she comes to a problem in her story, she'll pull a strand of hair out of the clip and twist it. She says the twisting helps her solve the problem, but I haven't found that to be a theory supported by mathematics. She does the same thing when she's worried, and today, her hair was mostly out of the clip.

"How—? What—?" She stopped and started again. "Calo—." She shook her head and sat on my bed. "When—?" She cut off and sighed.

"Just say it, Mom." Incoherence is very unmathematical.

She took a deep breath. "Alright, Lily. The thing is, Calo and everyone at HEA think you left work after Aven vanished."

I opened my mouth slightly. Was I seriously in trouble for leaving early?

"Did you leave then?"

"Yes, but—"

Mom interrupted me. "Right after he vanished or later? And how much later?"

I looked at my mother suspiciously. What were these questions about? "It was later," I said slowly. "Maybe ten minutes later."

"So you weren't there for the second vanishing?"

"What?"

"You don't know?" Mom swallowed. "Alright Lily, this is going to be difficult. I have some bad news." She started speaking faster. "I'll just go ahead and say it: Ella vanished this afternoon, also. It—"

"What?" I asked, this time confused about why my mother thought I didn't already know this. Did no one know I had been at Ella's? Shouldn't one of the trenchies or a Happiologist have been responsible for monitoring her castle?

A tear rolled down Mom's cheek. "I know it's a shock, Lily." She pulled me into a hug. "You two were close, huh?" Mom rubbed my back to comfort me. "HEA and the Agency are doing everything they can to get them back. Don't worry."

~~~

It was all very well for my mother to tell me not to worry. She had no idea that particular motherly phrase wouldn't work this time. She had no idea that I was deeply involved in this story. She had no idea that I was the cause of the vanishings. My interference led to Ella burning Aven's maps, which, no doubt, led to his vanishing. And, I was witness to the fact that his vanishing led to Ella's vanishing. I was a vanishing catalyst.

So for all my mother's motherly words, I *was* worried. I left a negative off an answer (and had to run back upstairs to replace it.) I went to bed without brushing my teeth (and then got back up to go brush them.) And no amount of counting squares put me to sleep (so I switched to fluffy illogical sheep at 312 squared). I was very worried.

My father didn't come home; Mom said he was in rescue meetings. She wanted me to go with her to the candlelight vigil for Aven and Ella, but I told her I didn't feel like it. How could I go and light a candle for the people I had vanished? I was as bad as Levi. Tandem Tallis should be hiring me as a Dark Mesa; I was such a lousy Happiologist.

I turned over in bed. Ella's words repeated in my head, "I let my selfishness ruin my story. I let my husband vanish." I was worse than that. I, a *Happiologist*, let my selfishness ruin their story. I let my *friends* vanish— all so I could prove they should be normal.

I sat up and looked around for something to distract me. I grabbed the copy of *Beauty and the Beast* I'd been reviewing from my work bag. Maybe a fairy tale could distract me where math had failed. It worked; I fell asleep, dreaming about Beauty selflessly (not selfish, like me) giving herself to the Beast so her father could be free.

~~~

Mom was gone when I woke up, or maybe she never came home. That's the thing about vigils. How do you know when you can leave? It seems kind of rude to leave before the person you're vigil-ing for is found, but who can just stay there indefinitely?

I went through the motions of getting ready for school, all the while thinking about Ella and Aven. Why did I have to get involved? Why didn't I suggest she paint maps for him? Why had I ignored the warning signs? Why hadn't I talked to Aven at the tea? Why? Why? Why? It seemed my questions were infinite.

And like infinity, the questions didn't stop at school. I felt like I was split in half. Half of me tried to be normal and pay attention. The other half was lost in questions and worry. I hated it, and I have never hated fractions before.

"Lily, dear?! We're waiting!" Mrs. Fox interrupted my thoughts.

"For what?" I asked, coming out of my stupor.

"Weren't you listening?!" She asked, rhetorically. "I asked you to read the first page of this obscure fairy tale we're studying today!"

I looked down at the page. The title of the "obscure" tale was *Cinderella*. Already one of the most well-known fairy tales was *obscure*. Somehow, I pulled myself together and mumbled through the page, without paying attention to what I read. My thoughts were on the obscurity of my friend Ella. I had made her obscure.

I hadn't been checking my shoe updates regularly because there was nothing to see. Ella had vanished, and Calo was steadily increasing ever since he started his condescending problem solving. But during the passing period before Algebra, I had to clean my shoe out. It was too full and becoming painful to walk on. I slipped into the bathroom to empty my shoe/communication device.

I pulled out the top sheet. Through the folds of the paper, I could see Doug had written something below the regular print out. Curious, I unfolded it. He had written **Come Quick!!** near the bottom and drawn a line to the top where he had circled:

Calo Miller   *Vanished*

~~~

Newton's life was changed by the realization that things fall toward the ground, Pythagoras's life was changed by traveling to discover secrets of mathematics from all over the world, and my own life was changed when I decided to skip Algebra and go back to Smythe's SFL.

Once my mind was made up, I acted quickly. I threw the remaining updates away; I wouldn't need them since everyone on the list had already vanished. I gathered my things, slipped out of the building without being noticed, and ran straight home.[57]

As I ran I thought about two things.

1. Why did Doug want me to "Come Quick"? What did he think I could do? I finally calculated that he must suspect I know something since I was receiving the updates on Calo.

2. Why had Calo vanished? Yesterday, Calo was barely Less than Less than Happy. Admittedly, not great, but pretty good for what Calo had been recently. What had happened?

3. I hoped Calo's vanishing was not in any way related to my meddling.

---

[57] Having never experimented with skipping school, running seemed appropriate. Besides, I was in a hurry.

I ran in the door and was about to rush upstairs when I was stopped by all the post-it notes. Mom had left a trail of messages for me. I went from "Awful news" to "Calo Vanished" to "We're staying" to "in the kingdom" to "Blaire will fix" to "some supper for you" to "Keep going to school" to "I'll come home when I can" to "Love you Lily!" The trail ended in the kitchen. The "Love you Lily!" post-it was on a bag of pretzels. Mom's distraction was off the charts today. Did she really think I was just going to stay home and *keep going to school* while all my friends and co-workers vanished away to languish with Levi and the Dark Mesas? I headed up the stairs to throw some clothes in a bag. I was staying in the kingdom, too. After all, I was the princess of that place. W here *else* should I be when my people need me?

Suddenly, I sighed. What was I planning? Rush into the HEA office and do what? Maybe I *should* just let Calo and his story be saved by Kara and the trenchies.

I jumped. Another update arrived in my shoe. It poked uncomfortably. I dug it out and saw Doug had written something on it as well. Great. Who else could be vanished? I unfolded it and read,

Hurry! Kara trapped in office. I have a plan.

How in Fibonacci's sequence did Kara get trapped? Wouldn't her security force have secured the perimeter or something? I started back up the stairs. Mathematical or not, I was going to help Doug with his plan. The conclusion was simple: these fictional people need me. The equation for their fictional, magical world was unbalanced, and Doug needed my help to balance it, and if I, Lily Sparrow, am anything, I am an equation balancer.

I was nearly to the top of the stairs when I heard my mother's voice. She was in her study talking on the phone. But her post-its had indicated she would be in the kingdom indefinitely. I went back downstairs and peeked in the study.

It *was* my mother's voice, but it was *not* my mother. Blaire sat in my mother's special writing chair, talking on the phone, imitating my mother's voice.

"No, David," she was saying. "I won't have the proofs ready by then...... Yes.... well, yes..... No, I'm going to have to cancel everything for this week and probably next." Blaire waved me into the room.

I assumed that she was talking to my mother's agent, David. I sat in one of the other chairs and waited for Blaire to finish her conversation.

"I know that, David, but it can't be helped. I'll call you again when I know more.... Goodbye." Blaire hung up the phone and said, in her *own* voice, "Sorry about that, Princess. Your mother didn't have time to make all of her calls before she portaled over, so I finished up for her."

"You sounded just like her."

Blaire nodded. "Of course, dwarves are good at more than singing 'Hi, Ho' and mining for jewels."

I had no idea what she was talking about, but I was beginning to get an idea of my own. "Blaire," I started slowly, "do you think you could call my school for me? As my mother?"

"Sure, what should I say?"

"Say there's a family emergency or whatever Mom's excuse to David was." I turned to leave.

"Wait a minute, Princess." Blaire hopped out of the chair. "What are you planning to do? Why aren't you going to school?" She stopped. "Why aren't you *at* school?"

"Three people have vanished in two days. I have to do what I can to help."

"But—"

I cut off Blaire's protests. "I *have* to. I am the Future Protector."

She looked at me and nodded. "Death of a close family friend it is." She picked up the phone and I went back upstairs, deciding that vanishing sort of equals death.

I went to the closet to get my Smythe's SFL bag. My mind was already creating a list of things to pack. As I pulled the bag off the shelf (in my distracted state), a file folder crashed onto my head. It was Ella's file. Her papers went everywhere. I hurriedly gathered them up and went to shove the file back into the bag. Then I noticed the bag was empty. There should have been another file there: the Candlemaker's Daughter. I had been keeping it hidden there, so my mother wouldn't find it, but it was gone. Did someone take it? Levi? Blaire? Or could it have vanished? Everyone seemed to be vanishing lately. But for the *file* to have vanished, the last person from *The Candlemaker's Daughter* would have to vanish. And I still didn't know who that was.

"Oh!" I realized suddenly that I *did* know who it was.

19

THE ORIGINS OF EVIL LEVI

Calo. It had to be Calo. It made mathematical sense. He had been adopted into *Puss-in-Boots*, but since his adoption occurred before the written part of the story began, it didn't matter. As far as the story was concerned, he was always the second son.

The evidence of Celdan's son's death was circumstantial at best and completely illogical. The queen didn't return to the hillside for a week. The miller (or his wife) could have found Calo and brought him home. The bloody clothes and entrails found a week later could have been from something else or put there as a decoy.

I stopped myself. That's an awful lot of work for a miller (or his wife) to do. Plus didn't the miller's journal indicate they found Calo on the doorstep? And

THE ORIGINS OF EVIL LEVI

how would they know to leave a death scene? It took sneaky spying to know what the queen intended when she dumped her grandson out there on the hill. And it required a fair amount of evilness also, to let Celdan and Colin think their baby was dead. The queen wasn't an option; she herself believed animals had eaten him. Only one other person satisfied that equation of spying and evilness.

Levi.

I bet there were grease stains on those bloody clothes. And hadn't Levi told me he was Celdan's Dark Mesa? That he's been working Celdan's case for a very long time? Not only did he make everyone vanish, he created the depressing end to her fairy tale.

I sighed. Great. Now Levi's plan was completed. Tandem Tallis would be pleased to have a fully vanished story languishing in his dungeons. Of course, I was probably the only one who knew that Calo really belonged to Celdan's story. Everyone else thought the story completely vanished hundreds of years ago.

I sat on my bed to think. So many equations were balancing now. Calo was always Less than Happy because his levels were affected by the fact his other story had vanished. No wonder he was grumpy all the time. And he wasn't muttering, "I'm a hot head" that day in the office (although he really is). He was muttering, "I'm adopted."

But Levi's timing bugged me. He could have pushed Calo over *anytime*. He obviously knew who Calo really was. Why not get him when he vanished the rest of the story? Why now?

~~~

Macon Mind was waiting when I arrived. "Good morning, Princess." He bowed. "I have been asked to give you this." He handed me a note. "I have several pressing matters to attend to, so if you have no further need of me..." Macon dangled his sentence, waiting for me to dismiss him.

"I'm good. Thanks, Macon."

Macon bowed again and started to walk away.

"Wait a minute, Macon," I called, hurrying after him. "I've thought of something."

"Of course, Princess. How may I serve you?"

"Could you," I stopped, hoping he would say yes. "Could you keep my being here a secret? I don't want my parents to know."

An odd expression crossed Macon's face. "Are you in danger, Princess? Is there not some other way I could assist you?"

I considered telling him. I considered saying, "Yeah, Macon, I'm on a mission to save the people I vanished." But instead, I said, "I just don't want them to know I'm here. I have to take care of something."

"And they want you to stay in the other world?" Macon's tone was even kinder than before.

I nodded.

"I will not openly lie to my king and queen, Princess, but," he paused, "I will not volunteer the information, either."

"Thank you, Macon."

He bowed and left.

I opened the note, which turned out to be another short and cryptic message from Doug.[58]

---

[58] I'm beginning to see a pattern (of short, cryptic notes) forming.

Don't come to the Observatory. I'll meet you in your
cubicle.

I ran upstairs to put my bag down, then I ran
back downstairs, hopped on my bike and headed for
HEA. I didn't leave my marble in the bowl for a very
good reason; I didn't want my parents to figure out I was
here. I would just have to be extra-careful not to lose the
marble. I certainly did not want to spend the rest of my
life in Smythe's SFL. I had brought Ella's file with me,
just in case I needed it. I planned to tell Doug
everything, right down to my need to make Ella normal.

But my plan failed from the beginning. As I
pedaled toward HEA, I saw my parents get off their own
bikes and enter the building. Not only that, but two
guards were now guarding the entrance. Security must be
heightened due to the vanishings.

I needed to recalculate my equation. I'm
technically skipping school and while I think I could
legitimately argue why I need to be here, I don't want to.
It has been my experience that when parents are already
under stress (from an illness, problem at work, or a
vanishing rampage in their kingdom) that being
disobedient (by missing curfew, failing to complete
chores, or skipping school to save vanished friends) only
increases their stress, which increases the potential
punishment. Since my ability to help Doug all depended
on my ability to (a) get to him and (b) not be sent to my
room or home by my parents, I was stuck. I hopped off
my bike and headed into the woods, far enough off the
path so I wouldn't be seen.

I sat on a large rock and thought. There had to be
a mathematical solution. There had to be some way I

could get into HEA without being seen. I exhausted the mathematical solutions first. No back or side doors. Only the main door.[59] And while some of the offices had windows, our cubicle didn't.

I sighed and said, unmathematically, "I wish I was invisible."

"Now, you're talking." Glenni hovered above me, plaid sparks dripping from her wand. "I do wish you'd wish more," she said, floating down to my level. "But fairy godmothers don't get to have wishes. We only get to give them."

"Why?"

"Well, it would be silly for a fairy godmother to have a fairy godmother. It doesn't make sense."

I nodded, careful to avoid pointing out that a fairy godmother doesn't make much sense in the first place. How are you supposed to learn to solve problems for yourself if you've got someone popping out of thin air every time you make a wish? How do you keep from being spoiled?

"So you want to be invisible?" Glenni was bobbing up and down slightly.

"Yes, I need to get into HEA without being seen." As long as I had wished her here, I might as well

---

[59] I know. Not a shining example of fire safety. When I mentioned this to Calo, he told me not to worry about it, that in the case of a fire, all the citizens inside would be transported to safety. Now, how illogical is that? Trusting magical forces for your safety. The magic didn't transport everyone to the fireproof room when Naga was attacking the castle. Shouldn't *that* protocol be in place?

use her. Spoiling or not, there was no other way into HEA. It would have to be magic.

"Well, invisibility has its uses, but you want to be careful with it. It can end badly if you do it wrong." She floated slowly in a circle, thinking. "Hmm. Yes, that would be the best." She stopped her circular motion in front of me. "Do you happen to have your key?"

"Which key?" I asked. "I left my house keys at home."

"Not *those* keys." She shook her head slightly. "Your key. Your key to the kingdom."

"Oh," I said, understanding. "You mean my marble."

"Yes, yes, your marble."

I pulled it out of my pocket and held it in my palm, offering it to Glenni. She pointed her magic wand at it, and said, "Float." The marble rose into the air.

I stared at Glenni. I wasn't shocked by the magic so much; I'd gotten somewhat used to that, but I couldn't believe there were no magic words. *Float* described what was happening, sure, but wasn't magic supposed to be something else? Shouldn't Glenni have said "Floatius," or "Floatia," or "Floatabracadabra"?

"Why in the name of Salt are you staring at me like that?" Glenni didn't look at me when she spoke. She was concentrating on the marble hovering slightly above her head. "It's quite difficult to perform any sort of magic while being ogled."

I shook my head slightly to break the stare. "I'm sorry, Glenni," I apologized. "But I thought you'd use magic words."

Glenni swiveled around to talk to me. She kept her wand pointed over her shoulder. The marble still floated. "What are you talking about? What magic words?"

"You said 'float.' I just thought you'd say something else like 'abracadabra, open sesame, float.'"

"That's ridiculous." Glenni turned back around. "Why would I say all that nonsense?" She moved the wand up and down slightly. The marble followed–in direct proportion to her wand movements. "I wanted the marble to float, so I said 'float.'"

"Okay, I get it." I got up and walked around Glenni so I could see her face. "I just thought magic words had to *sound* magical."

"Good grief." Glenni rolled her eyes. "That's more of that animated propaganda you get in your world. Next you'll be thinking we all break out into song, too." Glenni moved her wand from side to side, making the marble move horizontally also. "Words–magical or otherwise–only have the power you put behind them."

"What?"

"I mean, *people* give words their power. A taboo word is only taboo because someone decided that it was that. A magic word is only magical because I put magical power behind it. If you don't give words their power, they don't mean anything."

"So if I insult you, and you don't give the words any power, then you aren't offended?"

"That's the theory anyway." Glenni had the marble spiraling up and down and all around. "However, you very rarely meet with anyone who so completely retains their power. Most of us are all too willing to let the words have all the power."

I wasn't willing to continue this discussion. I didn't have time to mathematically determine how much of my power was tied up in words. And I was uncomfortably sure Glenni was one of those you "rarely meet with" who absolutely had all her own power.

"What are you doing?" I asked, to change the subject. Floating marble acrobatics doesn't seem to equal becoming invisible.

"I'm testing your marble's obedience."

"It's a marble. You can get them at any store."

"Not these you can't." Glenni made the marble do increasingly faster figure eights. "These were given to your father at his presentation by Jacomo."

"So?" I asked, a little tentatively.

"*So,* Jacomo only makes magical toys. For instance, he created Robert, the Steadfast Tin Soldier."

"So the marble is magic? Magic how? Like am I only a good marble player because I play with magic marbles?" Something else struck me. "Have I been cheating?" Cheating is *very* unmathematical.

Glenni looked directly at me. The marble looked like a hula-hoop spinning around her. "You are not a cheater. Only someone who knows the proper spells can use the magical properties of the marbles. The marbles were only ever regular marbles for you."

"What can they do?" I pointed to the blue whirl. "Can that one turn me invisible?" I asked, calculating the odds that the marble I had chosen as my key to the kingdom was *also* the marble that could turn me invisible. Assuming, of course, only one of the marbles could make me invisible. If all of my father's marbles had the capability to render me invisible, then it wouldn't have been difficult to choose the right one. That probability was 100%.

Glenni interrupted my math. "Yes and no. This marble *will* be able to turn you invisible. But only because it's a magical marble. Not because it's a marble that turns you invisible."

I blinked twice. "What does that mean?"

"Jacomo's marbles come with the potential to perform whatever task is magically assigned to them. If you had them adjusted to act as a flying aid, you would fly like a bird, or you could place one in your flour bin and be assured you would never run out of flour." She had my marble slow down. "Before your father left them for you, he instructed them to appear to be normal everyday marbles." The marble floated down into her hand. "But the effect isn't irreversible." She smiled and spoke to the marble. "When rubbed three times to the left, make the holder invisible. That should do the trick," she tossed the marble to me. "Give it a try."

I eyed the marble suspiciously. "So you were making sure it was obedient because as a magical entity, it might not be obedient?"

Glenni nodded. "Exactly. It's been fifteen years since any spell's been cast on them. They were bound to get a little rebellious in that time."

"Right." I nodded slowly. I took a deep breath and rubbed my rebellious marble three times to the left.

I said, "I can still see me," at the same time that Glenni was saying, "Ah! Perfect. It worked."

I stood staring at her incredulously for four seconds before I realized that if it *had* worked (like she said) she couldn't see my look of disbelief. "What do you mean it worked? I can still see myself."

"Of course you can. You're invisible, not non-existent." She made an exasperated noise. "Here." With a flick of her wand, a full-length mirror appeared.

I looked at myself in the mirror, but I suppose it would be more accurate to say that I looked at nothing. I had no reflection.

"Weird." This was very unmathematical.

Glenni smiled. "To become visible again, rub the marble three times to the right. Standard counter spell."

I rubbed.

"Ah yes." Glenni rose a little higher in the sky. "Very lucky you had the marble, dear. Becoming invisible by potion is just too time consuming to be managed. Say 'hi' to Cinderella for me. I'm glad you took my hint and became friends with her."

"Wait. What hint?"

"That day at the fork in the road. I just knew you two girls would hit it off. Good luck with the rescue!" With another flick of her wand, she and the mirror disappeared.

"What?" How did Glenni know I was on my way to save Cinderella?

I sighed. Nothing ever makes sense here.

I shoved aside the temptation to apply math to the situation and pushed the marble back into the safety of my pocket. Math would not always help me in this world. I hesitated before I spoke to my bike. "Go back to the castle please. You need to be there, so Mom and Dad won't know I'm here." I think the bike actually nodded with its handlebars, and then rolled slowly away. I rubbed myself invisible and headed for the main entrance to HEA.

Being invisible didn't prove to be an entirely perfect solution. For one thing, invisibility does not equal silence. I'm sure that a terrified (and probably talking) squirrel ran off at the sound of my footsteps. Also, being invisible seemed to equal being hot. If I had a decent Fahrenheit thermometer with me, I could prove that my body temperature had risen as a result of being invisible. It was as if something was literally covering me, hiding me, warming me.

Sweating, I arrived at the doors of HEA and was stumped by my first real challenge as an invisible person. I couldn't just sneak up and open the door, because there were people milling around inside (not to mention the guards) who would be (quite mathematically) surprised when the front doors of the building just opened by themselves.

I sighed, making one of the guards jump, which made me jump as I realized how loud I was. I should have wished for Glenni to just transport me directly to my cubicle. I stood impatiently near the doors, stupidly invisible, trying to think of a way into the building. Suddenly, the door flew open with such force that it hit the 180 degree mark and stayed there.

"Make way!" a messenger shouted. "Make way! Urgent message coming through."

I took advantage of the open door, slipping inside before the guards could recover. I headed straight for my cubicle careful to avoid people rushing by.

Doug sat at Calo's desk, tapping his thumb impatiently. When I entered, his eyes went straight to me. He looked me over suspiciously, then smiled. "Clever," he muttered. "Glenni's doing, I suppose?"

My jaw dropped. "I'm supposed to be invisible," I grouched, moving to my desk.

"You are." Doug turned to look at me. "I wouldn't be a very good Head Observer if I couldn't see through invisibility."

"I can't believe you can see me!"

"Well, I can't *see* you, in the strictest definition of seeing. It's more like I can sense you."

"Bizarre," I mumbled.

"It was your father's suggestion. He had all the Observers extra-visibly endowed a few years ago. Part of heightened security measures."

"Speaking of the Observatory, why aren't we meeting there?" The Observatory was a few floors above us. The odds of running into my parents there were significantly slimmer than here on the main floor, right down the hall from Grimm's office. I glanced nervously toward the entrance of the cubicle.

"We don't want to be overheard by any Dark Mesas."

"What?" I hadn't been aware evil Dark Mesas hung out in the Observatory.

"The receptors of the Observatory are set very high in order to 'hear' or receive the Happiness level information. Because of that it's easy for spoken conversation in the Observatory to be overheard or intercepted by Dark Mesas. They know we're using a high frequency. We're currently working on a more secure solution."

I understood Doug was saying very mathematical sounding words like "receptors," "level," and "frequency," but just because a sentence has mathematical words doesn't mean it makes sense. Doug seemed to realize I hadn't quite grasped what he was saying because he kept explaining it in different ways. I nodded occasionally, but I wasn't listening.[60]

---

[60] I still have trouble understanding how Happiness can be measured; I'm not ready to understand why it needs a high frequency.

I looked down at my desk so Doug wouldn't see my eyes glazing over. A note for me was placed in the center. I quickly read it.

Lily,
Listen, I'm pretty close to vanishing, so stop making equations. Stop trying to make a chart. I found out last week I was adopted (my brother told me). I don't want to get into a lot of personal details, but I haven't had much luck handling the news on my own. I'm not sure what other story will be impacted by my vanishment. Give this journal to Miranda. The page marked is where my father wrote about finding me. Maybe she can use the information to save the others. Okay, well, if I don't make it back–I wanted to tell you that I think you'll be a good Happiologist someday. Your ideas are good, they just aren't

"Aren't what?" I asked aloud.

"What?" Doug looked at me.

I ignored him and flipped the sheet over. It was just like Calo to leave half a note for me. Half a note does not equal an entire note.

"No wonder he vanished," I mumbled. "He was paying me a compliment. That must have made him really unhappy."

"What are you talking about?"

"This," I shoved the note and journal to him.

Doug quickly scanned the note. "Hmm. He's right about not knowing which story he came from. We'll have to alert the Observers. They can look for patterns, see if any story seems to have a downward trend. We already know the citizens from *Puss-in-Boots* will be affected. We sent out their Happiologists immediately; no one wants a repeat of the

Aven/Cinderella double vanishing. But it's odd that both Miranda and Grimm are unavailable though."

"Miranda?" I knew Grimm was a statue, but what happened to Miranda?

"She was in the office with Kara."

"So they're both trapped? Why won't the door open? And how did the trenchies let that happen? I thought they were all about security and body-guarding."

Doug smiled. "Trenchies? I guess you mean the Agents."

I nodded.

"Trenchies is a better name. I'll suggest that to Kara when we're finished. But to answer your questions: yes, they are both trapped. No, the door won't open. And all the, uh, *trenchies*, are trapped in the office as well."

I opened my mouth to ask another question, but Doug held up his hand and continued, "All their Super-Secret Beepers went off at the same time. They thought Kara was in trouble, so they rushed in to save her." He paused. "Now none of them can get out and none of us can get in."

"Can you talk to them through the door? And why won't it open?" There was no mathematical reason for the door not opening, unless the density of persons in the office was so great, the door could not swing inward.

"No, we've tried shouting through the door and slipping notes under it. Nothing's worked–probably for the same reason the door won't open." He shuddered as if he had touched something disgusting. "Grease. There's a thick layer of grease all over the door, dripping down onto the carpet. It's going to be a nightmare to clean when this is over."

That evil little sycophant. "Why is Levi harassing everyone?"

Doug looked surprised. "I've been wondering that myself, Princess."

"Oh, yeah?" I managed to say. I hadn't meant to ask the question aloud.

"Yes," Doug moved his chair up to Calo's desk. "Levi doesn't usually–that is–he isn't usually so involved on this deep of a level."

"What do you mean?" Everything I'd seen of Levi so far was completely in character for a man who stole a baby off a hillside just so he could make Celdan depressed enough to vanish. "He's evil."

"Well, sure, this does seem that way, but usually Levi just does prank stuff, like turning off the alarms at Marshall Road. I've never seen him mess with the Agency, not to mention Miranda and Grimm. Dark Mesas have rules, too, you know. They can't just be indiscriminately evil. They have cases assigned to them, just like we do."

"Are you defending Levi?"

"Of course not," Doug shook his head. "I'm merely exposing the inconsistencies in his behavior."

"Look," I interrupted. "I know for a solid mathematical fact that Levi's behavior is always this evil."

And for the next fifteen minutes, I explained to Doug everything I knew about Levi. The tango, the visit in the bathroom, the letters, the grease stains on the file folder, and the final proof–Calo's vanishing coinciding with the vanishing of the Candlemaker's Daughter file. Doug raised his eyebrows considerably when I explained my theory about Levi taking the infant Calo off the hillside and leaving him on the miller's doorstep.

"Did Calo know about any of this?" Doug asked, when I finally stopped.

"Any of what?" I asked cautiously. I hadn't got around to my part in the whole Cinderella/Aven mess.

"Secretly holding on to a supposedly vanished file? Being continually harassed by Levi?"

"Uh...no," I rushed on before Doug could say anything. "But there's some more stuff you should know." And before I could mathematically stop myself, I hurtled along and confessed to everything. I admitted to being the (rather unfortunate) variable in the lives of Ella and Aven.

Doug's mouth hung open for several seconds after I'd finished. "Two things. One: I'm glad I don't have to explain all this to Calo, because he is going to be very angry, and two: this doesn't affect my strategy at all–I think." He paused. "It just doesn't make sense for Levi to want Calo to vanish, to be actively involved in vanishing him."

"Why not? Don't Dark Mesas want all of us to vanish anyway?"

"In theory," Doug answered. "They're supposed to. But–I don't suppose you have any idea what the Sennish dungeons are like–do you?"

"No."

"Ella, Aven, and the rest of the regular citizens– Celdan, etc.–will just be tortured by things that make them unhappy forever. Aven might be lost without a map, and Ella will probably be watching him from her cell–knowing that she caused him to vanish."

I sighed. I am one lousy Happiologist. Why must I make everyone normal? I turned my attention back to Doug, who was hypothesizing in detail about the now miserable lives of my friends.

"But with a vanished Happiologist, it's different. Tandem Tallis gives them a choice: stay in the dungeon being tortured forever or become a Dark Mesa."

"None of us would do that," I said incredulously. "None of us would ever become a Dark Mesa."

"It's happened before. Many times. In fact, every Dark Mesa–except Tandem Tallis–was once a Happiologist. It is supposed that even your father's brother defected when he vanished."

"My father has a brother?" I paused to let that sink in. "I can't believe a Happiologist would switch sides. It's not mathematical. Why would they defect like that?"

"Think about it, Princess. Would you stay in a miserable dungeon working unsolvable math problems, knowing that if you *chose* you could be free?"

"Yeah, but—"

"Dungeons are dungeons. At some point, everyone wants out badly enough." He shook his head. "I don't like the choices some Happiologists have made– but I understand them. I hope you never have to make that choice, Princess."

I didn't say anything, but mentally I agreed with Doug. How could I make that choice? It's all well and good and mathematical to say I'd stay constant while I only hypothesized about it, but if I was *really* faced with torturous Geometry proofs that would not be solved, *could* I stay constant?

I didn't want to answer that question, so with mathematical effort, I turned my mind to another matter: Levi.

"So, Levi was once a Happiologist?"

Doug nodded. "An extremely good one, too." He leaned in to whisper. "Some say he was even better than

Calo or Grimm. Not that they ever worked together. Levi was way before their time. And he was being groomed to take charge of HEA, after the Head Happiologist retired."

"So what happened?" I asked. "How did he go from golden boy to grease bomb?"

"He got careless, I guess. Didn't keep up with his own happiness. And one day he vanished. Tandem Tallis was delighted with his luck. He had the best Happiologist in all of Smythe's SFL, locked in one of his dungeons. In those days, Tallis was the only Dark Mesa around. His strategy was simply to get the Happiologists to vanish. No Happiologists in Smythe's SFL would make the citizens easy to pick off. But the vanishing of Levi changed everything. Levi didn't like being in the dungeon and was determined to find a way out. He waited patiently, planning his strategy. In the end, he managed to get Tallis to agree to his release."

"How?"

"Levi agreed to become Tallis' lieutenant. In exchange for his release from the dungeon, Levi became the Dark Mesa he is today."

I didn't say anything for a moment. I was wondering how anyone could agree to betray their own country, but I was also wondering how anyone could willingly endure torture, knowing they had a way out.

"He's a traitor."

Doug nodded. "That's why he's so greasy. It's punishment for his treachery."

"What? Punishment from whom?"

Doug looked confused. "From the fairy tale Forces of Magic. You know, in all the stories good behavior is rewarded and bad behavior is punished, like Fanchon."

"Who?"

"Fanchon, the older sister who was rude to the fairy and was punished by having snakes and frogs come out of her mouth every time she talked."

I just looked at Doug.

He went on. "And the good sister had gems and jewels drip out of her mouth, because she was nice to the fairy. Good is rewarded; evil is punished. It's standard fairy tale philosophy. Didn't Calo go over that with you?"

I blinked at Doug. "I have no idea," I answered honestly. "Calo mentioned numerous things I can't remember." I looked down. "If you haven't noticed, I'm not very good at this whole Happiologist thing."

"Nonsense. You calculated why Calo vanished with astonishing accuracy, and you're here helping to save the kingdom." He paused. "I just wish I knew why Levi bothered Calo in the first place?"

"Other than the fact that he's evil, right?"

"Right. Calo's not even one of his cases. Besides Levi is competitive. He's been Tallis' number one for hundreds of years. He wouldn't want to give Calo the chance to become a better Dark Mesa than him."

"Assuming Calo would change sides, of course." I could not believe Calo would be so treacherous. He was an annoying, stuck-up jerk, but he wasn't a traitor. He was the one who stayed at work during my presentation ball to watch the monitors. He was the one who took offence when I didn't know anything about fairy tales. Calo loved E. G. Smythe's Salty Fire Land. He would never betray it.

"Of course." Doug didn't look like he held a lot of faith in Calo's constancy. "Just in case, though, we should get him out of there as soon as we can."

I thought about Levi's supposedly strange behavior. If he really was acting outside his limits, he was taking an incredible risk. Was his desire to vanish Calo greater than his need to be the best? It didn't seem to equal the image I'd formed of him.

Levi was ultimately selfish. He had selfishly chosen his own comforts over the greater good of the kingdom. Why would he go out of his way to vanish someone that could ruin his career? Why would he take the trouble of making sure Kara, Grimm, and Miranda couldn't intervene in his vanishing of Calo? If Calo isn't his true target, who is?

"It's me," I whispered.

Doug looked up from his notes. "What?"

"Levi's after *me*. It's basic mathematics. Why would Levi take such risks for just Calo? He's after a much bigger target. He wants the heir to the throne."

"I don't think that's true," Doug fumbled with his notes, making new stacks. "We can't assume—"

"There's no other reason. Why would Levi wait until now to vanish Calo? He thinks I'll be so saddened by Calo's vanishment that I'll vanish too."

"But you *aren't* living Happily Ever After, Princess. Levi knows that. You can't vanish." He cleared his throat. "I don't think you're the reason Calo vanished, but I do think you're the only one who can save him."

"Why am I the only one?" Being the *only* one greatly reduces the mathematical odds. The *only* one out of a hundred has a 1% chance of success.

"Because your Happiness levels can't be affected by Levi and Uppish Senna. You're not vanishable."

"Okay," I said slowly.

Doug rolled his chair over to me. "Look, we need someone in the dungeon to talk to Calo and Ella–to get them back to Happy so they will vanish out of dungeon. Since Cinderella is such a high profile story, we have to do this as soon as possible, before the whole thing vanishes."

"I don't—"

Doug held up his hand to stop me. "Let me finish. Any of us could go, sure, but our odds of success are only 10-12%. Your odds are closer to 57%."

"That's very specific."

"I was an accountant."

"Those aren't very good odds."

Doug shrugged. "If it were easy to get in and out of the dungeons, it wouldn't be so devastating when people vanish. Beside you may not be a certified Happiologist yet, but you have one major advantage."

"That I'm not vanishable?"

"Exactly. Any of the rest of us will begin to be affected by the sadness in the dungeon as soon as we get there. That will slow us down, impact our work, and if we're not careful, could leave us trapped there." He paused. "You, on the other hand, can't be bothered by the sadness, so you will be able to work at full strength for a long time–indefinitely, even. Plus, you won't be confined to your cell, so you'll be able to talk to the others."

"Why won't I be confined to a cell?" I interrupted, ignoring the question of how I got into the cell in the first place.

Doug smiled. "Didn't you know? The Sennish dungeons don't have bars or locks. The prisoners are locked in by the force of their own unhappiness.

Happiness is the only thing that gets them out. You will be able to move freely around the prison."

"Okay, but surely Tallis knows about that? It is his prison, after all. He's not going to let me just wander around."

"No. There are guards everywhere." He ran a hand over his bald head. "We really need a map table, but it will be tricky getting to the map room." He looked cautiously out the cubicle opening.

"Why do we need a map table?" Even though I was mentally reeling from the implication of his plan, I remained calm and asked rational questions. It sounded like this rescue equation was shaping up with me *in* prison. Prison is very unmathematical. Especially if there are no bars or locks.

"There are no paper copies of the Uppish Senna maps. The grease they emitted eventually ruined them. We had Aven commit them all to MTM a while back."

"MTM?"

"Map table memory."

"Oh." I nodded. "I have a map table." I opened my desk drawer and pulled out the one from Aven.

Doug grabbed it. "Excellent." He flipped the on switch.

The table began its rhyming speech.

> *"Need a map? Need a guide?*
> *Lost, no matter how you've tried?*
> *Here, let me show you! Here, let me tell you!*
> *I'll guide you through the land of the Zulu."*

"Hello, Map Table," Doug said politely.

"Hello, Douglas. Hello, Princess."

"Hello," I answered.

Doug cleared his throat. "Map Table, we need to bring the Sennish dungeons maps online, and we'll need tracking capabilities activated for the Princess."

"Hmm," The table paused, thinking, clearly unaware that tables do not, in fact, think. "Here are the dungeon maps. Four total: one basic, one showing heat, one indicating levels of happiness inside each cell, and one three-dimensional one. You can move between them using my toggle keys."

"Thank you." Doug started looking at the different maps.

"Does the Princess have any sort of enchanted device on her person?" The table asked. "That would be the easiest way to track her; we could follow her with the EOL map."

"EOL?" I whispered to Doug.

"Enchanted Objects Locator. It finds things that have magical properties."

"Oh." I was grateful Calo was gone. He has a very low tolerance for answering questions that I should already know the answer to. And, sadly, I actually knew about the EOL from when we had to find my bike.

"Hey!" Doug turned to me. "You're wearing your magic shoes, aren't you?"

"My dancing shoes?"

"No, the shoes I enchanted to receive updates from me."

"Oh, those." I blushed. "Yes, I'm wearing them."

"Great, we can use them to locate you."

"Wonderful," the Map Table joined in. "Please place the shoe on my screen, so I can get a reading of its magic."

"That's odd," I muttered. "When we used the HEA table to find my bike, it didn't have to have a reading." I started taking my shoe off. I continued wondering aloud. "Can a clearer picture be obtained by taking a 'reading' of a magical object?"

"Yes." Doug took my shoe and placed it on the map table. "If there's not a specific reading or request, the EOL map picks up anything that's magic. With a specific request, the EOL will only locate that object. When they looked for your bike, they likely looked for objects in the area, and then for ones that were out of place."

"Oh," I nodded, my understanding multiplying. "My bike was in the river, so of course, there aren't any magic objects in the water. That would've been a big clue."

"Well, except for the wish-giving fish. But they generally prefer saltwater."

"I am finished with the shoe," the table announced.

"Thank you." Doug handed the shoe back to me. "Ready to go?"

"Ready to go where?" I asked, putting my shoe back on.

Doug looked confused. "To save Calo and Ella."

"What? Wait a minute; there are some holes in your equation, Doug. You want me to save Calo and Ella, but you haven't told me what equals what. I can solve for one variable, but not two."

"Let me do the math for you." He grabbed a pencil. "In all the excitement, I forgot to tell you my plan."

He spent the next ten minutes going over the plan with me. It was dangerous, greasy, and involved a lot of work on my part. It was also the only thing that would succeed. Most of it was fairly straightforward: find

Levi, get him to take me to the dungeon, get "locked up," wander around talking to the other prisoners, getting them happy enough to vanish.

"Okay, after I get everyone to vanish back, how do *I* get out?"

Doug hesitated. "Well, the thing is, even though you can get out of your cell because you're not unhappy, and you can move around because of your invisibility marble, you're still in a fortress full of Tallis' guards, in the middle of the wilderness."

"Right, so how do I get out?"

Doug coughed. "The, uh, the best thing would be if you were to become Happily Ever After and then you'd vanish back."

I made sort of a half-laughing noise. "Is there a second best thing?"

Doug hesitated again. "Let's just say that if your odds of getting out by the first best thing are 50%, then the odds of you getting out by the second best thing are considerably lower."

"30%?"

"Lower," Doug whispered.

"15%?"

Doug shook his head. "You'd have to fight off the actual dungeon guards, get out of the fortress, and then make your way through thirty-four miles of dense forest before reaching Smythian safety."

"So more like 2%?"

"I'd calculate it at .4%." He forced a smile.

.4%? I sighed and shoved my hand in my pocket. My fingers felt my marble. I wondered vaguely if Glenni could improve .4% odds. Maybe I should just wish everyone out? Hey! That could work.

"Doug, I've got an idea! Glenni's my fairy godmother. Why don't I just wish for everyone to be free?"

Doug half-smiled. "That won't work. By law, all vanished people belong to Tallis unless their happiness level changes."

"Which won't happen, since they are in a dungeon surrounded by things making them unhappy."

"Exactly. Besides, fairy godmothers have three prohibitions about wishes: No wishing for extra wishes. No wishing for vanished people to return, and no wishing for ice cream."

"Ice cream?"

"It's too messy." He shuddered.

I sighed loudly. "I really hoped that would work." I closed my eyes. ".4%, huh?"

"You don't have to do this, Princess. I'll come up with another plan."

I looked at the map table. The heat sensitive map was showing. Twelve of the thirty-two cells had red in them. The red splotches equaled vanished citizens. If I didn't rescue them, how many more splotches would there be?

Calo was a terrific Happiologist; if I could get him almost to the point of vanishing back, I could use him to help me rescue everyone else. Calo at 75-80% efficiency was something like four times better than me. I would need a bit more information before I could work that equation with accuracy, but I felt confident my estimate was correct. Then when everyone else was safe, I'd get Calo to vanish back by groveling or flattery.

I wasn't confident that I would get to Happily Ever After—especially not after groveling to Calo, but…. I went over the numbers in my head again. It was the only way. I looked at the notes littered on Calo's desk. On his calendar, in the square for today, he'd written: *Lunch with Linda.*

"Who's Linda?" I asked aloud.

Doug was furiously scribbling alternative plans for rescue. He looked up. "Uh...Linda's the Beauty from *Beauty and the Beast.* She called earlier looking for Calo. I had to make something up." He went back to his planning and I tried to figure out why her name was Linda. Why wasn't it just Beauty?

I surprised myself by actually remembering her story. She had traded places with her father, so he could get out of the Beast's dungeon. She had sacrificed her life for his. Of course, it turned out rather well in the end, being a fairy tale and all.

And just like that, I knew I'd do it. Even if I wound up stuck in a room that was a geometrical impossibility–like those staircase illusions–I would do my best to rescue these stories. I would do it because of Beauty (or Linda, if that is her real name) and her sacrifice, I would do it because Ella offered me her friendship without expecting anything in return, because Aven took time out of his busy Atlantis campaign to make a map table for me, and because Calo didn't deserve to be vanished in Levi's attempt to get me.

I smiled weakly at Doug. "Okay, so how do I find Levi?"

20

THE QUEST CLAUSE

I stood at the edge of the Wildwood, willing myself to enter. "Darkness is just the absence of light," I repeated for the ninth time.

When I was little and light was just light and not something that traveled at the speed of 186,000 miles per second, I would run into Mom's room and cry because of the dark. She would give me a hug, read me a fairy tale, and put me back into bed, telling me "Darkness is just the absence of light." Then, she'd make some light: a night light, the hall light, or sometimes she'd leave a flashlight with me. But when I started school, I grew out of my fear. (Grew out of my fear = being able to sleep without supplemental light.)

I wasn't afraid to enter the Wildwood—well, not exactly. The problem centered more on the *degree* of darkness. At home, streetlights shined in my window, and the switch on my computer power strip had a light in it, plus I had glow-in-the-dark stars on my ceiling. It wasn't exactly the absolute absence of light.

The Wildwood was.

It was like staring into a black hole. There was nothing giving off light, nothing in the distance. The sun's rays didn't even penetrate the forest.

"It's a matter of will power," Doug had said. "The Wildwood wants to keep you out. You'll have to prove you want in that much more."

I didn't understand. "What do you mean? Like the woods are alive?"

Doug sighed. "Sort of. The darkness is one of the protections they have in place to keep people out."

"They who?"

Doug raised his eyebrows. "Well, there are lots of really bad things in fairy tales and legends. You know, like monsters, hags, and wicked dwarves. They need somewhere to live. Plus, all those questing princes need somewhere to go on their quests."

"Huh." I wanted to ask clarifying questions, but I was afraid more information might cause me to abandon the quest altogether.

"But the important thing is the darkness," Doug went on. "It's just an illusion. Once you've taken five steps into the Wildwood, you'll find the lighting to be just like any other place."

I stood at the entrance of the Wildwood preparing to take the five steps, thinking about how when I asked Doug if he knew about the change in lighting from personal experience, he'd taken a long time before saying, "No." He'd only read reports to that effect.

I mentally went over the directions from Doug one more time, then took a deep breath and stepped into the Wildwood.

"Interesting," I said, five steps later, blinking in the sunlight. I took a step back into darkness, then another step forward into light. I felt like I was standing on the International Date Line or the Prime Meridian, or like I had one foot in Kansas and one in Oklahoma.

I experimented a little with how far I could be in the dark and still have a foot in the light and vice versa. Then, I suddenly remembered why I was in the Wildwood in the first place. I took off down the path as fast as I could possibly go without missing the landmarks Doug had mentioned.

At the twisted oak tree, I turned left, and at the row of stumps, I took the road to the right. Then, at the abandoned hut, I stopped. This was where I would find Levi.

I remembered what Doug told me to say; I just didn't want to say it. I looked around the clearing. Maybe Levi would be here anyway. Maybe I wouldn't have to say it.

"You have to do whatever you were told to do." A low voice spoke.

I jumped and looked all around. Where was the voice coming from? Disembodied voices are highly unmathematical.

"The whole point of the quest is to follow the directions, you know."

"Where are you?" I asked, spinning around.

"Down here."

I looked down and saw an old turtle wearing glasses.

"Hello, Princess."

"Um...hello." I knelt down in the grass next to the turtle. "I'm pleased to meet you."

"And I, you." The turtle nodded. "Now, you should probably get on with your quest. You young people, always forgetting the important things. Always trying to get around the quest and do things your own way."

"Okay, but, um, if you don't mind me saying so, you don't seem very evil."

"Evil?" The turtle looked at me.

"I was told evil hags and monsters live in the Wildwood."

The turtle blinked. "They do. But they certainly aren't the only things that live here." He slammed his mouth shut.

I stood up, and dusted off. "How did you know I didn't want to follow my instructions?"

The turtle rolled his eyes. "Because you had that young headstrong look about you. I've seen it on all those young whippersnappers who turned into slabs of stone or frogs for not following the directions." The turtle made an annoyed sound as he continued ambling away from the clearing. "You just be sure to do what you're supposed to!"

After the turtle had gone, I looked around for anything else that looked like it might be capable of hearing and speech. I really didn't want anyone to hear what I was about to say.

I got on my knees and bowed my head. Contrition and submission were vital factors in this equation. Then I said, "I, Lily Elizabeth Sparrow,

Princess of E. G. Smythe's Salty Fire Land, crave the presence of Levi, Dark Mesa of Uppish Senna. I have need of his abilities. I need him for what I cannot do." A greasy hand tipped my chin up. "Fair Princess," Levi cooed. "It takes such a strong person to admit they need help. What can I do for you?"

After telling me the formula for getting Levi to appear, Doug made sure to tell me over and over to be servile with Levi. He had to believe he had the upper hand.

"Please," I whispered. "I need to see Lord Tallis. It is my only hope." I looked up at Levi, suddenly afraid I'd laid it on too thick. Too much groveling might upset the delicate balance of the equation.

"But, Lily, my dear, Lord Tallis is not known for his hospitality."

"It's the only way."

Levi cocked his head and smiled. "Very well." He removed a cloth from his pocket. It was damp with grease. "You'll have to wear this."

Levi tied the blindfold on, and once again, I was mentally repeating, "Darkness is just the absence of light." Levi's greasy hand grabbed mine and he led me deeper into the forest.

"Lovely weather we're having, isn't it?" Levi remarked.

"Excuse me?"

"We're having nice weather, aren't we?" Levi went on. "I mean, I vastly prefer this weather to an ice storm. Don't you agree?"

"Yes," I said, hesitatingly. Weather seemed like an odd conversation topic for a kidnapper to have with his kidnappee.[61]

"You know I knew your grandmother quite well."

"Oh? My mom's mom or my dad's mom?"

"Your father's, of course. It's not likely I'd know your mom's mom at all, is it?" Levi laughed.

I laughed a little too. Not that I understood what was funny. I was busy not tripping and making servile conversation. It bothered me, however, that Levi seemed to know about the mystery of my mom's parents.

"But, back in the day, I was almost exclusively assigned to your grandmother. Very cheerful woman. I thought I'd never get her to vanish."

I stopped shuffling along. "You vanished my grandmother?"

"In a manner of speaking." He grabbed my hand again and pulled me along.

We continued in silence for a few moments, then Levi's greasy hands removed the blindfold. "Here we are."

I blinked, adjusting my eyes to the sunlight. We stood next to a gnarled tree; its wood was very dark, almost black. But when I looked closer I saw that the tree was really split at the bottom and growing in six different sections around the original stump. (Six trees equaling one tree.) The space between the stumps was sufficient enough for a person to slip in between them

---

[61] I realize, mathematically speaking, Levi wasn't actually kidnapping me. I had *volunteered* to be kidnapped, but being blindfolded was the variable pushing me toward a kidnapping equation.

and stand in the middle, which is what Levi directed me to do.

"Now, dear Princess, we're going to jump down the hole like in *Alice in Wonderland*."

"What?"

Levi rolled his eyes. "Oh, I know, it's not really a fairy tale, since she's in a novel by that Dodgson fellow. You'd like him by the way, he was a mathematician, but fairy tale or not, though, it's still a good reference to what we're about to do."

"What? Do you mean Charles Lutwidge Dodgson?" Him, I knew. He wrote *Symbolic Logic Parts I* and *II*.

Levi nodded. "Right. As Lewis Carroll, he wrote *Alice in Wonderland* about his little neighbor friend, Alice. But since Alice is *his* created character, she's not a citizen of Smythe's SFL. I heard she's taken up regular residence in Wonderland, but Baldric is such a gossip, you can't believe everything he tells you."

"I don't understand what any of that has to do with the tree."

"We're going to jump in like the White Rabbit and Alice did." Levi looked at me a little funny, sort of like Calo whenever I don't know something about a citizen's story. "Oh, you're surprised I've read it. Trust me, Princess, we have an excellent library in Uppish Senna. (All the pages are laminated, of course.) And we have a brilliant section devoted to vanished tales. They can literally *only* be found in our library." He flashed his greasy grin.

I moved closer to the tree. "I'd be delighted to see it."

"I'm sure that can be arranged." He offered his hand and assisted me in slipping between two of the trees.

I looked down at the cavernous hole, calculating its depth. I stopped myself from figuring out my rate of speed and velocity. If I jumped down this hole, I'd have to do it without math. With math, all I had was an equation equaling my death.

"See you at the bottom," I called to Levi as I jumped into the hole.

Surprisingly, it was not dark in the hole. I tried to determine the light source based on the refraction and reflection of light in the cavern, but I couldn't pin it down. Also, I seemed to be defying the laws of physics. The speed of my descent was not increasing, nor was it slowing down. It was just the same as it was when I stepped off the tree.

"Having a good time?" Levi floated next to me. He was enjoying his fall/float from the comfort of a reclining arm chair. He laughed at my surprise, and added, "I didn't say it was *exactly* like *Alice in Wonderland*."

I didn't answer because I was suddenly aware of a new problem.

We were coming up on enough furniture to stock a small store.

Beds, bookshelves, lamps, desks, even a piano, slowly ascended. I wriggled to the left to avoid a burgundy ottoman. Then, I squirmed to the right to miss a flower-patterned love seat.

Levi laughed. "You'd better land in a chair. It will do the piloting for you." He pointed. "Look! That leather recliner. Aim for it."

I managed to direct my floating so I would be in the path of the chair. "How is it mathematically possible for the furniture to be rising?"

"Not everything is about math, Princess." Levi swiveled his chair so I could see him. "Now, put your body in a sitting position and—"

WHAM! I slammed into the leather chair with a grunt.

"Yes, exactly." Levi nodded. "It's Smart Furniture. All you have to do is assume the proper position above the piece and you'll find yourself in it. And once we get to the bottom, the chairs will float up again."

"Clever."

I spent the rest of the ride reviewing Doug's plan in my mind. Levi spent the free fall examining his finger nails and occasionally muttering things like, "I've got to get a manicure appointment," or "I must remember to pick up my dry cleaning."

I didn't really want to have a conversation with him; I needed the time to make sure the plan was firm in my mind, but still...if he *had* struck up a conversation with me, I would have asked him some questions about turning traitor and becoming a Dark Mesa. Had he really been a better Happiologist than Calo?

Eventually, after I'd had time to review the plan four and a half times, our chairs landed. Levi nonchalantly exited his chair and offered his hand. I knocked it aside and got up of my own volition.

Levi raised his eyebrows. "Independent, like your father."

"You mistake me, Levi." I smiled at him. "I just don't want to touch your greasy hand."

Our chairs started slowly rising back up the tree. Levi made a sweeping gesture with his hand, bowed a little and said, "If you'll just follow me, Your Highness."

I nodded regally and followed him through the rocky passage, noting mentally that all of a sudden I seemed to be the embodiment of all things regal. My posture was better, my speech took on a more formal, royal quality, and there was that random regal nod. I can mathematically prove I am not in the habit of nodding like a courtier in my normal life. In fact, in my normal life, I am not in the habit of using the word "courtier" or the phrase "not in the habit." Was Smythian magic finally affecting me the way it makes Mom less distracted when she's in the kingdom?

We stepped out of a cave, and Levi led me to a carriage. It was completely black, the driver was dressed in all black, and the horses were also colored with a touch of ebony. *Touch of ebony?!* I was turning into my mother! I quickly made a comparison of the two blacks and determined the black of the carriage was darker than the black of the horses. At least I can still do math. I started reciting squares to steady my nerves. (*Steady my nerves!*)

My malaise (!) was so distracting that I absently took Levi's offered hand as he helped me into the carriage. Its greasiness brought me crashing back to reality. "Am I turning into a fairy tale?"

Levi looked at me curiously, knocked twice on the ceiling to tell the driver to start, and asked, "What do you mean?"

I sighed, exasperated. "I don't know. My vocabulary is changing, my posture is straighter, and I'm acting rather regally." My hand shot to my mouth. "You see!? *Rather regally!* I don't talk like that!"

Levi stroked his chin. "You must have activated the Quest Clause."

"What Quest Clause?"

"Clause 981 of the Smythian Code of Laws: *If a citizen endeavors to complete a quest, but is lacking in some way, whatever he or she lacks will be magically endowed upon him or her.*"

"I understood all of that," I whispered. "It was full of jargon and was clearly not written in the best possible way, and yet, I got it."

"Precisely," Levi nodded. "You are embarking on a quest—futile, though it is—to save someone, aren't you?"

I nodded slowly.

"So the magic of your disgustingly happy Salt Land has enacted the Quest Clause. This is the sort of thing that is sure to be made into a legendary tale—not of victory, of course. It will be a lament for the lost princess. But, the main character can't run around with sloppy, unprincessly posture, saying things such as, 'It was like SO totally awesome, you know?'" Levi imitated what Corrie referred to as "people who waste oxygen in the tomes of history."

"I have *never* spoken like that."

Levi laughed. "But neither do you sound as you should."

I rolled my eyes. "How do you come to know so much about Smythian law?" I regretted my question as soon as I asked it. I already knew the answer. Levi knew about the law because he had once been a citizen, a Happiologist.

He made an impatient noise, and turned to look out the window. For a brief moment, as he turned, I saw not Levi, the villain, but Levi, the victim.

"You cannot be as ignorant as you pretend, Your Highness," he said quietly. "Even the most cursory inquiry into my background would have revealed my history."

Inexplicably and unmathematically, I felt sorry for him. Although I was sure it was mostly the result of the Quest Clause, I did think it would be unprincessly not to express concern for even the vilest creature. "Is there no way to take back your treason?" I asked. "Could you not undo it in some way?"

Levi turned to look at me. He began laughing. "You assume I *want* to take it back."

"Yes."

"Then your assumption is in error, Your Highness, and you do your mathematical background a disservice by pretending emotions you do not feel."

"I—"

He held up his hand to stop my protest. "You would do better to formulate an equation for the length of time it will take my Lord Tallis to bend you to his will. For whatever plan you have concocted will fail. And you, Princess, will be little more than another prisoner in his dungeon."

I looked out the window and ignored Levi for the rest of the journey. The greasy scumbag had tried my last sympathetic princess nerve. I hoped he was unhappy and haunted by his treason.

~~~

"Stand over there." Levi motioned to a dark area near the door of Tallis' throne room. "When I call for you, you can come forward, and," he smiled as if his mouth held laughter behind it, "have your *audience*. And remember don't say anything to Lord Tallis until he speaks first."

I nodded. Levi was a greasy, annoying, traitorous sycophant, but I had to play his game if I was going to get into the dungeon. And getting into the dungeon equaled freeing my friends, which also equaled saving Cinderella's story so little girls everywhere could hope for a missing gold slipper.

I mentally replayed the last part of the equation. *Gold slipper.* I reviewed Cinderella's story. "I think that's right," I whispered. "I think she really did lose a gold slipper, even though everyone thinks she lost a glass one." Apparently the Quest Clause made up for my lack of fairy tale knowledge.

I shook the shoes from my head and my eyes followed Levi as he walked down the strip of black carpet toward the dais and throne.[62] By the torchlight, I could see his greasy footprints sinking into the carpet. He bowed and generally sycophanted himself.

"May unhappiness smile on you forever, my Lord Tallis."

A tiny figure on the throne stirred. He was only inches taller than Peridiom, and Lubcker. It seemed strange that such a short person could be so evil–the sender of dead lilies and sparrows.

"Tell me, Levi, for what purpose have you disrupted my leisure? I was reading *The Raven* when I was called."

---

[62] In case you, like me, wondered what a "dais" is: it's a raised platform, often for dignified occupancy. It's a fancy Quest Clause way of saying "a little stage."

"I think, Your Lordship," (I could hear the arrogant smirk in Levi's voice.) "you will find my news far more pleasing than Poe."

"Enough with the riddling; get on with it, Levi."

The tiny man's voice was deeper than I had supposed. Two or three times deeper.

Levi bowed again and began, "Someone from E. G. Smythe's Salty Fire Land craves an audience with you."

Tallis leaned toward Levi; his eyes full of interest. "Who?"

Levi paused–probably for a smirk. "Princess Lily Elizabeth Sparrow–the Future Protector."

Tallis sat straight up and smiled. "I'll see her now. Tristen!" He snapped his fingers at a person in the shadows. "Clear my schedule and alert Malcom." Tristen made a shadowy bow and left the room.

During all of this, Levi stood near the throne like a puppy waiting to be praised. At a nod from Tallis, he gestured to where I was hidden. "My Lord Tallis, it is my unending honor to present: Princess Lily Elizabeth Sparrow, Future Protector of E. G. Smythe's Salty Fire Land."

I swallowed, made a silent wish that Doug's plan would work, and walked towards the dais. Tallis looked as if he were bouncing slightly in excitement and I didn't think Levi's smile could mathematically get any bigger. The ratio of muscle capacity to facial area was stretched thin already, and–

I stopped myself.

This was not the time for math.

I curtsied and waited.

"You may speak." Tallis moved an arm in a welcoming gesture.

I ducked my head a little in a slight bow and said, "Thank you for agreeing to see me, my lord."

"I always welcome my enemies into my home. Though I have heard my own emissaries did not receive an equally cordial reception."

I smiled. "No doubt our welcome was as genuine as yours is false."

Tallis laughed: a scary, deep sound. "Witty, like your father. And pretty, like your lovely mother, Ginnie." He shot a glance at Levi.

Levi turned and nodded at someone in the shadows.

"But surely you did not come all this way to verbally spar with me." He raised his eyebrows in anticipation.

"Your lordship speaks rightly," I swallowed, grateful for the Quest Clause's vocabulary. "I've come to ask that you release Ella, called Cinderella. Her story is of great importance to the children of the real world."

Tallis studied me for a moment. "No. Your request is denied. And you would do well to remember that while you're here, my world is the real and *only* world."

"Perhaps Your Lordship would be willing to bargain for Ella's release."

"Bargain?" Tallis smiled. "What could you offer me that would be worth the release of a prisoner? Worth emptying a cell?"

I returned his smile and answered, "Myself."

Tallis narrowed his eyes for a moment, studying me. "Done," he said, suddenly, slapping his leg. "I will empty a cell in exchange for your surrender. Levi, escort the Princess to the dungeon."

Grinning, Levi led me out of the room. His greasy hand held my arm tightly and as we left, I heard Tallis call out, "A pleasure doing business with you!"

Levi walked fast. I had to trot to keep up with him. I smiled to myself; Levi didn't know I had not the minutest intention of getting away. I was 100% glad to be going to the dungeon.

I mentally checked off another part of Doug's plan.

21

EVERYONE IS SAD

The cell door closed with a thud and Levi looked through the window. "Enjoy your stay, Princess." He flashed his greasy smile.

After his footsteps faded, I counted by squares to four hundred and let out a sigh. I was in. But would I really be able to get out?

I looked around the cell. Except for a pile of straw in the corner, it was less like a dungeon and more like a nightmarish classroom. An old desk sat in the middle, a chalkboard hung on one wall, and math books were stacked in the corner. That was the classroom part of the equation. The nightmare part equaled no chalk with which to write, the books were sealed shut, and worst of all was the art.

Framed and hung all over the walls were
equations obviously put there to annoy me. Every
equation was wrong and designed to look pretty. $7 + 5 =$
75 is prettier to look at than the accurate $7 + 5 = 12$.
Other such gems included:
$$6(6) = 66,$$
$$8 - 3 = 83,$$
$$4/9 = 49,$$
and $45 + 70 = 4570$.

I ignored the math art. This is the best they could
do at keeping me forever sad? I'm annoyed, certainly,
but not exactly morose. Great. I sighed. Another Quest
Clause word. I hope "morose" and "ebony" aren't
pushing vital algebraic equations from my mind.

Looking out the door window, I saw a guard
pacing the hallway. When he passed my cell, I glanced at
my watch: 7:45 pm. I sat at the desk and waited for his
return. I needed to calculate how long it took for him to
complete his rounds.

This was an integral part of Doug's plan. In the
HEA office, we'd studied my map table's heat sensing
map of the dungeon. I watched the dot that represented
the guard move around and around the dungeon, while
Doug explained the rest of the plan. He would send me a
map of the dungeon through my shoe. I had seen one
back at the HEA office, but we didn't know exactly
where they would put me. Because the map table had
heat sensing capabilities we could see which cells were
occupied. There were thirty-two cells total, twelve of
them were occupied before I arrived. I was the thirteenth
prisoner, but I expected Tallis to keep his word and

empty at least one cell. Then I would only have to rescue 12 people.[63]

I didn't think Tallis would actually free Ella. He had cleverly not agreed to that. He only agreed to empty a cell. I just hope he hadn't freed Calo. I needed Calo's help to get everyone else happy.

A sudden pain in my left foot meant Doug's first update had arrived. I kicked off my shoe and unfolded it. The map of the dungeon was clear. Doug had drawn a circle around my cell and marked it "Lily". On the other side of the hallway, six cells away, he had marked an X through a cell, with the notation, "Ella's birds–freed."

I slipped my shoe back on, without tying it. More updates were coming and they wouldn't hurt as much with my shoe loose. I tucked the laces in so I wouldn't trip.

I had hoped the evil stepmother or the evil queen from *The Candlemaker's Daughter* would be the freed prisoner, but on second thought, I was glad I wouldn't have to talk to birds.

Footsteps came from the hallway and I quickly sat on the map. I looked at my watch: 7:52. Seven minutes. I had no way of knowing if this was accurate. Any mathematician knows you must have lots of data to interpret from. What if he had been delayed on his circuit and it usually only took five minutes? I would have to get an average time.

As his footsteps faded, I focused on finding Calo. When I left my cell, I could either go left or right. 50% chance of choosing correctly. Going left meant another

---

[63] 12 prisoners + Lily = 13 prisoners – freed prisoner = 12 prisoners.

choice almost immediately as it split into two directions. But going right meant a long hallway, with only two cells to check, but it was the only way to get to one of the cells, unless I backtracked later. Where had they put him?

I decided to take the longer route to avoid the backtracking, which would waste time and be unmathematical. Also, I would be following the path of the guard and be less likely to run into him that way.

I smiled, confident in my mathematical decision and lay on the pile of straw, waiting for the guard to return. If he looked in, I hoped he would think I was lying there in a defeated position, thinking depressing thoughts. He returned at 7:58. Hmm. Only six minutes this time.

While he was gone the third time, I decided to test Doug's statement that I'd be able to get out of my cell because I wasn't unhappy. I quietly put my hand on the handle; it turned completely and the door pulled in a little. Inexplicably, and unmathematically, I'd be able to walk out into the hall whenever I wanted. I looked at the door more closely. There wasn't even a keyhole. Apparently, locking people up with their unhappiness was rather effective.

Next, I rubbed the marble to make myself invisible and slipped out of the cell. I closed the door and looked in my window. I needed to see what the guard would see; I needed to find a blind spot. After successfully discovering one near the door, I slipped back in, and returned to visibility.

I continued hanging out near the door. It was important that I look impatient when the guard passed next. He was back at 8:07. Nine minutes.

I thrust my arm through the window and assumed my princessly demeanor. "You there! Guard."

He stopped and raised an eyebrow.

I brought my arm back in. "Could I possibly have a blanket? This cell is quite chilly, and I'm ready to retire."

He brought the blanket back in seven minutes. As he was leaving, I called out, "As I'll be sleeping now, I'll thank you to step lightly as you pass my door."

He made a scoffing noise, stomping his feet loudly as he walked on.

When his footsteps had faded, I dashed to the straw in the corner and quickly made a pile that (when covered with a blanket) resembled a sleeping person. Taking a deep breath, I went to stand near the door and made myself invisible.

While I waited, I reviewed the route I would take. Out the door. Turn right, check second cell door on left. Turn left. Check second door on left again. Continue on. Turn left. Check first door on right.

I continued repeating the route until I was sure I knew it, and I heard the guard returning. I held the marble poised to reappear if necessary. He came to the window and looked around slowly. He was so close I could smell the fish he'd had for dinner. He narrowed his eyes as he looked at the "body" in the straw, but eventually he walked on.

When I couldn't hear his footsteps, I slowly opened the door and slipped out, closing it just as quietly. I walked silently to the left and checked the first occupied cell on Doug's map.

I stood on my tip-toes to see inside. Not Calo. I didn't recognize the occupant. I had no clue who this man was. I almost laughed when I thought of what Calo would say: "You didn't know who he was, Lily? How can you be so useless? Here is a perfect example of why you should have learned everyone in the kingdom on a facial recognition basis." I bit my lip, because it was true. I really should know who this man was, but I didn't. And I didn't have any more time to stand here thinking about this.

Just as I was turning away, a stroke of mathematical genius struck me. I may not know who he is, but *Calo* will. If I used my mathematical mind to describe whatever was making him sad, then Calo, the brilliant Happiologist, should be able to figure out who he is.

I looked in again. The man was trying to take a ring off his finger. There was an empty cradle in the corner, and on the wall hung a picture of a really beautiful, really evil looking woman. She reminded me of Potio Bane or Morgan Le Faye. I repeated the items again to seal them in my memory, then I turned the corner to the left.

The first cell on this hallway was empty. (The right hand side had no cells on it; apparently, it was just a wall.) I checked quickly anyway. Mathematically, it's always better to be safe than sorry.

In the second cell on the left, a woman sat on a low stool. She wore black mourning clothes. On the wall hung an embroidered sampler[64] that read, "Children are the comfort of old age." Underneath it were empty picture frames; one of them was engraved with the

---

[64] I suppose the Quest Clause enabled me to know what a sampler was.

words: "Mother's Pride and Joy." I memorized her sad
items and moved on.

The next three cells were empty—just as the map
had reported them. I walked as quietly as I could here.
This hallway formed a beautiful right angle with another
hallway. I peered carefully around the corner to see if the
guard was still in the intersecting hallway. He wasn't, so I
turned left and checked the first door. Hopefully it
would be Calo.

I peered through the window. A young woman
sat in a corner trying to sew by the light of a flickering
candle. She was quietly crying and whispering to herself.
I strained my ears to hear what she was saying: "Just
ignore it. Just ignore it. It isn't real. It's not really him.
There is no baby crying."

A baby crying? I didn't hear anything. I listened
for another moment, and still heard nothing. Obviously,
this wasn't Calo. I memorized her sad items and moved
on.

I walked very quietly; the perpendicular hallway
was short and intersected another hallway. I had studied
this hall very carefully on the map table. The guard
walked through it twice on his route. The first time on
the left side and the second on the right. I stopped to
calculate. He was about forty-five seconds ahead of me
anyway, since I had waited for his footsteps to fade.
Based on the data I'd gathered about his route, I knew
he took between six and nine minutes to complete it.
Twice he came back in seven minutes. So between three
hundred sixty seconds (6 minutes x 60 seconds) and five
hundred forty seconds (9 minutes x 60 seconds), I could
expect him to return to a given spot. I would, of course,
use the lower end of the equation; better safe than sorry
as Newton would say—if Newton had ever done anything

like this. I spent a moment imaging Sir Isaac Newton finding a way to use the law of gravity to free Calo.

Then I returned to calculating; I was already forty-five seconds behind (360 − 45 = 315 seconds). I estimated that each door stop had taken about thirty seconds for me to observe and memorize, so three stops at thirty seconds each equals ninety more seconds. (315 − 90 = 225 seconds until the guard came up behind me.) Additionally, I estimated three seconds each for the empty cells that I checked. Three times six equals eighteen more seconds. (225 − 18 = 207 seconds.) Plus I had been moving slowing, so I subtracted another thirty seconds. (207 − 30 = 177 seconds.) Finally, I subtracted another ninety seconds for how long I had been standing there calculating. (177 − 90 = 87 seconds.)

I was just wondering if the guard had already walked this hallway for the second time, when he suddenly came around the corner. I flattened myself against the wall and waited quietly until he turned the corner to the right. As silently as was mathematically possible, I began my trek to the next occupied cell. It was on the left–three doors down. No one was in the first two cells, but the one of them was full of feathers.[65]

Just as I reached the third door, the guard re-entered the hallway. I sucked my breath in. I had forgotten that when he left this hallway, he only went down a short three-cell hall and doubled back to pass by my cell. When he had turned the corner, I let out my breath and took a hesitant step forward. The margin of

---

[65] So glad I don't have to talk to those birds.

error in this equation was so small, there was no room for my carelessness.

Ella was in the next cell I checked. My stomach twisted with guilt. My friend (I hoped she would still be my friend when this was over) sat at an easel, painting. But she wasn't creating her usual paintings of talking birds or cleaning supplies. Instead, whenever she put the brush to the canvas, colors spread in all directions melting together to make a complete picture. The first stroke I saw became Aven searching through his old map room–looking for his maps. When Ella, horrified by this picture, withdrew the brush, the picture vanished. She touched the canvas again and there was Miranda and Grimm looking very happy on their wedding day. Ella herself was in the background, looking very sad. She removed the brush again, the picture melted away, and she buried her face in her hands, crying.

I wondered why she didn't just stop trying to paint. I began putting together a formula for the probability of her being magically confined to the stool, when I noticed the rest of her cell.

It was filthy–disgustingly so. Its filth defied all mathematical laws. How could one room be so dirty? The *only* clean spot was the small circle in the center of the room where the easel stood. No wonder Ella was there. She couldn't bear being in any other part of the cell.

I sighed. Ella's unhappiness may not have been all my fault, but I certainly did not do all I could to stop her. I looked at her once more and made a promise to myself. *If I get out of this alive, I will do all I can to become a true Protector for these people. I will stop trying to make them what I think they should be, and I will stop being so selfish.*

Because I knew now. My selfishness had done this. I was so mad about my plans being messed up that all I could see was figuring out how to quickly deal with the new stuff (magic, fairy tales, measuring happiness), so I could get back to my mathematical plans. A princess should be more than that.

I tore myself away. Calo was more important right now, and I needed to stick to Doug's plan. The next two cells were empty, but the third was not. When I looked in, I saw Calo reclining in his pile of straw. Every inch of wall space was covered with screens, playing fleeting clips of Calo's unhappy past: Thomas and Calo fighting as children, a lonely, younger Calo walking alone. Then the screens shifted to a scene of the HEA office without Calo–everyone looked glummer, Grimm especially. Then suddenly, the Happiologists started vanishing and Levi was there greasily running things.

Calo sighed deeply, and I looked to see what had equaled that response. There, strangely, on the screen was *me*, working alone in our cubicle, dancing with various citizens, walking through the castle, laughing.

22

THIS IS A RESCUE

W hy am I making you sad?" I asked aloud, without thinking. Calo turned toward the door; his eyes were wide and fearful. "Lily?" he whispered.

"Oh, right," I muttered, realizing I should probably be in the cell while we discussed things. The guard could come at any minute. I opened the door and slipped in.

As the door opened, Calo jumped off the straw and backed away. "Lily? Is that you?"

"Of course it's me. I've come to rescue you!"

Calo shook his head, mumbling, "I must be hearing things. Tallis is pumping her voice in to torture me." He rubbed his eyes and turned away from me.

"No, Calo. It's me!" I grabbed his shoulder to turn him around.

He jumped and shouted.

"Shh!" I hissed. "You'll attract the guard and he'll come and see—"

"Come and see what?" He hissed back.

I opened my mouth and closed it again. "Oh."

Calo: 1, Lily: 0.

I rubbed myself visible and felt as if a heavy wool blanket had been lifted from me. I was covered in sweat. In all the excitement of escaping my cell and finding Calo, I'd forgotten how uncomfortably warm it was to be invisible.

Calo's eyes went even wider than before. "What are you doing here?"

"This is a rescue," I said, importantly.

Calo sighed and rolled his eyes. "I suppose someone told you about Matt's Law and you decided to come save everyone."

"What's Matt's Law?"

"You waltzed into the heart of Uppish Senna without knowing about Matt's Law?"

"I guess."

"Are you insane? Do you have any idea the risk you are taking? Do you even realize you have jeopardized the entire kingdom?"

"Shh." I held up my hand and listened. Footsteps. I quickly rubbed myself invisible, waited for the guard to pass, and rubbed myself visible again.

Calo flopped down on his straw. "The only way this could be worse is if you just walked right up to Tallis and volunteered to be his prisoner."

I bit my lip. "Perhaps, I should explain the situation before we two endeavor to save our companions in misery."

"*Before we two endeavor to save our companions in misery?!?* You invoked the Quest Clause?"

I smiled sheepishly. "Apparently."

Calo sighed. "But if you invoked the Quest Clause, someone had to have sent you on a quest. Who would be stupid enough to send the heir to the throne on such a foolish quest?"

I cleared my throat. "Uh, let me explain. Doug told me only I could save everyone because I'm not living Happily Ever After yet. And then we came up with a plan to rescue everyone. See, first I'll get you to Less Than Happy, then—"

Calo waved his hand impatiently. "Then, I can go around and cheer everyone up. I know that part of the plan, Lily." He sat down and sighed.

"How do you already know Doug's plan?"

"Because it's what I would do." He sighed again. "Did Doug happen to mention a way to get *you* home?"

"Not specifically," I mumbled. "He said the best thing would be for me to become Happily Ever After and vanish back."

"Which will be *so* easy to accomplish here in a dungeon." Calo started pacing. "Being here is really not safe for you, Lily."

"What's Matt's Law?" I asked, hoping to distract him.

"You're not allowed to know. Of course, since you're already here and the prohibition on telling you was to prevent you from doing something exactly like this, I'm not sure if it matters anymore."

Calo looked like he might be about to tell me, but shook his head instead. "I better not tell you. If we do make it out of here, there's bound to be some sort of inquiry."

"Do you think Doug will get into trouble?" I was surprised by all this forbidden "Matt's Law" business. After all, I had created this situation. Logically and mathematically, I had to be the one to fix it.

"Doug should be fine." Calo paused, then added, "So long as I get you back in one piece."

I nodded. I must have looked a little frightened about the prospect of staying in Uppish Senna forever, because Calo took me by the shoulders, looked into my eyes and said, "I promise you, Lily, I will not leave these dungeons unless I know you have found a way home as well."

I shook his hands off in time to rub myself invisible as the guard approached. Calo flung himself onto his pile of straw. After the guard had passed, I hissed at Calo "I don't have to go back. I'm not doing any good at HEA, but *you* have to go back. You are a brilliant Happiologist and HEA needs you."

Calo snorted. "If I'm such a brilliant Happiologist, then you should trust me to make the decision about you getting back. Make yourself visible and we'll compromise." He waited for me to rub my marble, then he stuck out his hand.

I took it and we shook.

"Neither of us will leave without the other," he said.

I nodded.

Calo ran a hand through his hair. "Right. Well, next we should come up with some sort of plan, and for safety's sake, you'd better stay invisible. I'll just shut up when the guard walks by."

"Fine." I rubbed myself invisible and then took off my shoe. An update from Doug had just arrived. "Hey, you're already up to Not So Happy. Just six more levels to go."

"How did you know that?" Calo spoke to the wall, so that if the guard passed it would look like he was muttering at the images on the screens.

"Doug is updating me through my shoe on any changes in levels."

"Clever." Calo smiled. "But we'd better not aim for Happy. Let's just shoot for Less Than Less Than Happy. I can make people Happy on that and then, when it's just us, we'll work out something else. I'll know when I'm getting close, by the way, so you won't need the updates for me."

"You'll know when you're getting close to what?"

"To Less Than Less Than Happy. I've trained myself to recognize the subtle differences in my levels."

"That's possible?"

"Lily." Calo's tone was patient. "You just turned yourself invisible by rubbing a marble. Anything's possible."

"Could I learn to do it?"

"Probably. It's still sort of controversial. Not all Happiologists like it."

"Why not?"

Calo cocked his head patronizingly. "If Happiologists can learn to do it, then why couldn't regular citizens learn it too? We'd be out of a job."

"Do you really think the need for HEA could be eliminated?" I tried to visualize Smythe's SFL minus HEA, but I couldn't get the equation to formulate.

"I doubt it," Calo went on. "It takes a lot of time and discipline to master your own emotions and happiness. Most people are perfectly willing to let external sources affect their happiness." After a moment, he added, "And unhappiness."

"But," I began and stopped just as quickly when I heard the guard outside the door. His footsteps reminded me that we were supposed to be getting Calo's levels up. The unasked question hung around me waiting to be asked like a math problem begging to be solved. "I've got one more question and then we'll start trying to get you to Less Than Less Than Happy."

"Don't worry about that, Lily. Talking with you has been helpful already."

"Really?"

"Well, to be quite specific," Calo spoke slowly, choosing his words as he went, "...instructing you improves my mood."

I scoffed. Of course. Calo liked showing off that he knew more than me. I just rolled my eyes and took out the latest shoe update. "Alright, Mr. Brilliant Happiologist, let's see if you're right about what your level is."

Calo tilted his head considering. "I feel like I've Been Happier."

I made a disgusted noise, balled up the note from Doug, and threw it at Calo. "You're brilliant."

Calo smiled, "You said you had another question."

"Even if mastering your own happiness is difficult, why wouldn't everyone want to do it? Isn't it a good thing? It's hard to learn your multiplication tables, but you've got to memorize them if you want to work with math on a higher level."

Calo smiled. "Yes, Lily. It's a very good thing. But not everyone wants to take the time and effort to learn their multiplication facts. They could just get a calculator. And it's the same for their happiness. Why bother mastering your emotions if you know a Happiologist will come along and make you happy?"

"That's awful and irresponsible and mathematically unsound. A calculator could break or a Happiologist might not make it in time." Or worse. I thought of Ella. Her Happiologist had failed her. I had failed her. My stomach dropped faster than an infinite slope as I considered telling Calo what I had done.

Calo was laughing. "Which are you more upset by? That people use calculators or that they use Happiologists?"

"You're okay with the citizens relying on us for their happiness?"

He sighed. "I don't have to be okay with it. I don't have to think about it at all. I just have to do my job and do it the best I can."

"But if they can learn how to be responsible, shouldn't they?"

"Let it go, Lily. When we're up against the possibility of Cinderella vanishing, I can't take the time to teach her to be happy herself. If I don't act, if I don't find her a cleaning job, she could vanish. I know you don't really follow fairy tales, but Cinderella is pretty well known. Here's a syllogism for you: Cinderella is to fairy tales what Pythagoras is to math." He rolled his eyes. "And please don't critique my logic. I'm just trying to point out that we don't have the time to make E. G. Smythe's Salty Fire Land a perfect world, we've got just enough time to make sure the citizens stay in it." He paused. "Do you see what I'm saying? I'd rather have a co-dependent Cinderella than no Cinderella at all."

I took a deep breath and said, "Calo, I have to tell you something." Then I rubbed myself visible, just as the guard passed. "I've had sort of a side project, recently, and...um...I decided to prove that being normal equals being happy. And to test my theory, I tried to make an unhappy citizen normal in order to make her happy."

Calo's eyes narrowed. "Her, who?"

"Maybe we should check your levels, Calo. I don't want to set you back."

"Angry is not unhappy, Lily. Her, who?"

"Well, I...I used Ella as my test subject."

Calo was silent for twenty seconds, but it felt *much* longer. "What were the results?"

"Um...she became happier, much happier, but I think it was superficial."

"Why?"

"Because she vanished," I whispered.

"*You're* the reason she vanished? Are you telling me that in your first month as our princess you managed to vanish the most well-known fairy tale of all time?"

"Yes." My voice surprised me. I didn't know it could be so quiet.

After a few minutes of uncomfortable silence, Calo said, "At least some good has come from your incompetence. I'm nearly happy enough to go rescue everyone."

"Glad to be of service. I also memorized everyone's sad items, so you'd know what we're up against."

"Exactly how many people are we rescuing?"

I did the math quickly and answered, "Ten. Tallis let the birds go free in exchange for my capture."

"You mean you really did just *volunteer* to be a prisoner and you ransomed yourself for some birds? I didn't know you liked animals that much." Calo smirked, obviously feeling better.

"Very funny. The exact terms of the agreement were that he would empty a cell. I didn't know which one he would choose. I just hoped it wasn't you, because I really needed you for the plan."

"Tallis wouldn't be foolish enough to let me leave. He desperately wants me on his side."

"He's already asked you?"

Calo nodded. He went thoughtful and pensive for a moment. I wondered how I knew the word pensive and would my Quest Clause vocabulary be available to me when this was all over.

Calo came out of his reverie (!) and asked, "Who are we rescuing? I want to start formulating plans."

"Okay. Well, there's Ella and Aven obviously. Ella's stepsisters."

"Adelaide and Amaryllis," Calo interrupted.

"And her stepmother."

"Agatha."

"Then just your grandmother, grandfathers and your parents." My eyes darted to Calo to see how he would take this news.

"I don't have grandparents. My story opens with my father dying."

"Your story opens with your *adoptive* father dying," I corrected.

Calo stared at me. "You mean my birth family? You know who they are?"

"I'm 97% sure."

"Who?"

Calo's usual logic and reasoning seemed to have left him. If he'd been in a proper state of mind, he would have realized there was only one other tale in the dungeon. HEA and the Agency kept up with all that. But perhaps he thought I'd left a wave of vanishing behind me in Smythe's SFL.

"*The Candlemaker's Daughter* is the tale you started in." I went invisible as soon as I heard the guard coming.

"But everyone vanished from that story, there was no one left. The file disappeared," Calo hissed to my invisible self.

"The file was stolen, by the same person who kidnapped you and gave you to the Miller family." I rubbed the marble so I'd be visible and looked directly at him. "Levi stole the file. Levi kidnapped you."

"Kidnapped me? What is that story about?"

It was my turn to be shocked. Calo didn't know a fairy tale. "You don't know the story?"

He shook his head. "It was vanished long before I started working for HEA. We all just assumed the file was gone too. Our rescue plans were always more of the brute force "get in and grab everyone" variety since we had no way to make the citizens happy without invoking Matt's Law."

"What *is* Matt's Law?" I asked again.

Calo looked at me a long time, considering. "I will tell you, *if* you promise to tell me the story of *The Candlemaker's Daughter*."

"Okay," I nodded. I had planned to tell him anyway, but he didn't have to know that.

Calo began, "When your mother and father first began dating, she was kidnapped by Tandem Tallis and his forces."

"She knew about the kingdom, then?"

Calo tilted his head. "It's sort of how she found out."

"What?"

Calo ignored me and went on, "Your father wanted to rescue her. Everyone was against it. No one wanted to risk one of the princes on a fool's errand. Your father and Grimm met secretly, defying the king and queen, and came up with a plan to get your father into Uppish Senna."

"*Grimm* was a part of a plan to defy the king and queen?"

Calo nodded. "He said it was a matter of honor between partners. He managed to get your father smuggled into the dungeons. But your father was captured pretty quickly." Calo paused while I went invisible. After the guard passed and I'd returned, he went on. "It's important to note that no one who wasn't sad had ever been held in these dungeons before. Your father tested the strength of the door as soon as he was left alone and to his surprise, the door opened. He found your mother and her cell was unlocked as well. They managed to escape and made their way back to Smythe's SFL. Your father called the phenomenon of the unlocked doors 'Matt's Law'. Your father's parents were not thrilled that he had risked himself like that, and when the kingdom was preparing for your arrival, a new law was passed forbidding anyone from telling you about Matt's Law in case you tried to do the same thing he did."

"Are there other things my parents aren't telling me? Why is my Mom lying about her parents?"

"I'm not telling you anything else. Now, tell me my story, Lily."

"Okay." I briefly told the tale. I was worried how Calo would take the news. It wasn't a happy story. He listened quietly and said nothing until the end.

"So Levi took me off the hillside?"

I nodded. "It's the most logical analysis of the facts. Besides, he practically told me so."

Calo sat in silence for a moment and then stood up suddenly. "Let's go rescue my family, Lily."

23

AND THEY ALL LIVED
HAPPILY EVER AFTER

We didn't actually leave as soon as Calo's tone had implied. First, we finalized our plan; Calo did most of the talking. His new-found family was the last variable of the equation to make him Less Than Less Than Happy. He was like the old Calo: direct, bossy, arrogant. It was good to see him back to his usual self. I told him all the things that I had observed about his fellow prisoners. And I would even say his tone was complimentary when he said, "Well done, Lily. It's good to know where everyone is so we won't waste time trying to find specific people."

His plan was fairly simple. He thought just the explanation of the truth to *The Candlemaker's Daughter* citizens would be enough to send them back, with the possible exception of his grandmother, who had tried to kill him. My job was to stay invisible and when the guard came by, grab Calo and pull him into the "circle of invisibility" as Calo called it. Also, while he talked to the citizens, I would be busy making a dummy in the straw to be covered with the prisoner's blanket after they had vanished back. We needed to trick the guard for as long as possible.

"But will seeing your family make you too happy?" I asked.[66]

"I'm planning to focus on all the years I was deprived of them by my evil, sadistic grandmother."

"And Levi," I added.

"Yes, and Levi."

~ ~ ~

The first prisoner we came to happened to be Calo's (evil, sadistic) grandmother. We knew it was her because the cell was cluttered with photos of Celdan, Colin, and Calo together and happy throughout all of Calo's life.

"Where did the pictures come from?" I asked as we peered through the window.

"Magicked up from Tallis's twisted imagination, no doubt," Calo muttered absently as he studied the cell. "Alright, Lily, how should I approach this situation?"

---

[66] Lily and Calo's rescue plan – Calo = one big mess of unhappiness.

I turned sharply to stare at him. "Are you testing me in the middle of a rescue? We don't have time for this!"

"Just consider it. This is an interesting case. Pretend I need your help."

I shook my head and turned to study the cell again. We were both invisible, and the addition of Calo made it even hotter than before. The sooner I solved this, the sooner I could cool off.

After a moment of study, I said, "Okay. The queen is kept prisoner by the idea that Celdan and Colin have somehow escaped the dungeons, found you, and are living Happily Ever After. You should tell her the truth, that you've never met your parents and that you're all still languishing in the dungeons."

"Very good. And nice use of *languishing*." Calo nodded. "Let's go."

We slipped into the cell, splitting up to do our jobs. Calo surprised the queen, as he became visible.

"My lady," he bowed and began his explanation. I started making a straw-dummy. I only had to interrupt Calo once to turn him invisible.

After the guard passed and Calo was visible again, the queen asked, "Then, these pictures are false?"

"Yes, my lady."

"And my son and *common* daughter-in-law are wasting away in this prison?"

"Yes, my lady."

The queen began to laugh. "It's all too wonderful. They are unhappy. They have been robbed of their Happily Ever After."

And then she was gone. Calo rushed over to be included in my invisibility.

"Pleasant woman," he said under his breath.

~~~

Ella's stepsisters were next: Adelaide, followed by Amaryllis. They were similarly easy to return to Happy. Calo just told them Ella was in the dungeon and that Aven was free to be snatched up.

"Should we be lying to them?" I asked as we stood, invisible in Amaryllis's empty cell.

Calo didn't look at me as he answered. He was listening for the guard. "Don't think of it as lying. Think of it as rescuing. People who are so unhappy will believe anything to have happiness—even if they know deep down it's probably not true."

"But won't they all just fall into the depths of despair after they realize the truth?"

"The *depths of despair?*" Calo was grinning.

"Quest Clause," I muttered.

Calo chuckled. "I like this new facet of you. Lily-of-the-prosy-word-picture."

"Ha, ha. Can we get back to my question?"

"Fine. They won't fall into the *depths of despair*. As soon as they vanish back, they are met with specially trained Happiologists who help them debrief and come to terms with their lives and happiness apart from whatever we had to say to get them back."

"How do the Happiologists know where they are?"

"We've managed to make sure that everyone vanishes back to the eleventh floor of HEA. It's written into the accords we have with Uppish Senna."

"So that makes it okay to lie?"

"It's a necessary evil. If we don't lie, they don't go back."

I dropped the subject. The morality of lying to our citizens was an issue for another time, and I couldn't deny the fact that the lying *was* working.

After the guard passed, we gave him a bit of a head start before we continued on our way. Aven's cell was nearest, but as part of our plan, we purposely left Aven for later. Calo's royal grandfather (Colin's dad) was next.

Calo seemed a little nervous, but wouldn't go for any deviation from the plan. (I had offered to do the talking and let him stay invisible while he made the dummy.)

He pulled the king into one of the corners and talked quietly to him. I couldn't hear what they were saying, but the king hugged Calo right before he vanished.

"How are you doing, Calo?" I asked as he came over.

"Cinderella's stepmother is next, isn't she?" His voice was his old, arrogant self. He took two steps toward the door, then he stopped and turned around. "Sorry, Lily. I know what you're trying to do. I appreciate it. And after I've had some time to process it, I'll be glad for a friend to talk to." He smiled.

"We're friends? I thought we were just partners." I smiled, too.

"Partners *and* friends. Now, get over here and turn us invisible."

~ ~ ~

Cinderella's stepmother, Agatha, was delighted to learn that her daughters were free and had a chance to marry Prince Charming after all. She happily vanished back to Smythe's SFL to help the girls win the prince.

Celdan's cell was next. Calo planned to bring her to Colin's cell and reveal himself to both parents at the same time.

One part of this plan jarred with my mathematical mind. "How will Celdan be able to leave her cell if we're not going to get her Happy until she's with Colin?"

"How am I able to leave my cell? I'm not Happy yet."

"Huh." I had not considered that. "Why *are* you able to leave your cell?"

Calo shrugged. "I don't know. That's why I asked you."

"Why would I know? You're the brilliant Happiologist."

"Because I think you're doing it." Calo flattened us up against the wall in preparation for the passing of the guard. While we waited until it was safe, I calculated why Calo would think I was the cause of this phenomenon. Was I suddenly in possession of some sort of magical ability? Could the Quest Clause be responsible for this?

"Why do you think I'm doing it?" I asked, once it was safe to talk again.

"It's just a theory I have. I think the fact that you aren't unhappy sort of projects on to other people. Just like we can share in your invisibility, we can share in your Happiness."

"Interesting."

"Well, it's just one theory. It could also be that you have been endowed with some sort of magical power or the fact that you're in the royal family or that we've been misled by Tallis into thinking we're all trapped in our cells." After a moment, he finished with "Or...you're just a freak."

I sighed. "I love the *exact* precision offered by the magical world."

Calo chuckled. "Alright, let's get my mother."

Celdan was surprised to see us—well Calo, I was invisible.

"What is the meaning of this? I have been alone these many years. Why should Tallis send someone to torture me now?"

Calo made a slight bow. "My lady, pray give me the opportunity to explain. I have—"

Calo was interrupted by Celdan, exclaiming. "Good heavens! What is happening to the straw?"

"That is my partner, Lily. She's making a dummy so the guard will think you are sleeping long after we have rescued you. Now, my lady, we intend to convey you to your husband's cell."

"Colin? Colin is here?"

Calo nodded. "Yes, my lady."

Celdan sank down onto a stool. "I didn't know he had succumbed. I hoped he was still free."

Calo stepped over to Celdan and helped her stand again. "We must go now. The guard will pass again soon. If you please, do take my hand. Lily will hold your other hand, and we will all be invisible."

"You look a little like my Colin," Celdan said, taking Calo's hand.

~ ~ ~

We made it safely to Colin's cell. Calo and Celdan became visible and I went to work on the straw, thankful all the citizens had blankets. Straw-dummies minus the blankets would just equal piles of straw.

"Celdan!" Colin rushed to her side.

"Colin!" Celdan threw her arms around him. "Oh, my love."

"But how can this be?" Colin looked confused.

Calo coughed discreetly. "Please allow me to explain. Lily and I are here to rescue you."

"Lily?" Colin asked.

Calo gestured in my direction, and I stomped my foot.

"She's invisible," Calo added.

"Ah," Colin nodded. "Continue, please."

Calo took a deep breath. "As you no doubt know, the best way out of these dungeons is simply to become Happy. And besides reuniting yourselves, I have something to tell you that should make you quite Happy."

"You seem like a well-qualified Happiologist." Colin smiled faintly. "I'm sure you have thoroughly researched our sad history. We are delighted to be reunited with one another. But we have found it difficult to be Happy since we lost our children."

"I am aware of that, sir." Calo took another breath. "We have recently discovered that your first-born son did not die on the hillside."

Celdan gasped; Colin steadied her.

Calo continued. "He was rescued and adopted by a miller's family. He grew up and is alive even at this moment." Calo swallowed.

I tried to mentally send him courage to complete his equation. But he didn't need it.

Celdan ran to him. "You're my son, aren't you?"

After his nod, she held him tight and was soon joined by Colin.

"I should have recognized you immediately," she whispered.

I watched them for a moment, happy for Calo. Then I heard the guard's footsteps, and I rushed over to them.

After the guard passed, Celdan clasped Calo's hands and said, "I'm feeling so Happy." Her eyes filled with tears.

Colin put his hand on Calo's, "You do have a way home, don't you, Redmond?"

"Redmond?" I mouthed to Calo. He could see me because we were all still invisible. I stood behind his parents.

He shrugged and turned back to his father. "Yes, of course, sir. Happiologist technology has come a long way since you've been in the kingdom. Lily and I will be able to transport back."

"Oh good," Celdan sighed and she vanished.

Colin smiled, embraced Calo again and said, "It's so good to see you, my son." Then, he vanished.

I grinned at Calo. "Well, *Redmond*, I hope you don't get in trouble for lying to your parents."

Calo made a noise. "That is a uniquely disturbing name." He chuckled. "You know, when I found out I was adopted it never occurred to me I might not be named Calo. That's just always been my name. *Redmond*," he said, making a face.

~~~

Calo's other grandfather, Celdan's father, was another quick vanish. He was all too willing to believe that Celdan was happy again and that Calo was his grandchild.

"Are you ready?" Calo asked as we made our way to Ella's cell. Ella was our next to last stop. Our plan was to get her a little happier and finalize her Happiness by having her help rescue Aven. I just wasn't thrilled about my part of the equation: telling Ella the truth. About how I had used her, how I had tried to make her normal.

I looked through the window. Ella still sat in the middle of the room. I eased the door open and we slipped in; Calo held my hand tightly. Ella's eyes widened and she stopped crying.

Calo nodded to me, smiling encouragingly. I rubbed us visible. Ella's eyes exploded in width, "What—"

"Quietly, if you please, my lady." Calo shushed her and went to stand by the door.

"What are you doing here, Lily?" Ella offered me her stool.

I shook my head to decline the offer and said. "I've come to rescue you."

She gave me a weak smile. "Lily–I–I can't be rescued. It's hopeless."

"It's not hopeless." I sat on the floor beside her stool–trying to ignore the unmathematical filth everywhere. "Ella–you and I have both messed some things up. We created this equation."

"That's not helpful or cheerful, Lily. You Happiologists usually just talk to me about cleaning or birds." She looked to Calo in confusion.

I nodded. "And that never made you lastingly happy. Today we're going to."

Ella glanced again at Calo. He nodded and continued watching for the guard. Ella sat back on the stool.

"So," I took a deep breath. "I have a confession to make. I don't really understand the fairytale world. I like math. I like things that make sense *every single time*. I like knowing how to solve an equation." I swallowed. "I don't understand portaling through a bathtub. I can't understand the logic of this world. I just decided it was all abnormal. And I had to make it normal." I looked at Ella. "I gave you advice that I thought would make you normal. I encouraged you to paint and to get out more, and I went out of my way to be friendly to you just to make sure you were becoming normal."

"I don't understand, Lily. What do you mean?"

"I ruined your life, Ella. I made you unhappy." Inexplicably, tears were forming in my eyes. My descent into unmathematicalness was complete–crying about a fairy tale. "But while I pretended to be your friend, I really became your friend, and I'm so sorry. You have to come back, Ella. Aven needs you. The world needs your story."

Ella slipped off the stool and sank down beside me, wrapping me in her arms. "Lily, you didn't ruin my life."

"Yes, it was *all* me. You were better off before. The whole kingdom was better off before I came," I sobbed.

"I may not have *vanished* before, but I still wasn't Happy. Your suggestions were not harmful. *I* chose to burn Aven's maps. *I* made my husband, my true love, Unhappy. *That's* why I vanished. I made myself Unhappy."

We were silent for a moment. Calo rushed over to become invisible with me. Ella scrambled up onto her stool. After the guard passed, Calo made the straw-dummy.

"I've been unfair to Aven," Ella whispered. "I blamed him for leaving me behind all the time. But he always asked me to come with him."

"Why did you never go? You hate being left behind."

"I felt a real princess shouldn't go traipsing about the countryside. A real princess should stay at home and wait for her prince to come back. I hate that. I like to clean, but I felt I shouldn't as a princess. I love Aven, but since we married, I've been so unhappy."

I thought a moment and carefully examined the advice I was about to give. I was sure it was good advice and wouldn't make matters worse. "Ella, don't focus on what you think a real princess would do. You *are* a real princess. Whatever *you* do is what a real princess does. Ella, you've got to take control of your happiness. Paint your paintings, go with Aven on his trips, clean the castle yourself. Be the person Aven fell in love with. That's the princess in you." The last words were a little hard to get out, since they were somewhat illogical, but this day wasn't exactly a shining example of mathematical reason.

But strangely, I *could* see the math. In Ella's situation,

$$1 \text{ prince charming} + 1 \text{ misused girl} \neq \text{Happily Ever Afte.}$$

Ella only had to alter something about the equation, the situation it occurred in or the parameters of the misused girl....

"Lily?" Ella touched my arm.

"Sorry!" I snapped out of my calculations. "I got distracted. What were you saying?"

"I think I'd like to talk to Aven. Can you take me to him?"

I smiled. "We can do that."

~~~

Calo and I stood near the door, invisible and a little away from Aven and Ella. They were talking quietly. We'd already made the straw-dummy and now we served as the lookouts. I estimated it would take us two seconds to get to them if the guard came.

"You did a good job with Ella," Calo whispered.

"Yeah," I nodded. "I did an excellent job of solving my unbalanced equation."

"Lily." Calo tilted my face up so I had to look at him. "You will be a good Happiologist. Look what you did today. *You* saved *The Candlemaker's Daughter* and you've almost saved *Cinderella*. You *are* good at this. You used your math to get us in and out of the cells. You observed the items in the cells so we'd know who was where. Your calculations kept us one step ahead of the guard this whole time. Our kingdom needs you as its Protector. *All* of you, even your logical, mathematical side." He paused. "You should really take your own advice, Lily."

"About?"

"Don't try to make yourself into the princess you think Smythe's SFL needs. Be the princess that Smythe's SFL has. You *are* a princess. Be who you are."

"Thank you, Calo." His praise equaled a warm feeling inside of me.

"Excuse me, Princess, Calo?" Aven was looking in our direction. "I think we're about to leave. Thank you for all you've done. I hope you two will be able to find your way back."

"Don't worry about us," Calo answered. "We have a plan."

"Oh, good," Ella smiled at us, took Aven's hand, and they both disappeared.

"So, what exactly *is* our plan?" I asked Calo.

"To get home, of course."

"How?"

"That's open for discussion. I didn't actually think we'd make it this far."

I laughed a little. "It is pretty amazing, isn't it? We rescued everyone." I smiled. "Should we try to make each other happy?"

"I don't think that would work. You've got to start living Happily Ever After, not just get to Happy. I think we should try to stay invisible and sneak out of the dungeon."

~ ~ ~

Sneaking out was easier than we thought. We waited until the guard was well past the area, and since we had seen no other guards in the dungeon, we simply opened the door and traveled along a passageway for four and a half minutes looking for the stairs to the main floor of the fortress. Then we came to a figurative fork in the road. The passage split into two hallways.

"I think we should go right," Calo whispered.

"I think we should go left," I whispered back. It's not mathematical, but if I truly don't know which way to go, I like to go left.

"You just want to go left because *left* and *Lily*
start with the same letter."

I made a face. "And you just want to go right
because *right* and *Redmond* both start with an R."

Calo sighed. "I really dislike that name."

I laughed a little. "We need to pick a way to go."

"Yes, you do," said a greasy voice behind us.

I sucked in my breath and spun around. Levi had
a smirk on his face and a dozen guards behind him. Calo
grabbed my hand, and then we witnessed Newton's third
law of motion.

Newton found that for every action there is an
equal and opposite reaction. For instance, when we step
out of a boat onto the shore, the boat tends to move in
the opposite direction. And when Calo grabbed my left
hand, I was so surprised that I dropped my marble from
my right hand.

"Oh no," I breathed, watching it roll away,
leaving us visible.

Calo's eyes went wide.

We both moved to grab the marble.

"Looking for this?" Levi held my blue—the color
of the April sky—marble in his greasy fingers.

"That's my marble. Give it back," I said stupidly.

"Tsk, tsk, tsk, tsk." Levi shook his head. "There's
magic associated with this marble beyond its obvious
power of invisibility."

"Give it back, Levi."

Calo touched my arm. "Um, Lily. I think we
should go," he whispered.

"Not without my marble!"

"Princess!" Levi looked at me in mock surprise.
"I'm so shocked! Who let you take your key out of the
castle?"

"That's your key?" Calo nearly shouted.

I nodded. "I didn't want my parents to know I was here, well there. I skipped school, you know."

Levi laughed loudly.

I threw him a disdainful look. "Why are you laughing?"

"It's all too entertaining. The heir to the throne, trapped in my lord's castle and even if you do escape, you're trapped in your kingdom. Without your silly marble, you'll never be able to go home."

"What? Is that true? Never?" I turned to Calo. He nodded slightly.

"They can't just issue another one, like a new passport or driver's license?"

Calo shook his head. "Magic is a bit more black and white than that. You only get one key."

"Give it back, Levi!" I tried to snatch the marble from his greasy hand, but he held it high out of my reach.

"Let's see: what happens if I rub it three times to the left?" Levi rubbed the marble and disappeared.

"Run!" Calo grabbed my hand and took off to the right. We could hear Levi laughing behind us.

As we ran, the updates we'd been ignoring began jabbing even more painfully into my foot. That should have been factored into the equation when I agreed to turn my shoe into a magical mailbox.

We passed door after door. Calo didn't seem interested in any of them. I wasn't interested either. My foot was in serious pain.

"Do you know where we're going?" I asked him, panting.

"Not a clue." Calo ran faster.

Soon there weren't any more doorways, but Calo kept running. I kept running and the updates kept hurting. Finally (and thankfully), my foot stopped hurting. Of course, I realized, five strides later, my shoe had come off.

"Calo, I lost my shoe."

He didn't acknowledge my words. He just kept running. Running with only one shoe is a seriously unbalanced equation. I had to stop. When I stopped, Calo jerked back because his momentum had kept him going. (We were still holding hands.)

"Why did you stop?" he hissed.

"Shh." I put my hand on his mouth. "Listen!"

Levi was laughing. "It's a dead end, you know. I'll just wait for you to come back when you're ready."

Calo sighed. "What are the odds that we would pick the dead end?"

"50%."

He looked at me and rolled his eyes.

"There were two ways to go, so 50%. Although, if both passages lead to a dead end it would be 100%."

Calo sighed again.

"You were asking a rhetorical question, weren't you?"

He nodded.

"I really don't like rhetorical questions."

Calo leaned against a wall, trying to catch his breath. I stood there off balance because of my shoe. It's very unsettling and unmathematical to be off balance. "I need my shoe," I said to myself.

"What?"

"My shoe. I lost it while we were running. Now I'm off balance–like a scale with a badly placed fulcrum."

Calo rolled his eyes again. "I'll go find it."

I used the time he was gone to count by eights. I was at one-hundred sixty-eight when he came back.

"Give me your foot," he said, knocking out several shoe updates. I leaned against the wall and stuck my foot out. "It fell off because it wasn't tied, Lily. The next time we run for our lives, please have the courtesy to tie your shoes properly." Calo slipped my sneaker on. Then he looked up at me. "Just like in *Cinderella*. That might work. It would just need one of us."

"Um, Calo." He was still holding my foot, so I shook it a little to remind him.

He released my foot slowly and stood up. "Look, Lily. I think I've found a way to get us home. I'm not sure it will work, but we have to try."

"Yeah, whatever, Calo. I'm willing to fit into any equation that will get us home."

"Good." He nodded, smiling.

"What do I need to do?"

Calo took a deep breath, put his hand on my mouth and said, "Just listen. I'm in love with you."

My eyes widened beyond mathematical parameters. I tried to exclaim, but Calo's hand was firm.

"I fell in love with you by seeing your pictures in Arrivhall and reading the reports your mother submitted to the papers about what you were doing. I thought anyone with such a logical mindset would be the perfect worker at HEA, a terrific Protector."

What? *What?* WHAT?

This was not at all equal to anything Calo had ever said about me. He had never complimented my logic before. Usually, he hated it.

"I never planned to tell you. I'm just a commoner, a poor miller's son, after all. You're a princess and the Future Protector. But Levi and Tallis included you in my cell of unhappiness because they knew seeing you work alone would make me sad. That I would want to be with you. That I would want to take care of you." He swallowed. "I lied to you. I told you instructing you improves my mood, but really, *you* improve my mood. I love being around you and seeing our world through your eyes. I love watching your passion for our kingdom grow. I love you, Lily Elizabeth Sparrow."

Calo quickly removed his hand from my mouth and pressed his lips on mine, kissing me. A warm, cinnamony feeling overcame the shock. Suddenly, I felt happier than I'd ever been. I felt I would always be

Happily Ever After

EPILOGUE

What in the names of Pythagoras, Newton, and Descartes was that?" I shouted when Calo took his lips off my mouth.

"I can't believe it!" Calo smiled and hugged me. "It worked!"

"Calo!" I started to yell again, but became aware of the cheering all around us. We were not in the dungeon passageways anymore. We were in a place full of inexplicable sunlight. I could see Ella, Aven, Celdan, Colin and all the others we had rescued in the crowd. Miranda and Doug were there along with my parents.

"What happened?" I looked over to Calo.

He gave me a big smile. "We did it!"

~~~

After that, I didn't have a moment alone with Calo for a week. There were five full days of celebrating and the telling (and retelling) of the whole story.

My mom hugged and cried all over me. My father walked about proudly, reminding everyone his daughter had saved the story of Cinderella. If I was with him, I pointed out I had vanished it in the first place. But if Ella was near she would deny that and proclaim I was a true friend, I just didn't know it at the time and she was sorry she let things with Aven get so bad. She and Aven spent the nights dancing and the days chatting, laughing, and planning in a secluded corner.

Colin and Celdan never let Calo out of their sight, calling him Redmond all the while. Calo's (evil, sadistic) grandmother tried to stay for the celebrations, but she got so fed up the first evening that she left in a huff. Miranda assured me that she wasn't in danger of vanishing. The evil queen was happy to have Celdan around to torment again.

After the celebrations, when Grimm returned from being a statue and Ella's stepsisters truly accepted that Aven was still in love with Ella, things returned to normal. Or at least what equaled normal for Smythe's SFL.

A special delegation was sent to Uppish Senna to get my marble back. When they returned, they said Tallis thought the whole thing was a joke and he never meant to keep me in the dungeon for more than a few hours. He happily returned my marble, which had to be degreased. Horrible little man and his greasy sycophant.

My parents worried about the fact that I was now living Happily Ever After. My monitor worked and

364

Miranda was assigned as my Happiologist. I had to go to a special training to learn how to cope with my emotions now.[67] Mom told me no one had wanted me living Happily Ever After as a teenager.

"The ups and downs of the teenage years are a dangerous time if you're capable of vanishing, which you are now," she said one night, as we sat in the living room on Marshall Road. "You'll have to really guard against letting yourself get down over little things. Like fights with friends or a boy who doesn't like you."

"Mom. That's completely irrational."

But my mind kept replaying everything that happened in those last moments in the passageway. Did Calo really love me? Or was he just trying to create a Happily Ever After for us?

That's what he said in his official report. He testified my shoe reminded him of Ella losing her glass (or gold) slipper. He stated that all the stuff about love was just to make sure we were creating the conditions of a Happily Ever After. As proof, he pointed out there were *no* reports about me from my mother in the papers. But there were *numerous* reports from Calo, indicating that he disliked my logic and rational mindset. He further stated he'd only kissed me so we'd vanish back.

But was that true? Calo didn't have to make himself Happily Ever After. He just had to get happy. And by the crazy logic of fairy tales, could I live Happily Ever After if my "prince" didn't really love me? Because I had become Happily Ever After. I was this way *because*

---

[67] That was a super mathematical day, let me tell you. (Read the previous sentence with sarcasm.)

of what he said. Could Calo *lie* to the magic? Could the
magic know he was lying and still work?

I felt deep in my mathematical core that it
couldn't work that way. He couldn't lie to the magic. In
the fairy tales I'd studied, good was rewarded and bad
was punished. For crying out loud, Cinderella's birds
flew down and sang a song to the prince just to prevent
him from marrying the wrong girl. If the fairy tale
universe would go out of its way to make sure the right
person got their Happily Ever After, I don't think they
would just hand them out based on what a person said.

I had to conclude Calo had some feelings for me.
And the last part of his speech (*"You improve my mood. I
love being around you and seeing our world through your eyes. I
love watching your passion for our kingdom grow. I love you, Lily
Elizabeth Sparrow."*) had seemed sincere.

And the kiss. Well, it was a *very* nice kiss. Not that
I had anything to compare it too, but, I mean, it *did* have
some pretty amazing consequences.

Besides, I had other stuff to worry about. I had
missed six days of school, including the day I'd ditched,
so I was behind on my homework. Mrs. Fox excitedly(!)
let me have an extension on my paper. That was rather
beneficial since I needed to change my whole
assumption. I rewrote it and concluded that fairy tales *are*
important to study because the characters end up happy
and if you are happy, you are normal. My friend Ella
became a princess on her own terms, not a "normal"
thing to do, but it made her happy and being happy is
the missing variable in the equation of what is normal.

Of course, I didn't put the part about Ella in.

Mrs. Fox loved the conclusion. She thought it
was a unique perspective on the human psyche and

human emotions! I accepted the A and brought it home to show my parents.[68]

All the equations in my life were adding up again. If I could only get the Calo equation to balance, everything would be perfect. I decided not to talk to anyone about the Calo problem. I would solve that on my own…or maybe I'd let him help.

---

[68] They gave a copy to the court historian who keeps up with the chronicles of each ruler. I was a little disturbed to find out that everything I'd done would be written down and retold for generations. Maybe it was a good thing I'd enacted the Quest Clause for at least part of it.

Copy of a letter intercepted by Agents at the Agency:

My Lord Tallis –
May you be unhappy forever! Your Lordship will be delighted to know that all is exactly on schedule. As–according to my plan–Lily became more and more involved in the mystery of The Candlemaker's Daughter, *she found success and satisfaction which lead* so *easily to happiness. I am now, my Lord Tallis, able to report that Dear Princess Lily has reached Happily Ever After. She is ripe for vanishing.*

Your willing and humble servant,
Levi

Read on for a sneak peek of Lily's next adventure,
Calculating Christmas

"What exactly does 'dress warmly' mean?" I muttered to myself as I stood before my closet. Sweater warm? Jacket warm? Mittens and scarf warm?

Should I have checked a weather report for today? Does Smythe's SFL even have weather reports? Or weather, other than the changeable Fisher King weather? So far it had always seemed the same to me (a nice 70 degrees or so), but I knew some fairy tales had seasons and storms.

I filed the issue away in my "Things to ask Calo" mental file, and smiled. I would get to ask him some things today. I was finally going to see him!

Then I checked myself, a little embarrassed at how giddy I'd become. "Rational and logical," I said. "Rational and logical."

Rationally and logically, I chose to wear a pair of jeans, a sweater combined with a thermal undershirt, and my sneakers. A perfectly warm outfit.

I redid my ponytail, grabbed my marble off the dresser and portaled over to the kingdom. Beryl handed me a baggie of pretzels as I hopped on my bike. I'd become quite adept at eating pretzels and riding my bike at the same time. One of the many non-mathematical skills I'd acquired since becoming (or rather finding out I was) the princess of E. G. Smythe's Salty Fire Land.

But in this equation, being a princess does not equal wearing fluffy dresses, practicing dancing, and marrying a prince. It does equal working at HEA after school, having a father who is alive instead of dead, and dealing with fairy tale people in a myriad of situations. So it's sort of a modern princess thing. Although, I have worn a fluffy dress or two, danced in magic shoes, and am currently living Happily Ever After as a direct result of kissing a (handsome) prince. (Yes, Calo does = handsome.)

"Rational and logical," I muttered again and focused on getting to work on time.

Calo was standing beside my desk when I got to our cubicle. His dark curls were tousled across his forehead. Tousled? Tousled? I turned the word over in my mind. Ever since I had enacted the quest clause a few weeks ago, some residual vocabulary cropped up. Grimm said it would fade over time.

I smiled at Calo, trying to be rational and logical, of course.

He did not return my smile. In fact, he looked annoyed.

"I thought I told you to dress warmly." He walked past me and out of the cubicle. "Come on. We don't have all day."

Grimm frowned at me as we entered his office. "I

thought you were going to tell Lily to dress warmly."

Calo huffed as he sat down. "I did."

"I dressed warmly!" My voice was louder than I'd intended it to be. "This is warm." I pulled at my sweater. "I'm wearing a sweater and a thermal undershirt, plus jeans, and sensible shoes." I plopped down in my chair. "This is warmer than what would normally be worn in October."

Calo rolled his eyes. "Where we're going we need to be dressed much warmer than an extra shirt."

"It's not just an extra shirt!"

"Alright, you two." Grimm calmly held his hand up. "I'm sure there's something for Lily to wear in Wardrobe or maybe even in lost and found."

"Or maybe she could just summon her fairy godmother and wish herself a parka and snow boots."

I rolled my eyes. Leave it to me to get the one Non-Charming Prince Charming in the fairy tale world. And was there something wrong with using your fairy godmother? (I did feel a little weird for thinking that. After all, I had only used my fairy godmother twice and both times, it felt a little unethical, but still who was Prince Calo to judge me?)

"Enough," Grimm said firmly. "I want to explain this assignment to you both. I hope you understand that it is vitally important this case be handled with extreme delicacy and caution. This is a very unique situation that we are faced with and if we fail, there will be dire consequences for not only E. G. Smythe's Salty Fire Land, but for the real world as well."

"For the real world as well?"

Grimm nodded. "Carole Claus needs some space from her family."

Calo raised his eyebrows and then returned to his

professional attitude of listening.

"Who's Carole Claus?" I asked.

"Santa Claus' daughter," Grimm sipped his coffee.

"Have we found her a suitable foster home?" Calo took a small notepad out of his pocket and a pen off of Grimm's desk.

Grimm nodded. "Yes, the—"

"Wait," I interrupted, leaning forward. "Santa Claus exists and he has a daughter?"

"And two sons." Grimm smiled kindly.

"Okay. If she's unhappy, why aren't we just cheering her up? Why are we moving her out? And does Santa Claus even count as a fairy tale?"

"He's a legend. And I didn't say she was unhappy, Lily. I said she needed space from her family."

Calo made a coughing noise.

"Oh." I felt my face getting warm with embarrassment. You would think I would eventually learn to wait until all of the illogical fairy tale stuff had been explained before I started asking questions. "Why don't you finish your brief?"

Grimm chuckled and went on. "As I was saying, the Sparrow family has offered to welcome Carole into their home."

"Oh, that'll be great," Calo said sincerely as I processed that last piece of data.

"What Sparrow family? My Sparrow family?"

"Lily," Calo hissed, wanting me to be quiet.

"Yes," Grimm nodded. "Your Sparrow family."

"She's going to live in our house or in our castle?" I ignored Calo's look and kept interrupting.

"Carole will be living on Marshall Road in your house, Lily. She will enroll in Franklin High School and hopefully be able to get the normal teenage experience she's looking for."

"What's the cover story going to be?" Calo's notepad was filling up.

I looked back and forth between them. How could they calmly be discussing a total stranger moving into my house? And going to my school?

The Cinderella Theorem

I hope you enjoyed reading *The Cinderella Theorem* as much as I enjoyed writing it! Please let me know what you thought of the book; I love to hear from fans. You can contact me through my Facebook site: The Lily Sparrow Chronicles.

The best publicity a book can get is from people like you who have read and loved the book. Here are some ways to help promote *The Cinderella Theorem*:

Review the book—on Amazon.com, on Goodreads.com, or on your blog if you have one. If you do a review on Amazon, copy it to Goodreads as well. Also, Goodreads has an option where you can simply rate the book without writing a review.

Ask your school or local librarian to stock *The Cinderella Theorem* so others can read it.

Spread the word about *The Cinderella Theorem* to friends and family!

Like "The Lily Sparrow Chronicles" page on Facebook and invite your friends to like it as well so you can stay informed about what's happening with *Calculating Christmas*.

Thanks again,
Kristee Ravan

ABOUT THE AUTHOR

Kristee Ravan lives in Oklahoma with her husband, daughter, and pet cat, Kasidy. She wanted to be many things as she grew up including a general, an artist, and an architect. But she never bothered to say, "I want to be a writer when I grow up." She was always writing stories and thought of herself as a writer anyway. She sent her first story to a publisher in the sixth grade. (It was rejected - in a nice way.) When she is not making up stories in her head, she enjoys reading, juggling, playing games with her family, and hearing from her fans.

You can contact Kristee at the Facebook page for her Lily Sparrow books:

The Lily Sparrow Chronicles.

Made in the USA
Monee, IL
07 July 2021